GW00866408

To Kate with love at
Christmas 1977.

Mick.

973

# A Song for Every Season

# A Song for
# Every Season

## A Hundred Years of a
## Sussex Farming Family

BOB COPPER

HEINEMANN : LONDON

William Heinemann Ltd

15 Queen Street, Mayfair, London W1X 8BE

LONDON   MELBOURNE   TORONTO
JOHANNESBURG   AUCKLAND

First published 1971
Reprinted 1972
© Bob Copper 1971

Collection and arrangement of the songs in Jim Copper's
Song Book
© Coppersongs 1970

434 14455 X

Printed Offset Litho and bound in Great Britain
by Cox & Wyman Ltd,
London, Fakenham and Reading

# Contents

# List of Illustrations

*Between pages 66 and 67*

# Author's Note

Two persons in particular deserve my special thanks: Mrs Toni Russell who cast an expert eye over the text and laid a healing hand on the fractured infinitives and other literary discrepancies, and Comtesse Pierre d'Harcourt without whose invaluable help and encouragement it would probably never have known the dignity of print.

B.C.

To Jo, Jill and John

# Foreword

## by Ralph Wightman

I met Bob Copper first in 1950 on the 'Country Magazine' programme which he describes in his book. At that time I usually introduced the programme and acted as a link-man between speakers. This meeting was brief and my sole memory of it was to fix the Coppers in my mind as real countrymen in very raw, new-town surroundings, near Brighton.

Our next meeting was in 1953 when I sought them out for reasons which had nothing whatever to do with folk songs. Indeed without writing further I feel that I should confess that I know nothing about music, and cannot sing a note in tune. This may seem a strange qualification for writing a preface to a book on songs. Actually it is because I share with the Coppers a long country history, and these are country songs.

That second visit to Rottingdean in 1953 was when I was doing a radio series called 'Rural Rides'. A reader spoke the comments of William Cobbett concerning his travels through England in the last century, and I followed with what had happened to the land and people since then.

Something has certainly happened to the land at Peacehaven. Bob's old father described it to me in words I was quick to record—'All you can see is houses, houses, houses, it makes me prostrate with dismal, it's neither begun nor finished.' Bob, on the other hand, had grown up with it. Like me he had learned all the old farm crafts as a lad, but had taken better-paid work in his young manhood.

In 1953 my business with Bob was to trace any memories of Cobbett's visit in 1823. There had been a stormy meeting at Lewes the night before Cobbett came to Brighton. A Mr Ingram, farmer, of 'Rottendeen' had tried to have Cobbett thrown out. According to Cobbett 'I rose that they might see the man that they had to put out.' This, the old man claims, was enough for Mr Ingram and his Brighton friends. My question for Bob was if his family had ever had any knowledge of the farmer. 'Rottendeen' was almost surely Rottingdean near Peacehaven.

Bob's reaction was immediate. 'Well, Ralph, in Cobbett's time—you say about 1823—my great-grandfather, no, he'd only be six or so, it would be his father, John Copper, he had a small holding near by and a pig-pen in Rottingdean itself. There is no Ingram here now, but I know where he used to farm.'

That is a perfect example of the way memories go back in the country. I can remember in great detail how my grandfather described the cutting of the railway tunnel through the ridge between Dorchester and Weymouth. The extra link with the past possessed by the Coppers is a delight in singing the old songs.

A few of these old songs I heard in my boyhood but not in pubs, since mine was a strong Nonconformist village, and there was a connection between rejecting the Established Church and fighting 'the drink'. It must be sixty years ago when my elder sister was married, and Father provided a cold supper for all his employees and their wives. Beer was in open laundry baths behind the eaters, and each man helped himself by dipping in his pint mug. After an hour or so some of our non-chapel-goers were singing the old pub songs, and this is the first time I remember such favourites as 'Brennans on the Moor', and 'Wild Rover'.

Bob Copper is absolutely correct in his description of public-house singing. Looking back to more recent days, I had a few trips with Francis Collinson when he was collecting folk songs. It was always old men who could help us, but there was never any certainty that they would produce a real old tune, or one of the music-hall songs which had been popular in the 1914 war. Both were welcome in pubs before modern pop had swept the country.

The Coppers are unique in having preserved an astonishing number of very old songs. I think it underlines something which Bob barely mentions. Like my own family they were always just above the poverty line. The fact that there is a Copper's Corner of headstones in the churchyard is proof of this. The pauper poor had no memorials. No, grandfather managed a farm, great-grandfather had a small holding, father went to 'Dame School' and great-uncle ran a pub. They were never starving as plenty of farm labourers were in my youth. I do not think a man sings with an empty belly, although he may well go to a pub.

This book is a genuine bit of old Sussex. In many ways the farming of the land has changed out of all recognition. Slow toil has been replaced by the strain of nerve-racking concentration and the need for swift action. The men and their songs are faithfully remembered. Bob Copper's concern in writing the book is mainly to make sure that the tunes and words are not lost. What prompted me to write this introduction was to point out that the way of life was worthy of record. In this book such recording has been done so well that you need no knowledge of music to find it fascinating reading.

# Introduction

I remember as a small boy of about five lying on a heap of straw on the granary floor watching Grand-dad mend holes in an old corn-sack draped across his knee with a curved packing needle threaded with twine that smelt like turpentine. I lay there watching and listening intently as the ancient story unfolded, for the old man was singing, in a deep, resonant bass, a song he had heard from his own grandfather when he had been my age. The dog curled up beside me in the hot morning sunshine that slanted in through the large, open double doorway feigned sleep. Only the twitching of an ear or an occasional half-hearted attempt to wag his tail when Grand-dad's voice swelled to a higher note gave away the fact that he was alive to all that was going on.

I am quite sure I was not aware at the time of the full significance of such moments in my boyhood but somewhere deep down inside a chord of sympathy was being plucked which still rings clear to this day. That was over fifty years ago and it is by such slender threads as these that we are still connected with English village life of a couple of centuries ago.

That song is only one of many that our family have loved and kept alive down the years and now, in addition to the more durable things that remain in our village to remind us of days gone by—the church, the gaunt, black windmill on the ridge of the hill and the sturdy, flint farm-houses and barns built in the seventeenth century—we have something more fragile and far more likely to perish with the passing of the years than these monuments in stone and seasoned oak. It is something also that is more intimately connected with the lives of the villagers for, until comparatively recently, it has existed only in people's minds, having been handed down orally from one generation to another. We have a heritage of traditional songs.

Up until about the turn of the century these songs were sung frequently at the recurring village merry-makings that cropped up from time to time as the year ran its course. 'Spud-planting Night', sheep-shearing suppers and 'Hollerin' Pot' at harvest time gave the local songsters regular chances to give voice to their favourites. But as other interests came along and the old men passed away there was a sharp decline in the number willing or able to sing the old songs and also in the opportunities for those remaining to do so.

Our family has always had a built-in love of these songs and have therefore been slower than most to forget them. In fact my father, Jim, made a determined effort to ensure that they would be remembered by writing down the words of over sixty of them in what he called his 'Song Book'. He did this in 1936 and I have always looked upon it as a legacy. He was a great songster. No matter where he was or what he was doing, if the job in hand was conducive to singing he seemed to find it went along easier with a song. When I was a boy we lived in a farm cottage at the north end of the village, and whether he was lighting the fire in the kitchen range in the morning, working at his carpenter's bench during the day or hoeing between his carrots and onions in his garden in the evening, he was seldom without a song on his lips. He was also a determined singer. A mere snatch of a verse here or an odd chorus there were just not good enough for him. Once he started a song he had to go on until he reached the end. This may have been due to the the fact that many of them had a story, and having a tidy mind, he liked to see it carried through to its conclusion whether the subject was the farming year, a courtship or a battle at sea.

These songs were very old when he was a boy and although it is always difficult to date songs of this vintage with any certainty one could say that the majority of them are from a hundred to a hundred and fifty years old while some are very much older. They are the songs that used to be sung in Rottingdean, Sussex, by the men who struggled to lift a living from the shallow top-soil of the surrounding hill country or from the deep, salt-sea waves of the English Channel that almost lapped their doorsteps, and by the women who brought up huge families in the tiny cottages huddled together down in the High Street. In singing them they expressed their joys and sorrows, their hopes and fears and so the songs themselves reflect the way the villagers lived, loved, worked and played in those far-off days.

Life has changed so drastically in the last few decades that it must be almost impossible for anyone under the age of thirty to imagine what it was like in the days when these songs were still being sung in the ordinary course of events and not as the result of a folk song revival. But in the nineteen-twenties a few of the old timers were still alive and, for those of us who had direct contact with them, it was easy to recapture the moods and feelings of the mid-eighteen hundreds from their very presence. Once they started singing the years seemed to roll away; with their heads inclined and eyelids tightly shut they would be transported back to the days of their youth. The sweet simplicity of the songs, the sincerity with which they were sung and the complete lack of any twentieth-century sophistication combined magically to take you back with the singers.

I became aware at an early age that I was witnessing the very last chapter of a long story and that what I was seeing and hearing would quickly be finished and gone for ever. This made me doubly anxious to absorb everything I could while there was still time and in this task I had the indispensable help of my father. I have been lucky enough to gather together a collection of tales and information invaluable to any lover of the old songs, for to fully appreciate these it is necessary to know something of the type of men who sang them and of where and when they found an opportunity to do so. It helps, too, to know more of the part of the country where they lived, the details of their work and how they spent their leisure. The songs need the human background draped like a tapestry behind them to add another dimension and bring them to life.

It is with these thoughts in mind that this book is being attempted. It is the story of our family and the songs we sing.

# James Copper (1845–1924)

With a family name like Copper I suppose it was inevitable that sooner or later someone down the line should become the butt of Sussex wit and be dubbed 'Brasser'. This distinction fell upon my grand-dad, James. Born in Rottingdean in 1845, he was the son of a conscientious, forthright farm carter, or waggoner, known locally as 'Honest John', who lived with his family in one of the tiny 'two-up two-down' flint cottages just off the High Street within a stone's throw of the sea.

Rottingdean in those days consisted of little more than the cottages and shops that flanked the High Street, the large properties around the village green, the pond and the church. The High Street runs at an obtuse angle from the coastline, so if you stand looking down the street and see a ship out at sea it is not directly off the village but actually opposite Salt-dean, about a mile or so to the east. From the High Street the road runs northward out over the open hill country to Falmer on the Brighton/Lewes Road and at its lower end near the cliff edge it is bisected by the main coast road called, in those days, Brighton Road to the west and Dover Road to the east. The village itself lies sheltered in a combe on that section of the coast between Brighton and Beachy Head that consists of sheer, white-chalk cliffs which are a clean-cut cross section of the South Downs where they run into the sea.

Although there was a certain amount of fishing done by a handful of longshoremen the main support of the village was farming and all John's working life had been spent on the farm. Life in a carter's cottage in the 'hungry forties' was unremarkable enough. Hard, heavy work and the endless

struggle to maintain a decent level of honesty and respectability filled every day. Wages were low and food was dear
and as a boy young James used to hear his father sing:

> 'Provisions you buy at the shop it is true
> But if you've no money there's none there for you.
> So what's a poor man and his family to do,
> And it's O, the hard times of old England,
> In old England very hard times.
>
> 'If you go to a shop and you ask for a job
> They'll answer you there with a shake and a nod.
> It's enough to make a poor man to turn out and rob,
> And it's O, the hard times of old England,
> In old England very hard times.'[1]

When there was work to be done, however, they set to
with a will. 'We bean't afeard o' wark nary one an us,' they
said and took pride in their feats of strength and endurance.
A strong arm was a working man's stock in trade and John
was well equipped in this respect. It was his proud boast that
once, arriving at one of the barnyards just as the men were
knocking off for dinner, he loaded a waggon single-handed
with twenty sacks of barley, weighing two and a quarter cwt
each, in just under an hour, carrying each one almost fifty
yards from granary to waggon. A man's ability was reckoned
by the strength of his muscles and if a lad could lift a hundredweight he got a job and no other qualifications were considered necessary. Strong men were admired and tales of their
achievements lived on. Old Alfie Teale was a man of remarkable strength and stood almost as wide as he was high.
'He was a short-arsed little bugger—'e'd 'ave to climb up a
ladder to look down a well.' But with his exceedingly long
arms—''E could button up 'is leggin's without bendin' 'is
back'—he could carry a two and a quarter cwt sack of barley
under each arm.

The village was self-supporting to a great extent but if you
wanted anything that was unobtainable in the village store it
meant a four-and-a-half-mile walk along the coast to Brigh-

[1] 'Hard Times of Old England.' For full text and music, see Jim Copper's Song
Book, page 193.

ton. There was no resident doctor at that time, but, by sending a 'runner' off two and a half miles along the cliff-top to Newhaven, medical help could be summoned in the dignified shape of Dr Noakes, who would saddle up his cob and usually be in attendance at the sick-bed before the messenger had returned. He was much respected and as he rode down the village High Street in his all-weather smock and tall, beaver hat all the men would doff their caps and the ladies curtsey. His methods, it seems, were a little unorthodox but nevertheless effective. He is reputed to have cured a small boy of thirteen of asthma by recommending that 'he should smoke the strongest shag in a clay pipe'. The lad was rid of his asthma but became addicted to the pipe, which he smoked profusely until the day he died some seventy years later.

Such was the farm and village life into which James had been born. His education was scanty but he did attend a Dame School for a while where he had to 'say his book'. Pupils were each given a horn-book which consisted of a piece of paper printed on both sides with the numerals from 0 to 9, the alphabet, the vowel sounds and the Lord's prayer. It was set in a wooden frame and protected on each side with a sheet of transparent horn. A handle was attached and the overall shape was not unlike a square hand mirror and it was held in the same way. The scholar was made to read and memorize what was printed on the book and then, with it held behind his back, repeat out loud what he had learnt. This was termed 'saying his book'. One night the whole family was sitting at the fireside when a neighbour called in to complain to his parents about young James's mischievous behaviour that afternoon. The young offender sat in the corner earnestly reading his book and effecting complete oblivion to the goings on around him and the neighbour, growing exasperated, turned to him and shook his fist. 'A-agh! Ye young monkey!' he threatened. James's mother sprang to his defence. 'Don't you call my Jim monkey when he's saying his book,' she cried. This survived as a family saying even down to when I was a boy, when the most effective way to chide anyone for interrupting was to say, 'Don't you call my Jim monkey when he's saying his book.'

The Dame who ran the school was an ardent needle-worker and even moving about amongst the children in class she was always busy with her needle and thread. To maintain order when the chattering and giggling seemed to be mounting above a controllable level, she would punish the guilty ones by tapping them smartly on the head with a thimbled finger.

Honest John and his wife Charlotte did a sterling job in bringing up their large family in those difficult times. By discipline and example they created a strong family bond and earned from their children a love and respect which endured throughout their lifetime. There were six girls and three boys and James was the second son. The family Bible tells us this. There, on pages specially provided for the purpose set between the Old and New Testaments and headed 'Family Register', are the fading but still legible, steel-nibbed entries. The earliest entry in the Bible is the birth of John in 1817, but examination of the Parish records in Rottingdean Church shows that the family have been in the village since at least 1593. In that year the marriage is recorded of Edward Coper, so it appears that in the three hundred and seventy-odd years since then we have at least acquired another 'p' to our name if little else.

In the churchyard, down in one of the less frequented corners where the grass grows tall under the ilex oak trees, there is a group of lichen-splattered, weather-stained headstones that bear mute witness to the fact that we have never wanted to travel far afield in search of fortune and have always been content to call Rottingdean our home. Some of the older villagers used to call this part of the graveyard 'Copper's Corner' and as children we used to count up the 'Coppers' to see how much it would amount to in cash. Someone would be sure to remind me that when the time came around for me to make my contribution the total would be increased by one shilling and one penny.

When James left school he followed his father on the farm and in time also became a farm carter. But that is not the only paternal example he followed. Honest John had a reputation for singing and it was upon this more than anything else that his fame rested. A songster was welcome in any company for there was nothing like a song to cheer flagging spirits and what's more it was cheap. All you needed was a stout heart, a good pair of lungs and an ear for a tune, and audiences were appreciative and uncritical. James inherited his father's love of the old songs and in this he forged the strongest link in the chain that connects us with those distant times.

He was renowned for the depth and carrying properties of his voice. When later he had become farm bailiff and in the early mornings gave the men their orders for the day's work from his office at the northern end of the village, the cries of 'You go down New Barn and muck out, Jesse. You carry on where you left awf up Slonks, Woblow. Dido and Shirty, you go down the mow at Newlands,' carried to their wives, lying in bed and listening half a mile away, and they would know where to send the children out with food at lunch-time.

Grand-dad was a man who commanded a good deal of respect. He was, after all, the bailiff of a farm that employed nearly sixty men and boys the year through, providing work for the biggest portion of the employable males in the village. It was a position that demanded a certain amount of dignity and he conducted his life accordingly. In a parochial poem about local characters he was described as 'the bold and stately Brasser' and this is exactly what he was. I remember him well in his latter years and, although rheumatics had robbed him of some of his poise and he was reduced to walking with the aid of two sticks and riding his horse side-saddle because the effort of getting astride proved too much for him, he was still dignified and the power of his voice was undiminished. Even normal, indoor conversation would boom out from the great vaults of his chest filling those small, cottage rooms with ringing sound and, for a small boy, being lovingly dandled on his grandfather's corduroyed knee could suddenly turn into a terrifying experience. Tearfully, one day, I am told, I went to my mother and said, 'Why does Grandy shout so? He froughtens me.' His kindly and well-meaning attempts to send his grandchildren to bed with a lullaby were similarly heavy-handed, and a blood-curdling rendering of 'Admiral Benbow' ensured that haunting visions of the unfortunate Admiral, who 'lost his legs by chain-shot' and 'down on his stumps did fall and so loud for mercy called', would cause fretful dreams on a tear-soaked pillow.

Not only his voice but everything else to do with Granddad was on the large side. Even his features, while being somewhat roughly hewn, were saved from any hint of severity by a wide, generous mouth. In his pocket he carried a gigantic watch about three inches across which was tethered to his waistcoat by a solid silver chain as big and clumsy as a stud-stallion's curb-chain. The watch and chain together weighed just over a pound. It was almost as if a lifetime of association with huge, lumbering farm-horses had helped to set the pattern on which his life was moulded. He even used horse medicines to cure life's little ills—horse liniment to ease the crippling aches of rheumatics, or the 'screws' as he called it, and horse pills to deal with internal irregularities.

'Work hard and play hard' was one of his mottoes, and his philosophy was summed up in a verse which he was very fond of quoting:

> 'The world is round as a wheel,
> The sting of death we all must feel.
> If life was a thing that money could buy
> The rich would live and the poor would die.'

When walking about the farm from job to job to see that the men kept their backs bent and good progress was being made—for it was reckoned that the bailiff's boots were the best dung—he habitually wore a 'pepper and salt' mixture Bedford cord jacket, corduroy trousers and a bowler hat and always carried with him his old muzzle-loader shotgun in case Providence should throw in his path a dinner in the shape of a hare or a brace of rabbits or partridges. One day up the Saltdean Valley near Slonks Hovel he stopped to reload and carelessly left the hammer cocked and a percussion cap in position. He had poured a charge of powder down the muzzle and was ramming the wad home when the gun fired, shooting the ramrod straight up through the brim of his bowler hat. The flange at the end of the ram-rod whipped the hat away off his head and up out of sight. He returned home hatless, his composure badly shaken and firmly resolved to be more careful in future. Three days later the local postman picked up the hat a good half mile from where Grand-dad had lost sight of it, and delivered it with the next morning's letters. The old man wore it for years after that with the hole still in the brim.

His younger brother, Tom, also inherited the love of the old songs and together they sang them all the time they could. Tom, like James, spent his early life as a carter on the farm, and by hard work and thrift later became the landlord of the Black Horse, the sixteenth-century white-washed public house in the High Street which now enjoys the distinction of being the only one in the village that has not been entirely re-built. There he formed a team of hand-bell ringers, kept the traditional Mummer's Play alive, and was the host to a gathering of all the old village singers every Saturday night. He was a non-smoker but when every other man in the company was smoking a clay tobacco pipe, not wishing to appear unsociable by not having one, he would 'smoke' one with an acorn or a cob-nut stuck in the bowl to constrict the draught and make it more comfortable to suck on.

He was a genial man and popular as a landlord. With his head of white hair and fringe of white whiskers bristling out from under his chin and stretching from ear to ear, he bore a distinct resemblance to his brother, James, but he had a lighter voice and was, I think, a little less stolid. They were great friends and with their repertoire of songs they were always good company to be in. Their singing brought them a certain amount of renown, locally, but in 1897 they were instrumental, although I do not think they ever realized it, in furthering the cause of the preservation of English traditional songs on a much wider scale. In that year, Mrs Kate Lee came to the village to stay at Sir Edward Carson's house up at Bazehill. She had heard of James and Tom singing their old songs down in the Black Horse and, wishing to learn more about them, invited them up to the big house one evening. They put on their Sunday clothes and went along. Any embarrassment they might have felt at being asked to sing in front of a lady in an elegantly furnished drawing-room instead of at home in the cottage or in the tap room of the 'Black 'un' was soon dispelled by generous helpings from a full bottle of whisky standing in the middle of the table with two cut-glass tumblers and a decanter of water. They sang, they drank and sang again and all the time Mrs Lee was noting down the words and music of their efforts. They kept this up all evening and were not allowed to leave until the bottle on the table was empty and the book on Mrs Lee's lap was full. After several more evenings, proceeding on the same lines as before only with different songs, she returned to London with what was later referred to as a 'copper-ful' of songs and it was, we are told, largely as a result of her great enthusiasm about her meeting with them that the formation of the English Folk Song Society came about in the following year. At the inaugural meeting of the Society, Mrs Lee read a paper which said:

> . . . I shall never forget the delight of hearing the two Mr. Coppers, who gave me their songs, and who are now members of the Society. Mr. James is a Foreman of a farm and his brother is the Landlord of the Black Horse Inn, a very small public house. They were so proud of their Sussex songs and sang with an enthusiasm grand to hear and when I questioned them as to how many they thought they could sing, they said they thought about 'half a hundred'. You had only to start either of them on the subject of the song and they would commence at once. 'O, Mr. Copper, can you sing me a love song, a sea song or a plough song?' It did not matter what it was, they looked at each other significantly, and with perfectly grave faces off they would go. Mr. Thomas Copper's voice was as flexible as a bird's.

He always sang the under part of the song like a sort of obbligato, impossible at first hearing to put down. I hope to show you the beautiful variety of these songs which, by the way, I only collected in November last. . . .[1]

They were both made Honorary Members of the Society in recognition of their contribution of songs.

Then Tom took a larger public house called the King's Head at Chailey some fourteen miles away, and at least once every summer a trip was made by family and friends in a farm waggon pulled by two horses to visit him in his new home. These outings were well conducted but rather noisy affairs. I can remember one of them made in later years in Arthur Dilley's coal lorry, which was a great step forward in the march of progress. It was a solid-tyred, chain-driven Napier and would rumble along at a breakneck speed compared with the steady plodding of the horses.

When the great day arrived the lorry rolled up outside the cottage at Northgate at about eight in the morning. The brass radiator and headlamps were specially polished up, the floor of the lorry was swept fairly clear of coal dust and clean wheat sacks laid down for additional comfort. Grand-dad's armchair was lifted up and placed at the forward end so that he could ride with his back to the driver's cab and forms were placed along each side for the rest of the company. We children sat on the floor. Food and drink in plenty for the journey were loaded on. Crates of beer and home-made ginger-beer were put under the forms in the shade to keep cool, together with sandwiches and cakes wrapped in clean, linen cloths.

After several stops at cottages along the road to pick up all the passengers, off we went up the road and out over the open down leading to Lewes Road. Clouds of dust whirled between the hedgerows as we spun along at a cracking pace with every one in the best of spirits. Grand-dad said, 'Let's have a song then. Any dam' fool can sing at night. That takes a good man

[1] *Journal of the English Folk Song Society*, Volume I, Number 1 (1899).

to sing a song afore brakfus'.' The singing had to be loud to rise above the general rumbling and chugging of our progress. So we crashed through the early morning peace of the hill country, a happy carriage full of folk in a clamorous little world of din while all the surrounding hills and sky remained still. The sheep looked up from their grazing and the skylarks were fluttering in the blue above but, for all that we could hear above the general racket, their flight might have been voiceless.

At the King's Head a warm, hospitable welcome awaited us and after a good lunch there were races or pony rides for the children while the men, in shirt sleeves with braces dangling, tried to throw a cricket ball over the poplar trees that marked the boundary of Uncle Tom's land.

That evening the journey home suffered a severe interruption when the chain broke. This was considered, particularly by the ladies, to be a very bad stroke of luck after such a wonderful day. It happened, however, conveniently close to the Newmarket Tavern which was thought to be a considerable consolation by the men. When we eventually took to the road once more the singing and harmonies were just a little looser than usual.

In 1922 Grand-dad was persuaded to write down the words of his songs by the daughter of the farmer for whom he worked. These were the old songs that he had loved all his life, songs that he remembered hearing as a boy in the 1850s and at the foot of one, 'The Shepherd of the Downs', he wrote, 'My Grandfathers used to sing this song.' With painstaking care and drawing on the scanty resources of his 'thimble-tapped' education, he sat at the kitchen table at night scratching out the couplets and stanzas—some of them pure poetry—that had delighted him as a lad and he had carried in his head for all those years. The spelling was laborious but effective and it is with respect, not ridicule, that we smile at some of his more ambitious efforts. Note this verse, particularly the third line, from a song which he called, 'Hears a Dew Sweet Loveley Nancy'.

And when the wars are all over their will be Peice on Every Shore
Whe will Drink to our Wifes and Children and the Girls wich
   whe adore.
Whe will Call for lickore mirrle[1] whe will spend our money free
And when our money his all gone whe will Boldly Go to Sea.

Over thirty songs were written out in this manner, taking
him several long evenings crouched over his book in the light
of the oil lamp. Usually the words came readily enough but
sometimes, when a line proved reluctant to be winkled out
from the recesses of his memory, he would go back to the
beginning of the song and hum the whole thing quickly
through up to the point where the difficulty occurred. Then,
sure enough, in its correct sequence out the fugitive would
come and he would pin it to the page with his pen before it
eluded him again.

Granny Copper died four weeks after I was born, but in
spite of this I have a very clear picture of her in my mind from
all that I have heard about her and from old photographs.
She bore the burden of no less than five Christian names, no
doubt inflicted on her in obedient respect and recognition of
aunts and other female relatives in various branches of the
families. But although she had been christened Frances Emily
Jane Mary Ann, she was always known as Emily. She was as
sweet and subdued as Grand-dad was strong and strident and
they made an excellently matched pair. She was subject to
frequent attacks of hay-fever and sneezed, it is said, twenty-
four times before breakfast every morning. Her life was tran-
quil and rewarding but her death was touched with tragedy.
It came about suddenly in a family drama that was still talked
about quite a lot when I was young. Of their five children,
two girls and three boys, Charles Spicer, the youngest, was
Granny's favourite. He grew into a fine man, six feet three
inches tall and with a physique to match, and like the rest of
the boys was brought up on the farm. I still have the flail
which he used for threshing out the corn when the season
came around. A few years back when I showed it to an elderly

[1] liquor merrily.

friend of mine who had been on the farm all his life and had often used a flail in his earlier days, he took it from the nail on the wall where it is usually kept, and holding it in the position as if he were about to use it, he exclaimed, 'What a monster. This must have belonged to a giant.' 'It did,' I said.

Charles left the farm and joined the Brighton Police Force where his physical strength and the ability to use it stood him in good stead when dealing with rough houses and brawls. He was still the apple of his mother's eye and she cut out and saved all the notices in the local press referring to her son's career as a constable. In 1913 the Brighton Police decided to hold their annual sports meeting at Rottingdean and one event in particular was looked forward to by Charles and his older brother, Jim—my father. They both excelled in the art of throwing, having had plenty of practice as lads on the farm where, as any country boy knows, flint-throwing at anything from a gate post to a sitting hare is a favourite pastime. They both duly entered the open competition for throwing the cricket ball. The eliminating heats were thrown and eventually Charles and Jim were left to oppose each other in the final. Jim, losing the toss, had to throw first and, putting everything he could muster into it, threw the longest distance of the day. This really gave Charles something to beat, but with a herculean effort he beat it by one yard. He won the first prize—a porcelain and Sheffield plate biscuit barrel with a pink rose pattern on the side which stood on the sideboard at home for many years as a reminder of the sad event—for sad it turned out to be.

Immediately after making his throw he walked across to the fence at the edge of the field where the family had been watching clutching his side and gasping with pain. 'What's wrong?' they asked. He shrugged it off with a grin. 'O, nothing much. I think I've twisted my gut. A few pints down the Black 'un drackly 'll soon put that right.' But three days later he was on duty in Castle Square when he collapsed and was dead before they could get him to hospital. He was twenty-eight years old.

His mother was inconsolable. The shock of the loss of the son who meant so much to her engulfed her life completely. She was a changed person, grieving continuously and attending his graveside daily to kneel in prayer. One day, only a matter of months later, she failed to appear back at the cottage at tea-time. Enquiries at various relatives' cottages in the village brought no trace of her. Where could she be? Then at 7 p.m. came a rap on the back door from a neighbour who brought the news that she had been found. She had died suddenly while kneeling at Charles's graveside and was found lying across it with her hands together as if in prayer. The family reeled from shock at this second tragedy following so soon after and so closely linked with the first and the villagers sighed and nodded their heads: 'She died of a broken heart,' they said.

This marked, if not the end, the beginning of the end of Grand-dad's long farming career. For over forty years he had worked on the same farm and for the better part of that time as bailiff—keeping the records, paying the wages, buying stock, cattle and draught horses, looking after crop rotation and diseases of animals and all the sundry jobs there are to be done on a farm of that size. It was 3,000 acres in all, about 1,000 acres of which were arable land, and to keep it in good heart it required the services of nine four-horse teams, two teams of eight oxen and fifty-five men and boys employed throughout the year. The total weekly wage bill, not including overtime at lambing-time and haying and casual labour at harvest, was a little over £30. I have a copy of a wages and farm detail sheet in which the farm-hands and boys, many of whom are referred to by their nicknames, and the teams of horses or oxen with which they worked are all lumped together under the general and somewhat ambiguous heading, 'Cattle on Mr William Brown's Farm, Challenors, Rottingdean. 1896.'

At the head of the list is 'Foreman James Copper. Wage 18/-.' Then follow the details of the nine four-horse teams which include:

Carter. 'Oistup' Read (William) Wage. 14/-. Boy. Jim Copper: 4/-. Team. Tommy, Tippler, Prince, Swallow.

The oxmen were paid a shilling more a week than carters while shepherds and cowmen, second only to the foreman, got 16/– a week. A labourer's wage was 13/–.

Grand-dad's office was in the store room opposite Challenor's farmyard, which has since become a bowling green. Inside the desk at which, seated on a high stool, he spent much of his time writing and reckoning, were knots of new whip-lash, horse and cattle medicaments and a box of frost-nails to be handed out to the carters on frosty mornings so that they could drive them into their horses' hooves to prevent them slipping on the icy roads. On the top of the desk was a sheaf of dog-eared invoices impaled on a wire filing device and a number of books on veterinary practice and horse and cattle management and there was about the place a peculiar, but not unpleasant, atmosphere made up of the various smells of cattle-cake, locust beans, new waggon rope and horse liniment all laced together with St Julien tobacco smoke. Behind the door, hammered up with a horse nail, was the annual Laine Acreage Sheet. The arable land was divided into forty-eight laines or fields many of whose names—like Slonks, Links and Loose—go back to Saxon times. The word 'slonk', I have read, is an ancient word meaning slaughter so it can usually be accepted as denoting the site of some battle, and this theory may well apply to Slonks Laine on the Rottingdean farm. Links Laine has been levelled to a great extent out of the surrounding slopes and on the east and south sides is bounded by a high bank some ten to twelve feet above the natural level of the ground. This seems to have given it its name as 'hlinc' is an Anglo-Saxon word meaning ridge of land or bank. 'Loose' might come from the Saxon word 'hleowth' meaning warmth or shelter, for Loose Laine is sheltered from the south-west wind by a steep hill.

In 1914 Grand-dad made out his last Acreage Sheet for in the following year he retired and handed the bailiff's job over to my father, Jim, who moved into his cottage. Grand-dad moved around living with each of his children in turn, all of whom by that time had families of their own. But his knowledge of farming the Sussex hill country was still respected and his advice sought by more than one farmer in the area.

Old Brasser died singing. In his seventy-ninth year he had lain abed for some while ailing—in any case his 'screws' would not allow him to get downstairs—and he had not felt much like singing for a long time. One morning his voice was heard loud and clear raised in one of his favourite hymns, 'The day thou gavest, Lord, is ended'. The family downstairs were delighted, it must surely be a sign that he was feeling better; but on going to his room some ten minutes later they found that his time had come. The old man had kept singing until the end.

# James Dale Copper (1882–1954)

My father, Jim, was born in haying time 1882 at Oving-dean, a tiny village two miles over the hill from Rottingdean. Grand-dad at that time was still a carter and was living in a little flint cottage at the end of a row of four next to Oving-dean Grange and almost opposite the church. There was a large old pear tree that had been trained up the end wall which reached to the ridge of the gable and gave the place its name—Pear Tree Cottage.

At the age of four Jim first went to school in the tiny one-roomed building up the hill on the road to Woodingdean where there were only seven or eight other pupils. Very soon after this, however, Grand-dad was promoted to Farm Bailiff and they moved back to Rottingdean into the newly built farm cottages at Northgate where the family has lived ever since. Here he attended the Church of England School where there were five classes under the headmastership of Mr Lloyd, who was referred to by the boys as 'Bandy'. The younger children sat on long forms or benches and learnt to write on slates with a slate-pencil tied to the wooden frame with a piece of string. They later graduated to sitting at a desk with a copy-book and pen. For the privilege of going to school a fee of one penny a week was payable each Monday morning when Bandy called the roll, in answer to which the children had to call, 'Penny present', instead of merely 'Present' as for the remainder of the week, and march up to hand over their pennies. Bandy had a unique but effective system of punish-ments and rewards. Naughty girls were severely reprimanded but the boys received a good pummelling in the ribs with his heavy fists and the cane was resorted to only for the more extreme cases. On the other hand he encouraged conscientious effort by awarding good conduct tickets with values varying from five to fifteen points. Virtue being rewarded in such a tangible form gave diligent pupils the advantage of being able to trade in the points they had earned in exchange for school equipment. A new slate-pencil could be obtained in return for twenty points, a pen-holder and nib for thirty, a one-foot rule for forty and an exercise or copy-book for fifty points. A new slate, which luckily was only required in the rare event of the original being broken, would cost three hundred points. These were the legitimate uses of the point system but it also lent itself to a certain amount of under-cover trafficking. As there was no form of identification on the tickets, they were negotiable and so, of course, became a form of currency and the more advanced and less scrupulous pupils could hoard up a wealth of points to be bartered for anything from a jack-knife to a kiss from a recalcitrant sweetheart. But whether the points system was used legitimately or otherwise it seemed to work very well.

The school curriculum was not confined to academic studies. No doubt Mr Lloyd reasoned that as these boys were the sons of working men and destined, in the fullness of time, to become working men themselves, some form of practical tuition should be offered them. The bigger boys could weed the garden, clean the windows or scrub out the school lavatories and in return they would receive at the end of the week a suitable number of mauve heart-shaped cachous which he kept in a large glass jar on the window-sill behind his desk. All the children, both boys and girls, were taught to knit worsted scarves and mittens and Jim continued to produce excellent hand-knitted cardigans, socks and gloves up to fairly late in his life. This talent proved invaluable in the shortages of clothing during the Second World War.

Youngsters were still brought up on strict lines of discipline and if respect for elders and betters was not always earned it was rigidly enforced. Jim and his contemporaries, being members of the cottage community, had to pay suitable salutation to the gentry who lived in the large properties round the village green. The parson, the doctor, the landowners and farmers all received due acknowledgement in the form of a doffed cap or a small, bobbing curtsey from the girls. The master of the locally-kennelled harriers, Mr Steyning Beard, also demanded to be recognized as he strode down the High Street. 'I've very often felt the draught of 'is riding crop across the back of me calves,' said Jim. ''Specially if 'e thought you'd bin scrumpin' his apples.' There was no resentment on the part of anyone, at least within our circle, at this order of things. It was accepted as the natural pattern of life; after all you sang about it in church on a Sunday:

> 'The rich man in his castle, the poor man at his gate,
> God made them high or lowly and ordered their estate.'

The penalty for not practising this code was well known to all and the offence dealt with summarily. 'Come out here, Jim Copper,' the offender would be summoned before the headmaster, 'you passed Parson Thomas on Pump Green yesterday afternoon and you didn't raise your cap.' Then, unless Jim could produce a 'ten-ticket' as a forfeit, the lesson that incivility to dignitaries would not be tolerated was driven home by Bandy's cane and carried back to Jim's desk in two stinging palms.

But no matter how stern the hand of discipline or how little the rod was spared nothing could entirely suppress the high, animal spirits of young country lads. When a few of them got together there was never any lack of ideas for a frolic or a bit of sport. With an ingenuity born of having a minimum of equipment, even the long, dark, winter evenings were beguiled with such games as 'Tickle-the-Spider', 'Dickie Dyke' and 'Looby on a String'. Their games, like their clothing, were by necessity somewhat rough and home-spun. 'Tickle-the-Spider' was a favourite pastime in the village street and was operated in the following manner. A button, suspended on about six inches of thread, was attached by a pin to the window frame of the victim's cottage and another long piece of thread attached just above the button would be led away to a convenient hiding place across the street. This, incidentally, is an indication of the absence of traffic, pedestrian or otherwise, in the High Street in those days. From this point the boys would jerk the thread back and forth causing the button to tap smartly against the window pane. The unfortunate occupant, thinking somebody wanted him, would open his door and peer into the darkness up and down the street for the non-existent caller. After several repetitions and when at last a prank was suspected by the long-suffering householder, the 'spider' would be retrieved with a sharp tug on the thread and, with a flurry of chuckling and a tattoo of hob-nailed boots retreating rapidly down the red brick pavement, the rascally band would melt into oblivion.

Another popular game was a variant of 'hide-and-seek' usually played in the all-encompassing dark of a moonless night on the open downs at the back of the village. The quarry, 'Dickie Dyke', was at intervals required to give some indication of his whereabouts by striking sparks from a flint with a piece of steel. In response to the call, 'Dickie Dyke strike a light', he would strike fire from his flint three times then immediately dash off from that spot to evade being captured by his pursuers.

A classic prank that must be centuries old remained a favourite when Jim was young. A bundle of firewood or some equally attractive 'bait' would be left in the roadway after dark but visible in the flickering oasis of orange light thrown by one of the three oil lanterns that illuminated the village street. Attached to it would be a length of black thread the other end of which was held by one of the boys where they lay in hiding and the next unsuspecting passer-by, stooping to grab the fortuitous gift that no prudent housewife could have resisted, would be astonished to see the bundle of wood suddenly whisked aside and disappear into the blackness. On one occasion this joke misfired for when Mother Murphy, wise in the ways of village boys, saw the bundle of pimps beckoning her at the street-side, she produced a large, black elastic-sided boot from under her skirts and planted it firmly on the thread before stooping down to take the coveted prize.

But back in the cottage the winter evenings would often see the whole family seated about the small kitchen. The girls and Granny were grouped round the table darning socks or busy with their needles, turning shirt tails into shirt fronts, their faces gleaming in the warm glow thrown by the oil lamp. Grand-dad was over in a gloomy corner with a last between his knees snobbing the family's footwear, while Jim held a tallow candle to give additional light. As he hammered he would most likely be singing one of his old songs with everyone joining in the chorus. A song seemed to make a task a little lighter and the long winter evenings a little shorter. That is the way Jim learnt most of the songs and sometimes, intent on the story of the song that his father was singing, he would allow the candle to wander till it threw shadows on the work. The song would be abruptly interrupted while Jim was reproved and then resumed at the precise point at which it had been left—often in the middle of a line. The overall effect was rather odd,

> 'So now he is a-living in his cottage contented
> With woodbine and roses growing all round the door,
> He's as happy—
>
> (Dam' boy, hold the candle so as you kin see the boot y'self then I sh'll be able t' see it too!)
>
> —as those that's got thousands of riches
> Contented he'll stay and go rambling no more.'[1]

After dinner on a Sunday Grand-dad would give the boys a halfpenny each and that was their pocket money for the week. Down at Miss Allwork's little baker's shop up the steps next to the Black Horse it would buy eight cannon balls or four black rounds or four pear drops. Chocolate at a halfpenny a bar was a luxury to be avoided, for 'two mouthfuls and it was gone'. As constant reminders of the outcome of bad or

[1] 'Spencer the Rover.'

good behaviour there was always a cane lying across two nails in the wall and a glass jar of boiled sweets hanging from a hook in the centre of the ceiling, from which the wages for any gardening done or errands run during the week were dealt out with the weekly halfpenny—one sweet for each job. They were doled out with so much ceremony and so many delaying tactics that you might have thought the donor was reluctant to part with them. But this was really just a little play-acting, partly because it amused Grand-dad but more to impress upon the recipient the value of what he was about to receive. The procedure nearly always followed the same pattern.

'I dug that bit o' garden, like you said, Dad.'

'O, did ye, mairt? All right, we'll see about that drackly.' Then he sat down in his chair and took the Sunday paper, slowly, selectively turning the pages. The minutes ticked by until,

'What are ye hanging about here for then, mairt?'

'I did the garden, Dad.'

The old man seemed not to hear. He lit his pipe and blew a long jet of smoke upward till it flattened out and billowed under the ceiling. Some seconds later,

'C'mon, c'mon, you'd better be gettin' along, hadn't ye? You'll be late for Sunday school.'

Driven by desperation Jim at last got down to the point and timidly announced, 'I'm waiting for my sweet, Dad.'

'O, damnation, yes. I forgot.'

Not until this little charade had been played out would he reach down the jar, carefully take out a sweet and hand it over.

With two compulsory visits to church and two to Sunday school every Sunday the spiritual welfare of the children, one would have thought, was amply provided for, but in addition there were weekly Band of Hope meetings and the occasional exhortations of a visiting lay-preacher at the little chapel just off the High Street. Regardless of denominational preferences these were regularly attended and formed part of the frame-work of social life in the village. As a family we were Church of England but Jim, as a lad, preferred to go to Chapel. When you walked in through the ancient doorway of the village church you passed into a world of oaken pews, starched surplices and droning incantations that was as far removed from your everyday life as the ancient building itself was from the contemporary farm cottage under whose roof you laid your head at night. But in the chapel there was a total absence of dignity and circumstance. It was furnished with kitchen chairs, the preacher wore ordinary clothes, the atmosphere was homely and, what is more, you were allowed to laugh. Laugh out loud and the preacher would laugh with you. One evening when the children were all assembled there awaiting the arrival of some strange preacher the whispering, giggling and chair-scraping was suddenly silenced by his appearance from a doorway at the back. His slow, dignified passage down between them and up the steps and on to the platform at the other end stunned them completely. He stood there and surveyed the room benignly. Tall, erect and with a mop of snowy, white hair and a patriarchal beard. 'This evening,' he boomed in a rich west country dialect, 'I'm a-going to talk to you about the gospel of the Apostell Paul.' Seeing the wide, incredulous eyes and the mouths dropped open in awe, he added, 'Now I don't want you to sit there and think that I ham the Apostell Paul.' Then he slapped his thigh and threw back his head and let out a gale of laughter which spread through the room like a gorse fire.

Down in a lean-to, wooden hut at the back of a cottage on the corner of the High Street and Malthouse Lane (now called Steyning Road) an enterprising businessman kept the only mangle in the village, for the privilege of using which he charged one penny. It was of stout timber construction with a flat table top about three feet high. On the table top, resting on two or three wooden rollers, was a deep box the same width as the table but about half its length. This was filled with beach pebbles to give it weight. With a system of chains and winding gear this box could be moved backwards and forwards lengthwise along the table top, moving smoothly along on the rollers. There were one or two spare rollers around which the laundry was wrapped and as one roller came out from under the back of the box with the clothes nicely pressed, another, loaded with clothing, was inserted in the front and so on, backwards and forwards. As this was heavy work the weekly mangling job was usually given to Jim and his older brother, John. Frequently there were two or three other boys there with their mother's washing at the same time. Then the task would lose some of its boredom and become an opportunity for a bit of fun. There would be attempts to break the speed record for rolling the box from one end of the table to the other and this almost invariably led to the box running off all the rollers and sitting flat on the table. Being full of beach and weighing the better part of two hundredweight it would resist all the concerted efforts of the boys to restore it to its proper position. One of them, usually the youngest, would have to go down to the cottage and incur the wrath of the owner by asking him to come up to the shed and lever the box up and re-insert the rollers.

Brother John was of a very different make-up from Jim. Where Jim was quick-witted and mischievous, he was tardy and steadier of nature. It was indicative of the quiet, peace-loving type of man he was going to be that he started keeping bees while he was still just a lad. One day he spotted a swarm in a fig tree just below him as he looked over the flint wall at the end of the cottage garden. On his side the wall was only about three feet high but it dropped about seven feet on the other side where the tree stood. He could see at once that taking the swarm would be a two-handed job so, invoking the authority that his superiority in years and strength gave him, he sent Jim round to the other side of the wall to stand under the swarm with a straw skep while he remained above and attempted to smoke them from the limb of the tree and make them drop. Jim hated bees but, being less frightened of them than he was of John, he went. Standing on tip-toe against the wall beneath the swarm he held the skep high over his head to catch the bees as they fell while John commenced smoking operations. Some of the swarm had dropped and John was delicately applying his smoke screen trying to induce the queen to fall when an errant bee started to buzz around Jim's head. Round and round it went, getting closer to his neck every moment. Both his hands were needed to hold the skep in position so swatting was out of the question. He shut his eyes and gritted his teeth and, flushed with fear, fought manfully to remain composed until he could feel the draught of the bee's wings just behind his left ear. That was enough. He dropped the skep, bees and all, and ran away as fast as his legs could carry him and did not stop until he was safely in the kitchen at home. He got a good hiding from John, of course, when Mother was not looking, but even that was preferable to the threat of a hovering bee. At any rate there was no suspense about the hiding—he expected it and he was not long in getting it, but with the bee, 'It was all that buzzing and hovering that did me,' he said.

The children were seldom bored or at a loss for something to do. For one thing their domestic duties, which ranged from getting the milk from the cowstalls in the early morning to shutting up the chickens at night with all the other fetching and carrying jobs in between, left them very little leisure time. But being bred in the lap of southern England with the broad, rolling downland on either hand and behind them and the wide expanse of the English Channel before them, they were surrounded by nature's gentlest attributes which offered many pleasant pursuits whenever time permitted. At the edge of the hayfield the young Lothario could thread wild strawberries on a long stalk of grass and offer his sweetheart a necklet of succulent rubies or gather a posy of summer sweetness to declare his affections. The more adventurous could snare rabbits on the hill or catch fish from the foreshore, go bird's-nesting in the woods or drop a starling from the top-most bough with a well-aimed catapult. They were brought up in close contact with nature and the moods of the sea and the wiles of the weather were all around them. The flowers in the field and the birds of the air were their daily companions and all the time the peaceful and patient tenor of life seemed to penetrate even the thickest of exteriors and leave some kind of mark on their hearts.

This was the sort of world that bred and moulded the old-time English countrymen. The moulds are lost and gone for ever and once the last of this sadly diminishing breed has disappeared we shall never see their like again.

# Robert James Copper (1915–)

Jim was very keen on keeping written records of various happenings in his life, and, having made the effort to note things down, he showed a marked reluctance to throw any of his writings away. I still have numerous books and papers containing his jottings that were found in his effects after his death. Not so very long ago I came across his diary for the year 1915, and as this was the year in which I was born, I opened the book with, I confess, a certain feeling of anticipation. It would be interesting, perhaps even flattering, but at least illuminating to learn, after all these years, his reactions on the day that his first-born and—as it transpired—only son came into the world. I turned the yellowing pages carefully until there, preserved to this day in his clear, legible handwriting, was his entry for the 6th January.

6ft. of 4″ × 2″—2 prs cross-garnetts Ct.Fm.C/sheds.

He was Estate Carpenter at the time on the Rottingdean farms and it refers to materials purchased in order to effect repairs to the cow-sheds at Court Farm. So much, then, for the impact my arrival on the scene appears to have had on Father.

I think it is permissible to take the charitable view and to assume that the omission was not so much an indication of the insignificance of the event as proof of the fact that Jim was a practical man rather than a dreamer. His concern with the cow-shed door at that moment was not dimmed in any degree by pipe-dreams of having sired a future prime minister.

At a time when world-shattering events were changing the map of Europe only a few miles away across the Channel this inconsiderable, almost non-occurrence, took place in the cottage next door to Grand-dad's at Northgate and, although Granny Copper was still alive and living in a state of mourning for her lost son Charles, her death was only four weeks away. After she died our family moved next door to live with Grand-dad and, as we have already learned, the responsibilities of the farm bailiff's job were passed down a generation on to Jim's shoulders. My mother, Daisy Louise, was born in London, and had met and married Jim while she was in the area working in domestic service at Sir Thomas Leonard's house at Woodingdean. As a family we were a small close-knit unit which never expanded in number after my arrival, my sister Joyce and I being the only two children.

The cottage was the end one of a row of four, all of which were occupied by farm workers, and life in this little community was still going on very much the same as it had for many years before; the old standards of behaviour and outlook were practically unchanged. A good, clean, well-nourished level of living was maintained but only by dint of careful planning, strict economies and hard work. The plumbing compared with present day left quite a lot to be desired. At No. 1, which had been built for Grand-dad as bailiff, we were lucky in this respect and had a water tap indoors fixed over the shallow, biscuit-coloured sink in the scullery, but the other three had a tap and stand-pipe fixed to the wall just outside their back doors and a communal sink, or 'slop-hole', in the middle of the back yard. The carter's family that had taken over occupancy of No. 2 when we left had a rickety wooden bench standing outside under the window upon which stood a galvanized iron bowl with a short wooden handle, kept upside down when not in use in order to prevent it from collecting rain and becoming a bird bath. On the window-sill was a large chunk of carbolic soap and day-to-day toilet activity was carried out, particularly in summer, in the open air. A large oval galvanized bath hanging on a nail on the wall was taken down only twice a week. Once on Monday for the weekly washing of the family's clothes and again on Saturday for more thorough personal ablutions. On summer evenings after a hard day in the hay or harvest field, the men could be seen washing outside their back doors with a great show of throwing cupped handfuls of water up into their faces while the soap-suds dripped off their elbows and a terrific amount of puffing and blowing went on. Seeing them bareheaded—for they were seldom hatless, even indoors—one noticed how the lower halves of their faces, scorched to a dark mahogany by daily exposure to the sea-air and sun, contrasted sharply with their snow-white cap-protected foreheads. Afterwards they would sit on their sun-warmed back doorsteps smoking their pipes and holding a desultory conversation interspersed with long, pipe-puffing pauses until the daylight had finally disappeared behind the windmill and the bare ridge of Beacon Hill in the west.

Among the many early perplexities of life, one of the most puzzling was Granny Copper's copper. It was built into the corner of the scullery, a huge block of rendered brickwork made white by weekly applications of hearth-stone. This solid lump of masonry housed the fifteen-gallon copper which was used to boil the weekly wash and was heated by a fire underneath, access to which was gained through a heavy iron door. The copper itself was a very old one and actually made of riveted copper, which must account for the name that has stuck to them long after these utensils were made of galvanized iron. It was some eighteen inches in diameter and was kept covered by a wooden lid made from one-inch thick boards with a heavy wooden handle. In those days in order to be strong and durable everything had to be large and heavy. But the impression firmly rooted in the mind of a small boy was that everything to do with it—the copper-fire, the copper-lid, the copper-stick—seemed in some strange and inexplicable way to be related to the family whose name they bore. Even those in other cottages in the village, and in those days very few homes were without them, seemed to come within the bounds of some vague proprietary claim.

The copper was an item of great importance in the household. It was, in some senses, the hub around which the entire wheel of respectability and decency revolved. If 'cleanliness was next to godliness' then the copper was almost in the nature of a shrine at which, every Monday, nearly every member of the family, to a greater or lesser extent, performed his or her weekly devotional duties. The copper had to be filled by bucket from the brass tap over the sink, the firewood chopped and stacked conveniently close to the copper-hole, the fire lit and three large galvanized bath tubs placed on the scrubbed-top table—one for washing, one for rinsing and one for the 'blue-water' to help whiten the whites. My favourite job was trailing and dabbling the cube of Reckitt's blue, wrapped in a piece of flannel and suspended on a length of string, round and round in the bath of clear water until, growing deeper and deeper in colour by degrees, it attained an exciting shade of Mediterranean blue. Most of these preparatory jobs were performed by Jim, who liked to have the fire lit by 5.30 a.m., and we children helped or hindered with slight, well-intended efforts. But the high priestess of this weekly ritual was Mother. Enveloped practically from neck to ankles in a coarse apron of hessian tied with tapes behind and with her sleeves tightly rolled to well above her strong, dimpled elbows, she would move energetically and methodically about the jobs of wash-day. She stirred the copper from time to time with the copper-stick, the middle of which was worn thin and splintered from much use in levering out the water-heavy contents on to the stout, circular lid to be carried, dripping and trailing boiling water, across the brick floor to the wash tub. Each time this was done great billowing clouds of steam filled the scullery, misting the windows and condensing in a rash of droplets on the lime-washed ceiling. There was such an air of bustling industry, such a smell of soapy steam, and usually cold meat for dinner into the bargain, that Monday was an unfavourite day.

It was proudly boasted, when everything had gone smoothly, that the entire wash would be washed, mangled and on the line before we had left for school at ten to nine and if it was a 'good drying day', it would be dry-mangled, ironed and airing before we got home for tea. But if there 'wasn't much dry in the air' or on those hopeless, drenching days in winter, the little cottage kitchen would be full of sodden sheets and garments suspended on a criss-cross line, and the fire in the kitchen range would be effectively screened for days on end by a wooden clothes-horse draped with wet clothes. But in any event, the copper itself would have done its job by midday Monday. The fire would be raked out, the whole structure whitened and the firedoor black-leaded, the lid scrubbed and replaced, tables and tubs returned to their usual positions and everything was normal again for another week.

So our young lives were regularly punctuated with wash-days; and early risings, smells of wood-smoke, steam and soap suds, cold meat for dinner and fractious parents were the price paid for the undeniable comfort of clean clothes and freshly laundered sheets.

In many other ways, too, cottage life was what today would be regarded as primitive. All the family's footwear was still repaired at home and on snobbing night Jim would take down the box of tools from the top of the larder and make a start immediately after tea, for it was an unwritten rule that by eight o'clock all the work should be done so as not unduly to disturb 'next-door'. They, of course, showed similar courtesy but Jim made a further concession to good relations by designing and making a special last to cut down noise when the work was in progress. Grand-dad's last, which had been until then in constant use, was mounted on a single, vertical piece of wood that rested on the floor, and when the hammer was swinging the thumping that came forth seemed to rock the very foundations of the cottages. So Jim mounted a last on a piece of horizontal timber with two semicircular pieces cut out of it to make it fit across his knees. Consequently his legs took the thrust of the hammer blows and acted as shock-absorbers, reducing the noise to a minimum. This was quite typical of him. He liked to live in peace and his love of harmony in his songs was extended into his life and became apparent in an oft-repeated expression that he 'liked 'armony in the 'ome.'

While Jim hammered at his work, armouring the soles and heels of our boots against the rough flint roads and trackways they would be expected to encounter with heavy metal tips, pelts, studs and hobnails, he would invariably start to sing and it was standing at his side while he was snobbing that I first heard and began to learn the old songs some thirty-odd years after he had done precisely the same with Grand-dad.

When the work was done he would sometimes take down his clarionet, which was kept suspended from two hooks underneath the lower shelf of the dresser, and after mouthing and licking the mouth-piece to moisten the reed, he would start to play. He favoured the jaunty, lively, Irish-jig type of tune which he played tolerably well but only at the expense of a great deal of concentration which was shown in his facial expressions. Apart from a rather disconcerting trick of suddenly and unintentionally jumping either up or down an octave, he had the habit of moving his eyebrows up and down his forehead as if following the shape of the tune, and a scowl on everything in the lower register would be followed by a look of surprise on every high note.

After supper, holding on to the waggon rope that served as a bannister rail, and carrying my candle in a chipped enamel candle-stick, I would climb the two steep flights of stairs to the attic. The floor space was large and covered the whole ground area of the cottage but the ceiling sloped sharply down to the eaves on either side. It was used partly as a store room, and at certain times of the year there would be a strong smell of apples from behind the curtain draped on one side of the room where they were being stored for the winter in shallow wooden trays. But always in evidence was the smell of camphor balls liberally scattered amongst the clothing and bedding stored there in tin trunks and wooden boxes to deter the ravaging moths. After gabbling prayers on the knee-cold lino, I would climb into the tiny bed close up under the eaves where the ceiling was at its lowest and lie there looking at the tracery of cracks in the ceiling like a map of some distant uncharted lands far beyond the scope of my guttering candle flame, or listen to the patter of heavy raindrops outside on the tiles no more than a foot away from my head. To hear the bad weather so near and yet seemingly so far away added to the sense of warmth and security that was associated with home and presently sleep dusted the eyes and my little world would be lost for a while.

There was another row of four, slightly older, farm cottages at Northgate and two more at Balsway, about two hundred yards along the road. At Hope Cottage, which was one of those at Balsway, lived Uncle John, Aunt Jenny and our three boy cousins, Charlie, Ron, and David, and sometimes on a Sunday we would visit them to have tea. In the cottage at home a strict code of discipline was maintained and we children were left in no doubt as to our place in the domestic scale by the constant repetition of such adages as 'Little boys and girls should be seen and not heard'. But on such occasions as these Sunday outings to Uncle John's, our very best party manners would be given an airing. They were, I fear, too often kept shut away in the chest of drawers with our Sunday clothes or, just occasionally, hastily called into service if the vicar or someone from one of the big houses stopped in the street to speak to us. But there was something about going out to tea on a Sunday in a white shirt, a tie and grey flannel knickerbockers that was conducive to a certain restraint in one's behaviour. In winter a fire would be lit in the front room and we would sit around in the soft glow of an oil-lamp that stood in the centre of the table and as the ladies ran in and out bringing in the teapot, the cups and saucers and plates of bread and butter and cake, placing them on the table round the lamp, their hideously exaggerated shadows would leap from the room's dark corners and dance about on the floral wall-paper and up on to the ceiling.

After tea the cover would be removed from the harmonium and Aunt Jenny, after filling the wheezy bellows with a piece of frantic foot-work, would play some of our favourite hymns while we all joined in singing quietly and reverently. Uncle John's shepherd's crook standing in the corner, and the knowledge that his sheep-dog was chained outside asleep in the barrel that served as a kennel, lent an impressive realism to singing:

'Loving shepherd of they sheep,
Keep they lambs in safety keep . . .'

The hymns would be followed, with an almost imperceptible change of mood, by solos from the women-folk each of whom in turn would sing their own personal party song, sweetly and simply. Mother would sing 'Down in the Valley where the Bluebirds Sing', and Aunt Jenny always obliged prettily with 'The Old Rustic Bridge by the Mill'. By this time John and Jim, both of whom, from the cradle up, had been steeped in the old singing tradition, and who had shown admirable restraint throughout the evening, were struggling manfully to refrain from singing something more full-blooded and more in character. When at last the dams burst, a song like 'Warlike Seamen' came gushing out in full flood.

'The first broadside we gave to them which made them for to wonder,
Their main-mast and their rigging came rattling down like thunder
We drove them from their quarter they could no longer stay,
Our guns did roar, we made so sure, we showed them British play.'[1]

From then on the evening was more relaxed and things were back to normal.

Living at Northgate, which was outside the village proper, and beyond the northern extremity of the High Street, we were called 'up-streeters'. This was a term used to describe the rural and farming community as opposed to 'down-streeters', who were the children of the shop-keepers or people who worked in the shops or in the builder's yard opposite the pond, and lived within the bounds of the village itself. The

[1] See Jim Copper's Song Book, page 193.

word 'opposed' is used advisedly for in any game like football or cricket the teams fell naturally into two groups—'up-streeters' against the 'down-streeters'. The 'up-streeters' were regarded by the village children generally to be slightly inferior and were frequently subjected to such jibes as 'clodhopper' or 'swede-basher' or greeted in the school playground by a chorus of 'To be a farmer's boy'. But one notable victory for the bucolic side took place on a Saturday morning near the windmill on Beacon Hill. The party had fallen into the two usual sections and the cross-talk and insults had developed into a pitched battle in which both sides pelted each other with cow-pats that had dried and formed crusty discs which could be picked up cleanly and thrown as missiles. After some time of heavy exchange we, the 'up-streeters', seemed to be losing a bit of ground, so Cousin Ron and I, inspired by the kind of inventive genius that is the hallmark of our island race, left our confederates temporarily and ran down to Uncle John's cottage to return with two coal shovels. With these we were able to scoop up the cow-pats that had not lain long enough to dry out. When slung from the shovels these proved to be a far more devastating form of ammunition and the 'down-streeters' to our great glee were routed.

The devil, who had pretty much his own way with us lads during the week, had an uphill struggle on Sunday, particularly with those of us who were in the church choir. On that day he had to repulse sometimes as many as five spiritual onslaughts in the course of the day. The battles were fought in the calmest of atmospheres and started off with early communion. The serenity of Sunday mornings in those distant days is almost impossible to imagine for those who are not old enough to remember it and it is recalled with intense nostalgia by those of us who are. The roads were empty of vehicular traffic and while the heavy shire teams munched and snorted in their muzzle-worn mangers and stomped on the cobble-stone floors of their stalls, their harnesses hung on the wall and the carts and waggons stood idle in the yard, providing playgrounds for families of farmyard kittens.

The only thing likely to shatter the Sabbath calm was the passing of Midget Cheal's milk float—and shatter it it usually did at about half past seven. Pulled by an angular, long-stepping cob proceeding at a vigorous trot, the two-wheeled vehicle would go lurching past, sending up clouds of swirling dust and followed by a pack of barking mongrels. The polished milk pail hanging from the large brass tap in the churn swung crazily from side to side and the small cans hanging at the sides rattled madly like rows of toneless bells. Midget himself, standing on the step at the back with his hat brim blown back, would slap the reins on his horse's flanks and shout like a Roman charioteer urging his steed to still greater efforts. Once the clatter of his progress had receded into the distance the road would be entirely deserted except for pedestrian churchgoers and the church bells would ring for morning service, pealing out loud and clear over the whole village. At first the big bell called slowly, almost casually, 'Come to Church, come to Church', followed by the little one's imperious reminder, 'Hurry up or you'll be late', until the church clock itself chimed in its signal for eight o'clock. Those tardy risers, who had not by that time reached the lych-gate, knew that their late arrival as they shuffled breathlessly into their pews, stumbling over the hassocks while the parson led the first prayer, would attract the critical stares of those already there.

Breakfast on a Sunday was a more leisurely affair than on week-days and even then there was still time to clean out your rabbit hutches before going to Sunday school. After twenty minutes of scripture readings and conscience-pricking moralizing by one or another of the lady teachers who gave their time so nobly in such a good, but admittedly difficult, cause, the forces of evil would provide just sufficient time for the ungodly to run up Whiteway Road and grab a pocketful of gooseberries from Sir George Lewis's garden before climbing the crooked stairway up into the choir gallery in time for Matins. The service proceeded but after a while the cultured tones of the Vicar and the droning responses from the body of the church ceased to hold the attention and the wayward eye wandered to the Rev. Hooker's bust over the pulpit. One would never have guessed from his benign expression that he had been a great crony of the smugglers in his day. Through the clear glass window on the north wall the sun could be seen striking down through the trees and throwing mottled shadows on the swelling green turf mounds of ancient and long-forgotten graves. The birds of the air flew where fancy led them and I felt complete creature sympathy for the tattered but lingering red admiral butterfly that made repeated but ineffectual efforts to burst through the thin screen of glass that alone separated it from the whole wide realm of God's free, breezy, sunlit world without. The turgid moments dragged on, but at last it would be time to sing again and the sound of the organ in the opening bars would provide a chance to indulge in the fruits of scrumping. Trying to sing the Te Deum with a mouth full of half-masticated gooseberries had its own technical difficulties, apart from the fact that it took a great deal of courage to maintain your own piping treble against the long, deep reverberating bass notes that came rolling out from under Mr Brooker's moustache. They filled the whole church with pulsating sound and even vibrated in my own chest as I stood close beside him, watching out of the corner of my eye his white, winged celluloid collar slip up and down over his angular Adam's apple and marvelling that such a vast volume of sound, vying with the organ itself, should come booming out from one small human frame.

Morning service over I would occasionally walk out to Hope Cottage, our second home, and offer to help Aunt Jenny in the house. This was a concession I would never have dreamt of making at home but helping other people outside your own immediate family held attractions that for some obscure reason were not found at home. For this behaviour, if discovered, we were always suitably admonished. 'That's right! You'll never lift a finger to do anything indoors but you'll run your backside off for anyone else.' But there was at Aunt Jenny's a certain good-natured laxity that was most appealing, and the pleasant task of sitting in the sun on the brick steps outside the cottage and shelling garden peas into a battered colander, while 'Boofer' the cat lolled back luxuriously on the warm brick pavement at your feet, making half-hearted dabs with a forepaw at the flies within her reach, would be rewarded with the offer of a home-made rock cake straight from the oven—this, at Northgate, would never have been tolerated so soon before Sunday dinner. Down at the end of the garden path beyond the neat, green lines of runner-beans, peas and potatoes, where the nettles and summer grasses grew waist high, Uncle John would be tending his bees. Wearing a straw hat, yellow with age, and draped round with a piece of lace curtain tied under his chin and pierced conveniently to admit the stem of his favourite briar pipe, he could be seen moving quietly and gently amongst the white painted hives, softly singing all the while one or another of the old songs.

'As I walked out one midsummer's morning
For to view the fields and to take the air,
Down by the banks of the sweet prim-i-roses
There I beheld a most lovely fair.'[1]

The calm of the morning and the tranquillity of the scene combined to print an indelible picture on my mind.

At that time there were many of the old characters still alive in the village. They were, purely and simply, the products of their own initiative and of their immediate locality and had consequently developed into highly individual characters. They were natural and unselfconscious to a fault and if they were a little bizarre it was not for effect but because that was the way they had grown.

Tommy Harwood was one of that school. He lived in a small, wooden shack tucked away from the south-west winds under the trees on the east side of Beacon Hill. He earned his living at part-time farm work and gardening at the big houses, and the tools of his trade—gardening fork, rakes and hoes— were kept in an old, six-feet-long, ex-army rifle box outside

[1] 'Banks of the Sweet Primroses.'

his shack to allow as much as possible of the space inside to be used for sleeping and cooking his frugal meals. In spite of his spartan existence he was a good worker and contrived to keep clean and tidy and, even if he did spend most of his spare time in one or another of the five public houses in the village, he commanded a certain amount of respect from many of the villagers. One night, having made his way home from his nightly peregrinations between the village pubs and carrying, it is safe to assume, rather more beer than usual in that short, stocky frame, his unsteady hobnailed boots accidentally kicked over the small Beatrice oil-stove which was his sole means of cooking and heating in the tiny hovel. The spilt oil flared up and in a very short time there was nothing left of Tommy's humble lodging but an untidy heap of blackened, smouldering debris. Undeterred, he threw out his tools from the rifle box and took up the 'vacant possession' thus afforded. Next day, for increased ventilation in his new home, he drilled holes in the sides and henceforth lay down each night in conditions that must have borne a remarkable and disturbing resemblance to the interior of a coffin. He showed no signs of ill-effects, either physically or mentally, and made the box his permanent home and continued to live there for a number of years.

Down at the southern end of the village where the street ended right on the cliff-edge and the 'Gap' sloped down to the foreshore, three or four crooked, wooden huts, leaning against each other for support, housed the knots of sisal rope, anchors, lobster pots, shrimp-nets, seaboots and other paraphernalia of the part-time longshoremen who owned them. There, in a strong atmosphere of Stockholm tar, stale bait and shag tobacco, they would sometimes sit mending nets or making up cork lines, and were a constant source of fascination to most of us boys. One of these boat owners was Bob Lively, a tall, lean, gangling figure of a man who as a lad had left the village, along with others, on a Government scheme to go sheep farming in Patagonia. He had returned some forty years later comfortably off in pocket but rich, too, in worldly experience. The years spent away from home in the bleak isolation of a remote hill sheep-farm station with a staff of gauchos had left its mark on Bob. His long straggling moustaches, drooping down below the level of his chin, gave him a sad and doleful expression, and during his years of riding on horseback over the Patagonian hills he had become adept at rolling thin, twig-like cigarettes with one hand and striking his vestas with his thumb-nail. He wore a battered widebrimmed felt hat and presented a figure far removed from the shepherds of his native downland. He had retained the peaceful, slow-moving tenor of the local sheep-men but, quite unconsciously, his Sussex accent had been adulterated with strong infusions of South American. He spoke softly and unhurriedly and had an odd habit of pausing in mid-sentence to whistle a few tuneless notes as if to add weight to what he was about to say. He was rarely seen without his capacious plaited-straw fish basket, the contents of which were a dark secret and could range from half a dozen lobsters to a brace of rabbits, but always included a bottle of Scotch whisky. He would frequently press the neck of the bottle to his lips and suck it like a greedy calf. His humour was dry and unsmiling. One day, when asked the basket's contents, he drawled, 'That bag, son, is a one-man business. But if you really want to know, I got in there—', and here he paused and whistled a couple of bars of some unidentifiable tune, '—the world's one and only troop of performing oysters.' Some seconds later, 'One li'l ol' fella, wal, he's worth a king's ransom, ol' buddy. He gives a perfect imitation of Caruso singin' under water.' Then his deadpan face would pucker again into a low whistle.

Down by the slipway where the dark green seaweed hung in lank, dripping tresses and the sand-hoppers skipped in the cracks in the concrete, Bob's boat could sometimes be seen lying aslant on the drying sands waiting for the returning tide. I would have everything ready for a trip out to lift his lobster pots or an hour or two hooking. The anchor with the cable neatly coiled would be 'stowed up for-'ard', 'thole pins' in the 'gun'-el', 'stretchers' in position, 'oars shipped and at the ready', everything 'shipshape and Bristol fashion' and all ready to get 'under way'. All that was missing was the ship's captain who would not, it was certain, put in an appearance until closing time at the White Horse, outside which I would wait for hours if it seemed there was the slightest hope of him putting to sea. Eventually he would emerge, slightly unsteady on his feet and blinking in the bright afternoon sunlight. 'All ready then, boy?' 'Aye, ready and waiting, Mr Lively.' At last everything seemed set to go. Down on the foreshore we would pull the boat across the flat sands towards the water until the tide washed around her keel and presently, with Bob seated slumberously in the stern, a final push from me would set her afloat and she would lift on the waves and become a vibrant, living thing. Taking the oars I would head her out to sea and pull out across the dark blue waters over the ridge of rocks we called the Bar until the figures on the fore-shore had grown small and lost their identity. In a panoramic view of the downland and sea, the village could be seen set in a gap in the long line of white, chalk cliffs that margined the water, while on the western hill the black hooded wind-mill, arms flung widespread, stood like a lonely outpost sentinel. Nothing would be said. Bob might even be asleep and there was no sound save the slap-slap of the water on her clinker-built sides and the rhythmic creaking of the oars in the thole-pins. Bob would sometimes scoop water over the side in an old bait tin to dowse the leather on the oars to stop the dry, monotonous sound, or, on a very hot day, remove his hat and cool his bald and sweating pate with a sea-soaked handkerchief. Soon we would drop anchor, throw our lines over the side and sit there while the small craft lurched and rolled beneath us and the afternoon sun scattered a path of glittering sequins from the far horizon to the spot where we lay. Sometimes we would catch fish, sometimes we would not, but there was always the incomparable delight of being out there, elevated to another realm above that of ordinary, shore-bound mortals.

The love of sport on the Sussex downland, particularly

that around our village home, was deeply ingrained in all our family. Jim and I frequently wandered over the hills in search of something for the pot, like rabbits, hares or partridges, anything that would earn Jim some beer money. But we also loved a walk over the hills in the early morning for no other reason than to appreciate the beauties of nature. On one occasion in the height of summer, which is the only time of the year that it is possible, he roused me at 3 a.m. to walk to Kingston Ridge, about three miles away, to watch the sun come up between Mount Caburn and Firle Beacon. He made certain we arrived there before first light and from the eminence of our position on the top of Kingston Hill we sat in the shelter of a clump of gorse bush in complete silence while the night sky was still peppered with twinkling stars. Jim lit his pipe and took an apple from his pocket and handed it to me to beguile the time until the daily miracle of dawn arrived.

Presently the faintest suspicion of a glow appeared far over in the east and as the minutes slipped past it grew in height and intensity until the horizon, low down and many miles away across the weald, was clearly defined. Slowly the glow spread upwards and outwards putting out the stars one by one and driving the shades of night back over our heads until the rim of the blood-red sun itself peeped over the edge of the earth and slowly gilded the crests of the downs to where we were sitting, while the village some 200 feet below us was still in semi-darkness. The skylarks had anticipated the sun's arrival and gone trilling up into the sky to greet the new day with a burst of song. How aptly did the poet, A. S. Cooke, describe this as the 'Gates of Dawn', for emerging gradually between the two prominent hills before us—Mount Caburn on our left and Firle Beacon over to the right—the light spilled across the flat floor of the wealden acres until it flooded right up to the foot of the ridge on which we sat, and the golden glory of day had arrived. With the daylight the wheel of life started to turn with more vigour. Cloddy birds[1] joined the larks in song and rabbits scampered on the steep hillside

[1] Corn buntings.

below us. A dog and a cockerel down in the toy village in the valley added to the rising tide of daytime sounds and not until then was our silence broken. Jim stood up, 'Well, boy, now you've seen something that you'll remember all your life.'

Any walk over the hills with Jim was made richer by the many tales he could tell about the various places we visited. One evening, climbing a steep, chalk cart-track and drawing near the top of a high hill, I noticed over the brow a small cottage, more of which became visible with every step we took. I had never seen it before. This part of the downland was particularly bare and you could walk for miles up and down the interfolding hills without seeing even a fence in those days. I was about to ask Jim what it was, when he said, 'There's old Baldy's cottage. Did I ever tell ye about him?'

It was a bleak, desolate spot and there was something in the tone of Jim's voice that made it seem even more sinister. 'No,' I said. We walked on for a bit in silence and I think he was getting the facts sorted out in his mind. There was a stiffish breeze blowing when we reached the top of the hill and as we approached the cottage we could see that it was empty. We came up to it and stood there looking down over the smooth hills that fell gently away to the sea, some three miles away. The wind moaned under the eaves of the slate roof and into the cottage through a broken window-pane. The sun was rapidly sinking in the west. It was deep orange in colour and split across horizontally by a narrow, solid bar of black cloud that ran right across the western sky. Twenty miles away the last visible point of land ran out into the sea, marking the end of the wide sweep of the bay. We turned and looked back and a small but dense plantation of wind-torn sycamores and beech trees was visible just below us down the north-eastern slope of the hill. 'That's Newmarket Copse,' said Jim, 'that's where he was going to bury 'im.'

'Bury him?' He had me intrigued, which was just what he had intended. 'Yes.' He paused. ''Twas like this—leastways this is what my old Daddy told me. When 'e was a boy, about

1850 time, there was an old fellow by the name of Baldy lived up 'ere all alone. Decent little old kiddy he was, about fifty-five years old, with bushy white whiskers; but 'is head was as bare as a badger's backside. 'E used to work at the farm down yonder in the valley.' He pointed with his stick, 'You can't see much of it from 'ere though, because of the trees. 'E was a carter and 'e'd been down there for years. 'E used to keep 'imself pretty much to 'isself, like, and I reckon that's what got the poor old bugger into trouble, really. Y'see the chaps 'e worked with used to pull 'is leg a bit about 'avin' a "tidy old stocking", 'cos 'e was a bit tight-fisted with 'is money. Mind you, they didn't mean no 'arm y'know—just used to tease 'im a little, that's all. But, look 'ee, there was one fellow there by the name of Jack—'e'd only been taken on as a casual to 'elp out with the 'arvest—'e used to sit and watch Baldy when they were sitting under the shocks of wheat 'avin' their bit of "bait"—just the same way as a stoat garks at a rabbit; only worse. Old Baldy was a 'appy, soft-natured sort of chap and didn't seem to notice it, but several of the other men—after it was all over—said they'd seed 'im sitting there sort of brooding, as if he was working something out in 'is 'ead.

'Well, one Friday night Baldy was mooching up the 'ill towards 'is cottage and just as 'e drew abreast of this clump of fuzz-bush'—we had been strolling slowly down the hill towards the trees and Jim indicated a patch of gorse on our right—'out jumps this 'ere fellow from the bushes, runs up to poor old Baldy and ups with a shot gun and lets 'im 'ave both barrels between the eyes. Kills 'im stone dead. 'E takes Baldy's money pouch, with two and a 'alf sovereigns 'arvest money, out of 'is pocket then carries 'im down this path where we're walking and into the copse.'

We entered the plantation in the fast failing light, Jim walking slightly ahead. He stopped at the foot of a beech tree and with his stick traced out a rectangle in the carpet of dead leaves. 'Next morning Baldy's body was found just 'ere!' He spoke slowly and I looked away from him for I could tell by the break in his voice that he had a bit of a lump in his throat. His mood was infectious and I jumped visibly as an owl crashed through the branches just over our heads. "E was laying alongside an open grave,' he continued after a while, 'and whether the other chap was disturbed or whether 'is nerve give out at the last minute, nobody knows. Any road 'e didn't bury 'im as 'e no doubt 'ad intended to, but the cottage was ransacked and even then 'e didn't find old Baldy's money what 'e kept in a large earthenware jar underneath the sink. About thirty-five pounds in golden sovereigns, I think there was. The only thing missing was 'is old muzzle-loader shotgun and that was found a week or two later in the dew-pond just down the 'ill below where we're standing.

'They sends the 'ue and cry out for this 'ere Jack—y'see they knowed it must 'ave been 'im what done it when 'e didn't turn up for work next morning—and by and by 'e was picked up at Portsmouth. Trying to enlist in the Navy 'e was, but they fetched 'im back and I 'ave 'eard tell 'e was the last man to be 'anged at the County Gaol at Lewes. So that was the fate of poor old Baldy—shot by 'is own gun for two and a half quid as you might say.'

His voice stopped and an unnatural vacuum of silence closed around us, broken only by the wind sighing in the branches overhead. The sun had quite disappeared leaving only a faint, rapidly diminishing glow in the west. Under the trees it was quite dark and I felt suddenly cold.

'There you are, boy,' his voice broke loudly on to the still-ness, 'now you know the story of Baldy's cottage.'

'Come on,' I said, 'let's go home.'

We boys did all the jobs on the farm that were usually allotted to those of our age, like being 'tar-boy' at sheep shear-ing time, 'stand-fasting' at harvest and 'bond-winding' and raking the chaff out at threshing time, but by the time I had left school in 1928 the last big farm had been sold and farming in the area on anything like its previous scale had ceased to exist. My first full-time job, therefore, was not on the farm but as lather-boy in the local barber's shop and as such I probably came into close personal contact with more of the older men of the village than most of my contemporaries. Many of them were of Grand-dad's generation and were still steeped in the manners and modes of fifty years before. The shop occupied a ground-floor room in a small cottage called the 'Nest', which lay just back from the High Street, close to the village school. Down that well-worn step through that little old doorway stepped a fair cross-section of the local male population. The shepherds, the racing stable lads, the longshoremen and the local gentry. There is no more effective social leveller than the barber's chair. Sitting side by side at any one time we might have a retired admiral from one of the big houses and a hog-man or a renowned poacher and one of the parish magistrates. Each in his turn would make a contribution to the conversation no matter what the subject and as that tiny room was too small to accommodate more than one topic at a time the talk was always common to all. Being totally enveloped from the neck down in the red and blue striped hair-cutting cloths, or with two-thirds of their faces completely hidden by an inch-thick foam of lather, there really seemed to me to be little to choose between the ones from the large properties bordering the village green, and those from the crooked little cottages huddled together lower down the street near the sea.

Being one of the social centres of the village, the little shop was often a hot-bed of local gossip and it was here that all the topicalities were exchanged. But at any time one of the older men could suddenly whisk the conversation back three parts of a century by telling of something that had happened in his youth. Old Jim Murrell, well on into his eighties, did just this one day. 'Old Mick Murphy', he said, 'was the only chap I ever knew to have his hair cut with a shovel.' Such an incongruous announcement was, of course, bound to put an end to all other conversation and we all listened while it was related how Mick, working as a navvy on the main coast road when they were making the cutting and building the embankment at Greenway, found that while working hatless because of the heat, his hair kept falling in his eyes. So he 'did no more' than up-end his shovel and, laying his hair across the edge of the blade, hammered away with a large flint until the offending fringe was severed.

One of the regular visitors to the shop for his weekly shave was 'Pup' Moppet. He was a teg shepherd, a kind of under-shepherd who looks after the young 'second-year' ewes. He was of indeterminate age and his tall, rangy figure could often be seen striding along the white chalk road out of the village up on to the open down. His approach was usually signalled by the stomping of his long-staffed crook on the road surface and the mad, reedy notes of a battered mouth-organ, which he played with great enthusiasm but with a total disregard for melody. Back and forth across his mouth went the instrument, letting out crazy arpeggios that seemed to put heart into his heels. ' "Territorial March", Bob,' he would holler as he passed, interrupting for a moment a wildly incoherent succession of chords that were quickly resumed to fade gradually into the distance as he strode on.

He was a kind man and a simple man, but an unfortunate impediment in his speech had earned him the reputation of being far simpler than he actually was. He was frequently the butt of sharper wits in the shop which caused a great deal of amusement to the company in general but, by accepting the jibes and insults with good-natured resignation, he invoked my boyhood sympathy. That is why I remember so clearly the time that Pup bit back.

One Saturday afternoon, above the snip-snip of scissors and the scraping of a keen blade over a week's growth of whisker-stubble, the talk—as it often did—turned to gardening.

'I could do with a pinch of cabbage seed,' said Pup to the company at large, 'if anyone's got a bit to spare. I only wants enough for about 'alf a 'underd plants.'

'Sham', the local bookie, pricked up his ears. His nimble brain saw at once the opportunity of yet another laugh at Pup's expense. 'I'll bring y' some tomorrow morning, if y' like. I've got a little left. 'Tis a lovely little drum-head cabbage—"Fish's Superb" they calls it.'

The following morning—barbers were open on Sunday mornings in those days—Sham delved into his waistcoat pocket and presented Pup with a small portion of seed screwed up in a little piece of newspaper. Pup thanked him and left. Directly he was out of earshot Sham, to the delight of all present, confided that what he had so generously given was nothing more than cooked herring's roe crumbled into the 'cabbage seed' it so closely resembled.

It was several weeks later that Pup amazed Sham with, 'I just 'ave got a nice row of stuff come up from that 'ere seed you give me.' Sham was puzzled, to say the least, and upon further enquiry was invited to look for himself when next he was up that way and was given the exact location in the garden where the crop could be found. 'Just past the onion bed, on the same side, looking towards the windmill.'

If Sham was puzzled, I was on fire with curiosity and on my way home to tea that day, I made a detour up through the Hog Platt to find out for myself what sort of crop had germinated from the peculiar seed.

I could hardly believe my eyes. There, emerging from the soil and pointing to the sky in a long straight row, were about two dozen red-eyed herrings' heads.

Pup was never again taken for quite such a fool.

# A Song for Every Season

Jim never tired of talking about the old days in the village when he was a young man, any more than I did of hearing about them. That is how I garnered such a rich harvest of his memories. The world those old-timers lived in always seemed to me to be more exciting, and more colourful and the men themselves more highly individual.

Village folk were insular to a degree that is difficult for us even to imagine. They had been brought up to grow their own vegetables, mend their own boots, bake their own bread and brew their own beer as well as to make their own amusement. They remained on the whole much the same as their forbears, uninfluenced by outside forces in their dress, their speech and their methods of work and ways of spending their leisure. Many of Jim's workmates in his earlier years had been born and bred in Rottingdean in the first half of the last century and they still had their feet firmly planted in that era. Men like Dave 'Monk' Moore, the old oxman, with his flowing white beard and gold ear-rings whose favourite song was 'Spencer the Rover'; Harry 'Hunter' Bishop, a general labourer and 'good old bacca-chower' who always sang 'The Pleasant Month of May'; Jim 'Comfort' Godden who earned his nickname by responding to any item of disastrous news with the compassionate remark, 'What a comfort there wadn't any li'l children.' Or 'Fodge' Goddens, the flail thresher, who loved to sing 'The Lark in the Morning':

> 'The lark in the morning she arises from her nest
> She ascends all in the air with the dew upon her breast,
> And with the pretty ploughboy she'll whistle and she'll sing,
> At night she'll return to her old nest again.'[1]

[1] See Jim Copper's Song Book.

They still wore their round frocks (or smocks), their boot-legs, their mole-skin caps, their mutton-chop whiskers and stout leather wrist-straps. It is true that some could neither read nor write but they could carry in their heads enough knowledge, and often wisdom, to fill a library. The very nature of their work demanded a detailed acquaintance with a very wide range of tasks together with a good deal of manual dexterity. From thatching a roof to laying a hedge, from shearing a sheep to draining a field, all jobs made claims on their various skills as the seasons revolved. Add to this a fund of tragic or amusing stories and in many instances a repertoire of old songs and spice the whole with a keen sense of fun and dry, almost sly, wit and you have some of the qualities that went into the make-up of the old-time farm-worker. Their slow, methodical way of approaching work concealed a deceptive expediency in getting a job done and in a like manner their slow, drawled-out speech was often the vehicle for surprising wit and sagacity. Jim himself had an amusing knack of playing with words and would deliberately introduce something very close to a malapropism just for the sheer fun of it. But the odd thing was that instead of losing its meaning the result often had an even greater impact. I stood with him one day looking southward down the Salt-dean Valley to the sea. In his day he had seen it green with downland turf and dotted with sheep, ploughed into rich brown ribs like corduroy and waving fair with yellow corn, but now the brick and mortar excrescences of speculative builders were spreading along the valley and up the hillsides at an alarming rate. He looked silently for a while, leaning on his stick, then, 'I dunno what my ol' Daddy would say, boy. Look at it. 'Ouses, 'ouses, 'ouses—that makes me prostrate with dismal.'

Progress in farming had not kept up with that in industry. Improvements had been made, like the introduction of steam power and threshing machines, but there was a certain tardi-ness in adopting them. Many of the methods employed were still precisely the same as they had been for a thousand years.

They ploughed their land with teams of oxen, sowed their seed by hand, reaped the corn with sickles and threshed out the grain with flails as their Saxon anccstors had. Their lives were hard but uncomplicated and through living and working close to nature they had a clearly defined and well-balanced sense of values. In the main they were content and were aware when they sang, in the words of one of their old songs, 'Peace and Plenty fill the year',[1] that it was not so very far from the truth.

They knew peace. The Crimean War was a distant and shadowy memory that had long since ceased to ruffle the village calm and the Boer War was yet to come. Although they still sang in praise of heroes or in glorification of the slain—Earl Cardigan and Lord Raglan figured in their songs and pictures of the Battle of Alma graced their parlour walls —their immediate horizons were unclouded by wars or threats of war.

They had plenty. Plenty, that is, in the sense that they had sufficient. The 'hungry forties' were forgotten and, providing they were willing to exercise strict economies, work hard in the garden and keep a few ducks or hens, they were rewarded with a constant supply of wholesome victuals throughout the year. Life, of course, was not easy and small expediencies which fell under the heading of 'self-help' were the necessities of a continuing existence. The contents of a frugal larder could be supplemented by the timely arrival of a rabbit caught with the full permission and encouragement of the farmer or an occasional hare or brace of partridges whose demise, had the farmer known, would not have been met with the same enthusiasm. Mushrooms and blackberries from the hills, and prawns, winkles, shrimps and the odd lobster from the foreshore, each in their season added variety to the diet.

On warm summer evenings when a flat sea quietly lapped the beach, shoals of mackerel would sometimes run close inshore after the myriads of whitebait that could be seen

[1] 'Brisk Young Ploughboy.'

flashing and curving in a quicksilver cloud just under the glass-like surface of the water. A look-out posted on the cliff-top would shout to the villagers who lined the water's edge and point towards any approaching shoals that came within his view and when the mackerel came streaking and thrashing into the shallows—so thick that they jostled each other out of the spluttering water—everyone would dash in knee-, thigh- or even waist-deep to scoop the fish up in wicker baskets, pieces of lace curtain or anything else that came to hand. Some of the women used their aprons or the long, voluminous folds of their skirts as make-shift fish nets. The Lord had been kind and thrust a tasty meal right under their noses and good food was theirs for the taking.

The opportunity to pick up something for nothing was seldom missed but the methods of acquisition were not always so irreproachable. 'The good Lord,' Jim used to say, 'helps them that help themselves,' and he was not above bending the meaning of the last two words until he felt free to indulge in what he regarded as a little mild, justifiable larceny. From time to time a sack of corn for the chickens or a basket of apples for the children or a piece of timber for a chicken-house repair would find its way up to the cottage, usually after dark, and I am certain no receipts could have been produced in respect of their purchase by legitimate means. Many and various were the means adopted for earning an 'honest crust' and I recall one instance of Jim's ingenuity.

He was a keen and accomplished bird-catcher and from time to time employed all the methods known in the district of snaring our feathered friends. He had all the devices of bird-trappery and a pretty formidable armoury they made. The contents of one corner of his garden shed would be enough to send waves of terror running through the entire bird population. The large silk-net to imprison skylarks, the clap-net used on the ivied house wall for sparrows and star-lings, and the wily trap-cage in the lower half of which sat his well-trained call-bird who, with a sweet, seductive song— like the sirens with the sailors—lured unsuspecting victims to their doom. Jim had all of these—not forgetting the catapult that he carried in his pocket with a supply of small round beach pebbles about the size of muscatel grapes for frightening the scavengers off the pea patch—and he was skilled in their use. He was also a dab-hand at the lowly art of bird-liming for linnets—the cottager's canaries—who adhered inescapably to sticky straws placed breast high around their drinking places. He knew birds' habits and where they fed and nested and he seldom missed an opportunity to catch anything that might earn him the price of a pint in a certain bird-shop in Brighton.

We were walking one day over the hill near the windmill when he spotted ten or a dozen 'branchers' feeding on a patch of seeding thistles on a piece of enclosed, private land belonging to one of the properties in the village street opposite the green. 'I'd like to get a net round that lot, boy,' he said with a gleaming eye, 'they're fetching eighteen pence apiece in Swaysland's.' ('Branchers' were young goldfinches before they attained their bright red and yellow plumage and if caught at this stage they adapted readily to cage life and developed into sweet songsters.) 'Well, I don't think there's much chance of you doing that,' I said, 'That bit of land belongs to Miss C. and being stuck up on the bare side-hill like that she'd be bound to spot you from the cottage if you tried without her knowing. And she wouldn't give you permission—that's certain.' 'Yeah, wal,' he smiled cunningly, 'we'll see.'

Miss C. was a prominent and respected resident. A councillor, a church woman and keenly interested in all aspects of the spiritual and social welfare of the village. She was also very concerned with matters relating to cruelty to animals, against which she sometimes voiced spirited protests which did little more than invite knowing smiles at her lack of worldly knowledge so far as the behaviour of animals was concerned. She was once the innocent witness of a duck and drake engaged in the mating act in the middle of the village pond, and being totally out of touch with such intimacies in the animal, or possibly any other, kingdom she rushed urgently round to the owner of the ducks and called, 'Oh, do come quickly, please, one of your ducks is trying to drown another one in the middle of the pond!' She most certainly would never have been party to a flight of wild singing-birds being netted to spend the rest of their lives cooped up in cages. So there they sat for the remainder of that week. Untouchable and gloating, it seemed, in a kind of diplomatic immunity. We passed them daily on our way home from work and as they twittered away and pecked at the thistle heads Jim glared greedily from under the peak of his cap like Colonel Blood looking at the Crown Jewels— and as far as I could see they were just as safe.

On the Saturday as we were having dinner, Jim had an 'old-fashioned' look. 'Comin' down Dale Cottage to 'ave a crack at them branchers s'arf'noon?' 'Not me,' said I, 'she'd be bound to see us.' 'That don't matter if she do,' he looked smug, 'I've got 'er permission.' I questioned the truth of this but agreed to go along with him after he suggested that, to put my mind at rest, he would go to see her again while I stood at the garden gate with the net and tackle.

Sure enough he walked up the garden path and knocked on the front door. Miss C. came out. 'Good afternoon, ma'am,' he touched the peak of his cap, 'all right if I go up now?' 'Yes, do carry on, Copper,' she said, 'and I *do* wish you luck.' Hardly able to believe my ears, I followed Jim up through the garden and out on to the rough ground further up the hill and to the patch of thistles. Luck was with us. We set up the net and well within the hour we had caught the lot. Eleven beautiful young birds. On the way home I was still very puzzled. 'How the devil did you manage to get her permission to do that?' 'Never you mind 'ow I got it,' he said, 'I *did* get it, didn't I?'

So for many years Jim kept me in ignorance and always my query, which would crop up from time to time, would produce nothing but a slow, cunning grin. It was almost twenty years later that he eventually decided to let me into the secret. 'Would you *like* to know, then?' he said one night,

'Wal, I'll tell you.' He sipped slowly at his beer, for we were enjoying a quiet pint at the time, and then methodically started to fill and light his pipe as a kind of delaying action to add emphasis to the occasion. I could see that he was enjoying every moment. 'You remember at that time I was a keen bird-fancier and used to do a bit of breeding. Wal, ol' Mum C. knew this the same as anyone else and I went up to 'er that morning an' sez, "When I was cleaning one of my birdcages out yest'y, ma'am, the little bird got out and flew away before I could catch 'im. Now I've bin very worried about 'im, dun't y' know. Y'see, ma'am, a little cage-bred bird like 'im would soon perish out in the open. T'other birds would set about 'im for a start and then, y'see, 'e aren't never bin used to getting 'is livin' in a natural state. 'E's always 'ad 'is dinner served up to 'im on a plate as you might say." "O," says she, "I *am* sorry, Copper." "But luckily," says I, "I 'appened to spot him on your bit of spare ground this morning, feedin' on a patch of thistles. I wonder if you would be kind enough to let me and my boy come along this arf'noon and try to catch 'im in a net."

' "O, certainly, Copper," she says, "and I do hope you catches the poor little dear." '

Jim drained his glass and pushed it forward to be replenished. 'We catched the 'little dear' all right, didn't we, met,[1] and some of 'is pals.'

One of the most amusing instances of Jim's genius in raising a 'latch-lifter' for the local pub came to light shortly before his death in rather peculiar circumstances. Colonel Moens, a local resident of many years' standing, was at the time collating material for a book on Rottingdean and I was happy to pass on to him several facts and tales that I had learnt from Jim. Included in these was the legend of Hangman's Stone. This tale, which Jim in turn had got from his father, concerned a character of ill-repute from nearby Brighton who walked over to Saltdean in the neighbouring valley and stole a sheep. Rather than kill the sheep on the spot and carry it the

[1] mate.

five or six miles home he tied a rope around its neck and started to walk along the cliff top. It was late at night as he went down the hill into Rottingdean but the pubs were still open and there were one or two villagers not yet abed. Not wishing to be seen in the conspicuous position of leading a sheep along the road at that time of night, he tethered it to a large stone about three foot high and went down into the High Street alone and into one of the pubs to fortify himself for the rest of his journey.

Alas, he stayed too long and drank too deep. He returned to the stone and slid down beside the sheep and fell into a heavy, drunken slumber from which he was never to awaken. During the night the sheep shifted around and struggled on its short length of rope until it had somehow looped around the man's neck and back over the stone. The red light of dawn revealed a gruesome scene. The sheep was grazing contentedly on the green cliff turf but on the other end of its tethering rope the sheep-stealer lay strangled. In those days his crime of sheep stealing was punishable by death and this little drama had been played out to the end. The crime had been committed, the criminal apprehended, so to speak, found guilty, sentenced and dispatched all in one act.

The Colonel loved the story and at his request I took him along to show him the stone where it stands on the cliff edge to this day. He was very impressed I could see and stood looking at it for a moment or two in complete silence. Then, 'I think that is the most astonishing story I've ever heard in my life,' he said. 'Incredible! Most extraordinary! You are sure this is the actual Hangman's Stone, aren't you?' I assured him Jim had been telling me the yarn and pointing out the stone ever since I could remember. He couldn't take his eyes off it. Walking round and viewing it from every possible angle and muttering to himself, 'So that's the Hangman's Stone.'

Frankly I thought his reaction to the story was rather odd—a bit overdone. But then he started talking. 'About forty years ago when I was living at Down House your father came to me with a large sarsen-stone in a wheelbarrow. He told me the story of Hangman's Stone, just as you have today, and said he thought I might like a little bit of local history in my own garden. He sold me that stone for a golden sovereign and for all these years I have been boasting to my friends under the entire misapprehension that the Hangman's Stone stood in the corner of my lawn.' The silence that followed seemed slightly strained. 'Oh dear,' I said at last, 'I seem to have let the old man down, don't I?' 'Not at all, Copper,' he laughed, 'I think it is a marvellous story. I wonder how many more innocents believe they have the Hangman's Stone in their garden.'

But Jim is best remembered for far better things. He and his brother John most certainly had the love of the old songs in their blood, not only remembering and singing all those Grand-dad had sung but adding to them many others that they picked up from the old characters with whom they worked. Most of them were about the beauties of the countryside, the joy of work well done or the perennial delights of love. It is significant that there were few songs of complaint or protest; even those songs about their work were joyous songs. With what enthusiasm they sang:

'When six o'clock comes, boys, at breakfast we meet,
And bread, beef and pork, boys, so heartily eat.
With a piece in our pocket, I swear and I vow,
We are all jolly fellows that follow the plough.'

In 1936, in the hope that they would not be allowed to perish, Jim wrote down the words of all his songs in a book. I do not think he realized that by doing so he was preserving a little piece of nineteenth-century England that might otherwise have been lost. In addition to these, I persuaded him in 1953 to write down what he could remember of farm life in those early days. His memory proved good and in a neat, legible hand, which spoke highly of Bandy's tuition, he wrote down many details of agricultural work, and headed it, 'Work on a Sussex Farm year 1900'. It covers all the more important jobs on a big farm as the seasons ran round but, as he wrote:

There are various odd jobs come along at odd times like cooching, dock-digging, kilk-pulling and thistle-dodging and I can truthfully say I have had a go at all the jobs mentioned.

When Jim sang—

'Sometimes I do reap and sometimes I do mow
At other times to hedgeing and to ditching I do go,
There's nothing comes amiss to me from the harrow to the plough
That's how I get my living by the sweat of my brow.'[1]

he meant it, for as we read:

... I started as a Shepherd-boy from that I went to Carter-boy and then I was groom to my old Daddy's cob and under ploughman. From this I started feeding the steam threshing machine aged 17 years and mate to the engine driver, Ben Hilton, who was Estate Carpenter. After a year or two he died so I took over his job as driver and carpenter, which was repairs to all implements, keeping the stalls in stables and cowsheds in order, repairs to all gates and fencing, wattle mending, making new harrows, sheep troughs, hay cribs and a thousand and one jobs wanted attention to keep them up to scratch.

I carried this on to 1915 when my old Daddy retired after 43 years with Mr. Brown. They used to ride round the farm horse-back and in the latter part he had to have a ladies' saddle and ride side-saddle and after 3 or 4 hours when he got home he didn't get off—he fell off. He suffered from rheumatism and at the finish he had to have old 'Duke'—a horse and cart. But it soon got like that he couldn't manage it any longer so I took the job on.

And at this time things were getting to a pretty queer stage. There was Worker's Union and the War being on made things very difficult and by the time I had been two years in charge they got much worse. The Army took a lot of our young men—five of them being carters—and eight of our best horses. They even took the hunter I used to ride so instead of three or four hours in the saddle I had to walk over the farm. This started us on tractors. We had a very powerful Titan to replace our best horses and being short of men I had to drive it and do all the threshing, a good deal of the ploughing and anything that came along such as rolling, cultivating, the binder, chaff-cutting and mills for grinding and crushing.

Many of the jobs and the old-time methods employed in

[1] 'The Labourer.'

doing them in Jim's earlier days were identical with those referred to in the songs.

The whole of Jim's writings, then, both his Song Book and that containing the farm detail, are closely inter-related. They speak eloquently of what life must have been like for the ordinary farm worker in this part of Sussex at that time, which seems now so far distant.

Let us go through the year with Jim, turning from time to time to his own comments on farm work and the detail of the task in hand and also to his Song Book for a verse or two of song that is related to the time of year, for, as he used to say, there is a 'song for every season'.

# ❧ January ❧

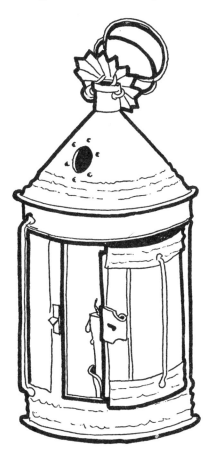

*horn lantern*

*'Twas down in the farmyard where the oxen feed on straw*
*They send forth their breath like the steam.*
*Sweet Betsey the Milkmaid now quickly she must go,*
*For flakes of ice she finds,*
*Flakes of ice she finds a-floating on her cream.*

'Christmas Song'[1]

One day just after Christmas when all the family were seated at the tea table, Grand-dad turned to young Jim and said 'You'd better learn all you can this wik, mairt. I want you to start shepherding next wik. I see Mr Lloyd down the Plough last night and 'e said t'would be all right.' The informal way in which Jim's schooling thus ended was typical of the age.

The next day he took Jim down to Charlie Reid's stores in the High Street and bought him a new overcoat, a plaited straw basket to carry his food in and a brand new jack-knife. On the following Monday morning, his hob-nails ringing on the frosty road, he clomped off out of the warm cottage into the early morning blackness with an exciting sense of self-importance. He had grown up overnight from being an eleven-year-old schoolboy into an eleven-year-old working chap with well-dubbined boots, a 'grub-basket', a nice straight hazel cut from the hedgerow, and able from now on to make his contribution, however small, to the household economy. In his book he wrote:

> When I left school to go to work in 1892 age 11 years, I started
> on a farm at Rottingdean as shepherd-boy with an old shepherd

[1] See Jim Copper's Song Book.

named John Henty. He had 2 lovely Scotch collie sheep-dogs fine dogs they were but apt to be a bit lazy in the summer. I would rather have the shaggy old English sheepdog for work and appearance. The collies names were Beauty and Lassie, Beauty was Lassie's mother and Lassie had a brother Laddie. He was a pet house dog at Challoners Farm House where Mr. Brown lived and I had to call at the house to take him with me on the downs for exercise but he was no good for tending sheep he was too fat, If I wanted him to head the sheep back (no not he) I had to run myself and if I swore at him he'd slip off home so he was more bother than good to me. But still he died.

John Henty was the head shepherd and as a younger man had served as a soldier in the Crimean War. He was a tall man with bushy sand-coloured side whiskers and in winter he wore a long cloak with a cape over the shoulders, boot-legs which were full-length button-up leather leggings, and a billy-cock hat. He was a methodical and slow-moving man, gentle with his flock but a fierce disciplinarian when it came to dealing with the conduct of a shepherd boy in his charge, and it was a rough life for a lad to be suddenly thrown into. In the depth of winter the hills were desolate and windswept and once you had left the shelter of the valley and climbed one of the white chalk tracks that led out up over the surrounding hills you were exposed to all the buffetings and drenchings that our capricious climate can contrive. Up there the long sere grasses were laid flat and combed in one direction by the persistent wind off the Channel, and the stunted gorse patches and scrubby blackthorns, sheared right down to grass level on the windward side, offered little protection from the squalls that run in from the sea. Aware of this, most of the downland shepherds carried large green or blue umbrellas which opened out to about five feet in diameter and could be bought at Lewes market for six shillings. But Shepherd Henty, quite oblivious of the ludicrous figure he must have presented, carried, in addition to his gleaming sheep-crook, a ladies' parasol, which was white on the outside with a blue lining and had a handle carved to represent the head of some obscure bird of the stork family. Out on the open downs this erect and otherwise rather regal figure made a comic sight standing with his back to the rain under the totally inadequate shelter of a parasol 'only just about big enough to cover his billy-cock hat'.

A shepherd boy's working life alternated between short periods of intense activity and long, lonely hours of boredom. Even the short-lived days of January can seem endless when you are alone on the hill with no other company than 'they ol' mutton'. A reluctant sun would struggle up out of the crimson sea, sneak across the far southern sky and, like a tired salmon, fall back into the water again all before Jim could think about making tracks for home. The chances are that he would not have seen a soul to speak to all day long. Even if the shepherd had been up there he would not have been very good company— '. . . a shepherd, he don't say nothing only swear at ye and I'd like as many ha'pence as times he's thrown his old sheep-hook at me.'

There was a 170-acre run of turf for sheep grazing and his job was to keep the flock off the growing crops. Laddie, as he told us, was little or no use to him in this respect and so he had only his two little legs and a stick. If he could not run fast enough he would resort to throwing a small flint at the leaders to head them back and sometimes he was a bit too keen on this for the shepherd's liking. He used to turn them back long before they got near the edge of the turf for, as he said, 'once you let them get the taste of a sweet crop like clover or sanfoin you would never keep them off. Leastways not without a dog. Old John was always rousting me about this, "Let 'em feed the turf down right up to the crop, cocky," he'd 'oller, "or else we sh'l 'ave to get a 'ay mower up yer t' cut it." '

So that was Jim's first job, tending the sheep up on the open downs overlooking the Channel. It was almost like working at sea. You could always taste the salt sea brine on your lips and many of the weather signs came from the sea. If you could see Highdown Clump at the back of Worthing, some eighteen miles away westward across the bay, that was a sign of rain. So, too, was the sound of the big combers

'Honest John' Copper (1817–1898).

James Copper 'Brasser' (1845–1924).

Uncle Tommy, Brasser's brother, outside the Black Horse Inn.

James Dale Copper 'Jim' (1882–1954).

ottingdean worthies of about 1880. John Henty, the head shepherd, is on the right, 'Mus' oppett is wearing the smock.

'Joe-'n-'Arry' time for the shepherd. Note piece of cheese as large as the bread.

Luke Hillman's cottage in the Saltdean valley.

A shepherd, 'e don't say nothin', only swear at ye.' *See page 66.*

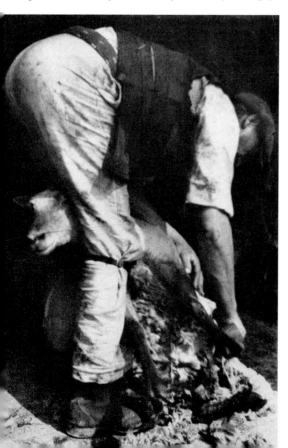

Jim shearing sheep.

A Rottingdean ox-man and his boy.

Steam-threshing gang about 1900. Jim is on the extreme left.

Sheep-dipping around 1920, with Bob assisting.

The Rottingdean windmill. The Heinemann Windmill colophon is a drawing of this windmill done by Sir William Nicholson in 1897.

Bob, Uncle John, Cousin Ron and Jim in 1951.

Jim with grand-daughter Jill and Bob.

raking on the shingle beach at night. If you saw a school of porpoises heading eastward you would move the flock away to some more sheltered combe for it indicated a good blow from the west. But if, on the other hand, they were making westward you could expect a reasonable spell of fine, quiet weather.

So the days went by. Sworn at, 'more cuffs than compliments' when the shepherd was up there with him, and bored to the teeth with the dead monotony of it all when he was alone. He would get up to all manner of tricks to help pass the time of day, knitting worsted mittens or scarves, playing a little tin whistle that he always carried with him or knocking out the tunes of some of the old songs with a couple of sticks on the sheep bells that were not in use. Once up at Vicarage Laine the flock was feeding on a piece of gratten and, intently preoccupied in cutting sticks for his mother's geraniums out of old wattle heads, he allowed several of the sheep to stray over on to a patch of clover. Suddenly looking up and discovering this he quickly got them off and although they had trodden the clover down in several places there was other, and far more conclusive, evidence of their passing, so he spent the next quarter of an hour frantically picking up their droppings and throwing them back on to the gratten before his negligence could be discovered.

Another time he made a sort of kite out of paper bags and flew it on a long piece of string but it zoomed and swooped about all over the flock, scaring them so much that they scattered away in all directions. The shepherd saw this from across the valley and when he came up Jim was left in no doubt as to what he thought about it. 'You young bugger,' he hollered, 'I can't leave you alone for two shakes of a nanny goat's tail without you're into some mischief or knitting your damned chemise or summat.' Then he sent him off with a flea in his ear to get out of the way and help the men bush-cutting over the brow of the hill.

They used to cut the gorse-bush in January and cart it to the lambing-yards in preparation for the first arrivals.

We always had three or four men on the hill bush-cutting. This was piece work and the days work was 100 faggots at 3/od per 100. These we had a good use for—in the first place they were taken to the lambing-yards for shelter. We always had 2 large pens outside the yard to work them out of the small pens to make room for newcomers as they got older—so it took a good amount of faggots to make a 5 ft. shelter around them. After the lambing was finished the bush would be loaded up again and taken to the grattens where the sheep fed, and stacked in a hedgerow (with a sod of earth on every 2 or 3 to hold them from the wind) by the side of the growing corn, as a shepherd could not tend 4 sides of a field and this made a good protection on 1 or 2 sides. When the corn was cut, away goes the bush again. It was picked up and carted out for foots of corn-stacks to keep the corn off the damp ground. You will think that was the finish of the bush (but no) when harvesting a stack into a barn, when the sheaves were all loaded up the 3 men and sometimes the carter would load home with all the strunks fit to burn and set light to the remainder.

'Bush-wacking' as it was called was a rough job, even for the men who were dressed for the purpose in their oldest clothes with plenty of protection from the spiteful gorse spikes, but for a little fellow of eleven it was 'like floundering about in a sackful of 'edgehogs'. But all that would be forgotten when he got back into the clock-ticking security of the warm kitchen at Northgate in the evening. With the curtains drawn and a good fire of gorse strunks in the grate, his wet clothes changed for dry and he himself safely on the outside of a good dinner, he used to come back to life again. Playing marbles with his brothers on the hearth-rug, or any other game for that matter, was permitted so long as silence was preserved. Observation of this rule, though mightily difficult to maintain from the boy's point of view, was strictly enforced by Grand-dad who, with his spectacles perched on the end of his nose, sat at the table scratching away with a steel-nibbed pen, keeping his records up to date and planning what was to be done in the coming year. The foundations of a farming season that produces good fat stacks and full barns in the autumn were laid during the previous winter's evenings in that small kitchen.

Presently the old man would say, 'Wal, I think that gits it pretty much up together.' Then he would get one of the boys to draw him some beer from the barrel that was stolleged up in the beer cupboard under the stairs and, after he had lit his pipe and drawn long and deep from the beer-filled mug, he would push his chair back so as to face the fire. After a while, when he had settled down again, he would say, 'Let's have a song then, shall us! Best have a Christmas one, I sh'ink, that ben't over yet. There be twelve days to Christmas dun't y' know.' Then he would incline his head slightly, and with his eyes tight shut, break into song.

'On the first day of Christmas my true love sent to me
A partridge in a pear tree . . .'

and so on, until

'On the eleventh day of Christmas my true love sent to me
Eleven bears a-baiting . . .
On the twelfth day of Christmas my true love sent to me
Twelve parsons preaching . . .'

Everyone would join in, mother as well, and that is how they would pass a winter evening away.

# February

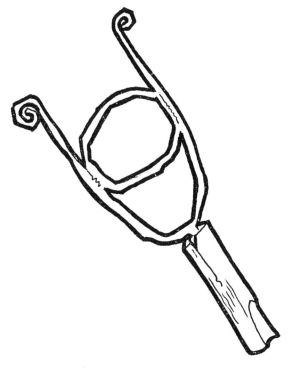

*balling or drenching iron*

*'Twas on the morn of Valentine when birds begin to prate*
*Dame Durden and her maids and men they all together meet.*
*There was Moll and Bet and Doll and Kit and Dolly to*
*    drag her tail*
*There was Tom and Dick and Joe and Jack and Humphrey*
*    with his flail.*

*Then Tom kissed Molly and Dick kissed Betty*
*And Joe kissed Dolly and Jack kissed Kitty*
*And Humphrey with his flail*
*And Kitty she was a charming girl to carry the milking pail.*

'Dame Durden'[1]


The counterfeit gold of February sunshine, making pale promises that can never be fulfilled, nevertheless infuses a little hope into even the most winter-weary heart. February was always a deceiver, to all but the country-wise, and although the yellow-brimstone, temporarily warmed by the brief midday glow, may be deluded into thinking that spring has arrived and stir prematurely from its winter state, the shepherd and his boy know better. They build their lambing pens thick and high against the biting north-easter and all-enveloping blizzard which can follow hard on the heels of a mild and golden spell. They know from experience that only too often there is truth in the adage, 'As the days lengthen the cold strengthens.'

In any case, this is a month of the highest importance to the shepherd. His ewes, heavy with lamb, must be closely watched and nurtured in preparation for lambing time, the

[1] See Jim Copper's Song Book.

shepherd's harvest. His portable hut, mounted on wheels like a caravan, would be drawn by a couple of horses up into the 'lew' of the lambing yard wall and that would be his home for the next few weeks. The shepherd has a wonderful knack of creating a little bit of warmth and comfort—both for his flock and himself—even out on these bleak old hills at a time of year when most of us will not venture from the fireside. Inside the hut there would be a little stove with a crooked tin chimney leading out through a hole in the roof, and the walls were lined with empty corn sacks nailed up to keep out the draught. Up at the far end, there would be a large poke of chaff lying on the floor where he would snatch an hour or so of sleep at night. But, of course, the sheep were his main concern. Inside the windproof pens the ground would be strewn with deep, clean straw into which the ewes nuzzled huge cosy caves where they and their lambs could lie safe and warm from the winter winds, snug as a podful of broad beans.

The shepherd with strong but gentle hands went about his rough and ready midwifery with a quiet, reassuring calm that transmitted itself to his charges. He knew what a timid lot his family were and how easily they could take fright, which would mean a crop of slipped lambs and still-births. Going his rounds at night, he would move silently about from pen to pen in the soft, yellow light from his old horn lantern, keeping a look out for difficult deliveries or any other sign of trouble. One eye and ear would be cocked, alert for any sign of the cunning and greedy fox. In a hard winter a fox's appetite will drive him to almost any lengths to obtain a meal and to him a penful of young lambs would appear to be just so many dinners on four legs. In the corner of his hut, the shepherd would have his faithful muzzle-loader, loaded, primed and cocked ready for the first sign of 'Maas Reynolds'. If he discovered a fox's run in the bushes or long grass near by, he would also set a large gin-trap in an attempt to dispose of the marauder. He had no scruples about using this method of dealing with the foxes for, cruel as it may have been, the sight of several of his defenceless lambs lying decapitated as the result of ten minutes' work by one pair of snapping jaws, and knowing the moments of terror they must have experienced, made the quick work of the steel trap seem quite humane and justified.

At lambing time Jim's duties increased both in number and variety—haying up the sheep cribs, fetching mangolds for fodder and keeping the fire going in the hut. If a ewe died, its orphan—or 'hob-lamb'—had to be fed with milk warmed up on the stove. One bad year there were so many hobs they even took a milking cow up to the barn near the lambing pens to provide milk for them. Sometimes another ewe who had lost her lamb and had plenty of milk could be persuaded to feed a hob if the skin of her dead lamb were tied round it so she would recognize the scent. It would only be left on for a day or so, of course, until the step-dam got used to and accepted the new lamb. One day the shepherd, John Henty, asked Jim to lend him his jack-knife so that he could skin a dead lamb for this very purpose. The newly acquired knife was the pride of Jim's life and he revolted at the thought. 'No, Maas Henty, I got this knife for cutting up my grub, not for you to cut up an ol' dead sheep with.'

When the shepherd felt the need for a drink of beer, a fairly frequent and recurring condition, he would send Jim down to the village about a mile and a half away to fetch him a quart in an enamel can with a tin lid, and he promised him a penny for every time he went. One day he said, 'How many times you bin down to Rott'n'dean to fetch beer for me, ol' cocky?'

'Thirty times, Maas 'Enty.'

'Oh no you en't. You're lyin', me ol' cocky. I han't drinked so much beer as all that.'

Jim took him over to a gate post where he had cut a notch with his knife every time he went.

'There y'are, lookee, there's thirty. That'll be 'alf a crown.'

'Oh damn,' says John, "ere, you take this florin and think y'self very wal paid.'

Then the lamb-tailing would be taken on. One day, after all the lambs had been delivered and had become established enough to be able to withstand the somewhat crude operation, a brazier fire was lit in the corner of one of the pens where the shepherd would sit astride a wooden bench. Jim had to round the lambs up and keep a succession of spade-shaped tailing irons hot in the fire and hand them to John, who grabbed the lambs one by one and, placing them in an ungainly straddled position on the bench in front of him, carried out the job with a deft thrust. There would be a few bewildered bleatings and a strong smell of singeing wool and soon the pen would be full of bob-tailed lambs while a pathetic little pile of cropped tails had appeared underneath the wooden bench. If the shepherd was in a good mood, Jim might be allowed the privilege of taking these home so that Granny could make a lamb-tail pie, which was considered quite a delicacy.

For three years Jim worked as a shepherd boy and it was during this time that he acquired his nickname, 'Tanty', or sometimes 'Tants' or 'Tanto'. To recall how it came about is to see how simply and spontaneously a name can be coined and appended to anyone—frequently against his wishes—so that it sticks to him all his life and is carried with him to the grave. Even then he is far more likely to go down to parochial posterity by that name rather than the one appearing on his headstone. One day Jim was sitting with the shepherd on the steps of the hut eating his dinner. Old John, who had eaten two cold mutton chops and the top of a cottage loaf, cleaned the blade of his knife by pushing it in and out of the ground, folded the blade away and put it in his pocket, then threw the two chop bones out for the dogs. Laddie lifted the lid of one baleful eye and decided that they were not worth getting up for, while Lassie slowly got up from where she was lying in the shade of the hut, walked over and sniffed them, rejected them out of hand, walked back and promptly went to sleep. Old John snorted, 'Tanty [dainty] young bugger,' he said, 'wun't eat mutton when lamb's in s'ason.' This amused Jim so much and he repeated the tale so often that he and not John Henty became known as 'Tanty'.

The longer time went on the more restive Jim got with his

job. He was altogether too lively a lad to settle down to this sort of work and it is doubtful if he would ever have made a good shepherd. Old John Henty summed it up very well when he said, 'I've had a lot of boys in my time. Willie Solomons was the best boy I ever had and your brother Johnny he was a nice lad, but you—you're a bloody twister. I never shall do anything with you.'

Jim kept worrying his father for a change. 'Git me down on the farm, Dad. I'm fed up with bein' up there on the 'ill with they ol' sheep. When I'm sitting there eating my Joe and 'Arry[1] at dinner time I can 'ear the other boys playin' down in the farmyard and it makes me wish I could be down there with 'em.' Eventually Grand-dad took him off shepherding and he started to work as carter boy at Court Farm, just behind the church.

The carter under whom Jim worked was named Bill Reid. He was a mild-mannered man of slight build and somewhat negative character. He wore a doleful expression that was heightened by his sad-looking moustache, whose wispy ends were permanently bedraggled by beer or tobacco juice or sometimes both, as he was 'fond of the hop' and an inveterate "bacca-chower' to boot. His appearance was not improved by an unfortunate facial affliction which the merciless wit of the farm lads seized upon and from which his nickname was derived. The lid of one of his eyes was what used to be called 'lazy'; he had difficulty in raising it, and when talking with anyone he had developed the habit of inclining his head to one side and winking the eyelid until he could 'hoist it up'. It seemed quite natural, therefore, that he should be called 'Oistup'. He was, nevertheless, a kindly man and Jim worked along with him very well.

His team of four heavy shire horses, Tommy, Tipler, Prince and Swallow, were stabled behind the churchyard in the low, flint-walled buildings, into whose pungent warmth Jim would creep on a winter morning to start his day's work, long before the clock on the church tower had struck six. He

[1] Bread and cheese.

would 'muck out' the stalls, rub the horses down with a dandy brush and give them their first feed, all by the light of the candle lantern that old Oistup preferred to the more modern hurricane-type oil-lamp. If this lantern were accidentally kicked over or knocked from its nail in the wall by someone going past with a prongful of hay over his shoulder, the candle would snuff out and there would be an end to the matter. But the spilt oil of the other type would have ignited all the dry litter on the floor like a tinder and the whole stable would have been ablaze in next to no time.

Jim wrote:

The Carter's day started in the stables at 5 a.m. to feed and clean his horses before the days work. This went on till 6 a.m. then home for breakfast returning at 6.30 a.m. for orders, bringing his lunch with him. Having got orders he was off to harness his team and after watering them he was away till 2.30 p.m. with an hour at 11 a.m. for lunch. After returning to the stable he then went to dinner. Back to the stable at 4 p.m. till 5 p.m. to feed and clean then home to tea, then back to the stables again at 6.30 till 7 p.m. and rack up. That is final feed and bed down for the night. The above would be winter times, but in Spring and Summer when things were growing there was his green-meat to get in. This was done between dinner and tea times by taking a horse and cart out to a field and cutting enough Rye, Tares or Clover or whatever was going for his team for one day. If the field of green-meat was in the same direction as his day's work he would take his cart with him in the morning and get his load on the way home before going to dinner. His day was work on the land, chiefly plowing and sometimes waggon work moving sheepfold or some odd job that wanted doing on wheels. When he went off to plough he knew he had an acre to turn over which meant walking just 10 miles behind a single-furrow Sussex Wheel plough.

The boy's hours were 5.45 a.m. to clean the stable out and stack the dung before breakfast and after dinner get in litter for bedding and chaff for feeding. If the carter had a 2 horse job ploughing, the boy, if man enough, would take the other two which were driven abreast and the boy also had to plough his acre. The best two ever I had was old Bung Dudeny's two odd ones, Captain and Steamer, they'd walk along and get over the ground. If it was 3 horse ploughing (which depended on the soil some was clay and some was chalk) they were drove single with the boy to drive and a labourer would take the odd horse from 3 teams to make another plough. With our 36 horses we could muster 18 two horse teams but we only had sixteen ploughs and I have seen them all in one field with bullocks and all.

Oh yes, Jim knew what it was all about when he sang:

'So early in the morning the plough-boy he is seen
All hastening to the stables his horse for to clean.
Their manes and tails he will comb straight
With chaff and corn he will them bate
And he'll endeavour to plough straight,
The brave ploughboy.'[1]

Many of the songs sung by those old timers were about the work they did and the fact that a singer was so well acquainted with the subject of his song gave it the ring of truth. You can really believe in a song about the plough when it is sung by a ploughman but, be it ever so sweetly sung by a man who does not know a share from a coulter or a whipple-tree from a pratt-pin, it will never sound quite the same.

Although his money dropped by a shilling a week from five to four shillings, Jim was much happier in his new job. He enjoyed the travelling about from farm to farm and the visits to neighbouring towns and villages. There was always plenty to do when they were on the road: jumping off to open gates that barred the way; fitting the skid-pan under to lock one of the hind wheels when travelling down a steep hill; or, when driving up hill, dropping the road-bat down to trail from the back axle and dig into the road surface to stop the waggon from running back when the team halted for a breather. There were very few dull moments. He also enjoyed the company of the other carter boys and many and varied were the games they invented for recreation during the dinner hour.

One rainy day when it was too wet to play out in the farm-yard, they hung a horse-collar by a piece of rope from a beam in the stable and had a competition to see who could stand farthest back from it and still manage to spit through it. Jim

[1] 'Brisk Young Ploughboy.'

won hands down but not without the use of artificial aids which had disastrous after effects. With his knife he had cut off a chunk of block-brine that was always left in the horses' mangers for them to lick, and he sucked it 'to make my spittle run'. This stimulated a fine flood of juices with a high velocity and excellent trajectory which left the other boys standing. But his joy in winning was short-lived and he spent almost the entire afternoon, until the emetic effects of the brine had worn off, disappearing surreptitiously behind the stable-yard wall.

Jim continues:

We always had one waggon on the road to Brighton, sometimes two or three with straw and corn and load back with dung. Straw then was 1/od per truss and we always loaded up to 100 trusses—£5 and dung was 7/od a waggon load so we used to take 107. One hundred to the merchants and 7 (wherever) for dung . . . as there was no motors they kept a good many horses which took the straw and kept us busy clearing dung heaps which is the only thing you can get a good natural crop from.

If we sent 3 waggons in with straw or corn it would perhaps be a job to find a load of dung, the Brighton carter (my Uncle Tommy at the time) would know within a little but he wasn't always quite sure. In that case a boy would go to mind the horses while the carter went and found a load. I have been myself many times and outside the Abergavenny Arms (now on the beach) and where they always used to pull up for lunch on their way home, I have seen eleven waggons, loaded with dung, from Rottingdean, Ovingdean and Telscombe. Boys were allowed in pubs in them days and I used to get a stone ginger and a ginger biscuit. The horses would look after themselves, they was alright with their nose-bags on and most of them were used to it.

The Abergavenny Arms Jim refers to used to stand at the south end of Rifle Butt Road, Kemp Town, but was eventually condemned and evacuated due to coast erosion. It gradually crumbled and fell over the cliff and finished up, as he said, on the beach. The Brighton waggon was Jim's favourite job, he enjoyed the sense of occasion and the feeling of importance that attached to it. Driving down the High Street, Rottingdean you knew people were pulling their lace curtains to one side and looking through their cottage windows to see it go by and saying, 'There goes the Brighton waggon.' A housewife might pop out and walk alongside, asking the carter to buy her a tin kettle or some other household necessity that was unobtainable in the village store. One day a request was made to purchase a pair of boots 'for Father, size 10'.

'What colour?' said Oistup.

'Just a minute, I'll nip in an' see.'

A few seconds later when the waggon had trundled some distance down the narrow street but was still within earshot, the woman's voice came loud and clear.

''E said 'e don't care what colour they are s'long as they're brown.'

Once on the Brighton journey Jim was with a carter known as 'Bishop' Hide. They had pulled up out of the village and on to the coast road that runs along parallel with the sea and never more than a few yards from the cliff edge, when an observant fellow carter who was chain harrowing the piece in front of the windmill shouted out, 'Got yer nose-bags, Bish?' The old man looked to the side of the waggon where the nose-bags containing the team's midday feed should have been hanging, 'No, buggered if a 'ave,' he cried. 'Whoa!' he called to his team and quietly sat down on the bank at the side of the road and lit his clay pipe while Jim walked over the hill and down the Hog Platt back to the stables to fetch them, a distance of about a mile. There was no sense of urgency or frustration, the carter and his team waited patiently for Jim's return, then quite naturally and with no fuss resumed the journey. After all, half an hour or so one way or the other did not seem to matter very much. It is doubtful if in those days they would have seen any other vehicles on the road, apart from the horse bus returning from the first of its two daily journeys into Brighton, but motor cars pass that same spot now at the rate of 2,000 an hour or more.

But Jim's proudest moments were in Brighton town itself —striding down North Street at the head of the leading trace-horse, a brass-ringed whip over his shoulder, his head held high. The harness jingled and the sets of bells in the hames sent peals of music rattling through the streets, making the townsfolk stand and stare and the town dogs bark like fury. That was a proud moment for any boy. 'Better than all your shepherding,' he said.

# March

*bird-scaring clappers*

*When sawing is over then seedtime comes round,*
*See our teams they are already preparing the ground,*
*The man with his seed lip he'll scatter the corn*
*Then the harrows will bury it to keep it from harm.*

'The Ploughshare'[1]

Although nothing in the countryside ever stands still, the change that takes place, usually during the month of March, is the most remarkable. For this is when the first decisive step forward is taken to leave winter behind. The transformation, not so much physical as of the senses, can come about quite suddenly and if you are lucky enough to be afield when it happens you will be aware that something really significant is afoot.

It may come early in the month or late, but it is quite unmistakable when it arrives. It is not just a change in the weather, for several fine days may have already come and gone with no particular significance; but when this day dawns you will need no telling. You will be suddenly aware that the day is not merely fine, but a part of the vast, upsurging change of mood in all the surrounding earth, sea and sky. Some early morning as the sun comes peeping up over the broad shoulder of East Hill a slight current of warm air, not really strong enough to be called a breeze, comes in from the south over the pale blue mirror of the sea, which is not even ruffled by its passing. There is a certain sweet softness about the atmosphere and the earth seems to stir from its winter slumber and start to breathe deeply again. Spring, moving up

[1] See Jim Copper's Song Book.

from the lower southern climes, is standing on the threshold of England, knocking at the door and waiting to be admitted.

When all the frost is out of the ground and the sun is growing stronger every day until the brown, ploughed lands on the southern slopes steam like fresh baked bread, the farmer knows it is time to start thinking about sowing his spring corn. When Jim was a lad quite a lot of this was still done by hand. Half a dozen or so men would work their way across a field, broadcasting the seeds in cants or strips. Their seed-lips, which were kidney-shaped galvanized containers curved to fit their bodies with a handle on the outer rim for extra support, would be slung across from their right shoulders on broad leather straps. They strode out steadily in a straight line flinging their right hands out each time their left feet went forward, with something approaching military precision, and letting the grain run freely and evenly through their fingers, one handful for every other step they took. It was an art which could only be acquired after a great deal of practice and needed ideal conditions to be successful. A gusty wind cutting across the field, for instance, would make it quite impossible to sow the grain evenly.

In Jim's book we read:

Well having got it ploughed which is Autumn and Winter work (except when frosty) we've got to set about putting the crops in. There wasn't any drills in them days for seeding, we used to use a machine called a scatter-board. It had no disc coulters like a drill but on behind was a narrow box with wires running through it, the corn was thrown into spouts which took it into the cage and scattered it evenly over the ground. We used to press all our land to be sown with corn with a five wheel presser which took three horses, a man and boy and the day's work was five acres. This was done to make a seam for the corn to lay in so that it would be buried nicely.

The scatter-board was $2\frac{3}{4}$ yards wide so you cover 1 rod of ground in a went or turn. A day's work with the scatter-board was 12 acres. If oat-sowing you would take 15 sacks of oats each containing 4 bushels (60 bushels) and sow the corn 5 bushels to the acre, 12 acres (60 bushels). Following would be a team of four horses abreast, each with a wooden harrow coupled together which took twice the width of the scatter-board. So the seedsman had to do one went before the harrows could start. Harrowing was always done twice in one place, you cross the field and come back on the same ground to bury, which was called 'wenting', if once in a place it was 'tinding', and you had to sow that 15 sacks before coming home, and to do this you walked 12 mile.

Our wheat we always sowed in cants behind the sheep-fold—in the same way but 3 bushels to the acre. We didn't grow very much barley in them days the only crops was in the Spring, if it was too late for oats, behind a bit of lambing rape. The middle of April is late enough for oats and sometimes then they are Cuckoo oats, they don't mature they are brown instead of black.

When all the seed was safely in the ground the next job was to try to keep it there, and that was not always as easy as it may sound. It was all very well to sing,

'The man with his seed-lip he'll scatter the corn
Then the harrows will bury it to keep it from harm.'[1]

But five or six hundred sooty, ragged-winged robbers, from the rookery in the neighbouring village of Stanmer over the hill, had completely opposite views. They used to fly down daily in droves at this time of year to raid the freshly sown fields. This was an annual hazard and, although there was a small colony of rooks in the trees in the Dene garden overlooking the pond, by far the biggest dangers came from the rapacious 'Stanmer Park' rooks who outnumbered the 'Rottingdeaners' by about ten to one. Following a particularly fierce March gale, old Sham the bookie said, 'Blow, I should think that did blow. That blew all the feathers off the Stanmer Park rooks and I'm baggered if they did'n 'ave to walk 'ome.'

To combat this very real threat to the crops, labourers, mostly the older men, and boys, were sent out into the fields bird-scaring, or 'rook starving' as they called it, and they used home-made pairs of clappers that rattled and clapped when shaken violently. These were made of a bat-shaped piece of wood—rather like a butter-pat—with two loose pieces of board wired on either side to form clappers. They were most

[1] 'The Ploughshare.'

effective when first used in the mornings but as time went on the rooks seemed to notice that, though a volley of what they first took to be gunfire rattled out at regular intervals, neither they nor any of their companions suffered any casualties. They presumably concluded that either the bird-scarer was a singularly bad marksman or, clever birds, that it was not gunfire at all. In any event, they gradually grew bolder and bolder and merely flapped languidly into the air in token recognition of the bird-scarer's efforts and then, after a brief circular flight, returned to their foraging with renewed vigour. This state of affairs developed until finally, clap as he may, the frustrated bird-scarer could do no more than induce only those birds in the immediate vicinity to leave the ground. To overcome this difficulty one man walked around with a shot-gun and from time to time a well-aimed charge would remind the rooks of the dangers of complacency and lend renewed significance to the sound of the clappers. One such gun-man, relating how on his rounds he had fired both barrels of his gun at a flock of starlings that went flying overhead, concluded his story '. . . but I didn't git ne'er one an 'em. I reck'n I must've aimed a liddle low, 'cos over in the next fiel' I picked up 'alf a bushel of legs.'

To make fuller use of the presence in the fields of these animated scarecrows, as they might be called without disrespect, for this is written by one of that ancient fraternity— they would sometimes be set on flint picking, which was a never-ending job on the shallow, flinty top-soil of the downlands. Every heavy shower of rain brought a new outcrop of flints to the surface of a field where the soil had been washed away, and one or two of the older men were firmly convinced that the flints grew like any other crop, not only in numbers but in size. All sizeable flints were picked up by hand and collected in a seed-lip to be deposited on the flint heap at the edge of every ploughed field. They were later carted away to be used as metal for repairing the rough roadways and cart tracks that networked the hills.

When Grand-dad was very old and crippled with rheumatics bird-scaring was one of the few jobs that he could still manage. They used to take him out in a horse and cart and sit him in the middle of a field in his favourite chair with his muzzle-loader gun, a pair of clappers, a jar of beer and his bread and cheese tied up in a red and white spotted handkerchief. There he would sit all day long until they came to pick him up at tea time. After all those years of riding round these same lands on his cob, bearing on his shoulders the full responsibility of a farm of that size, with its 1,000 acres of arable land and over fifty employees, he accepted without resentment that age and the 'screws' had brought him, in his retirement, to this the most menial of tasks on the farm. He was not even paid for it but he was amply rewarded by the knowledge that in spite of his physical incapacity he was still doing a worthwhile job. I was only about five at the time but sometimes I was allowed to go along with him with a miniature pair of clappers that Dad made for me, because I was not 'man enough' to handle a full-size pair. Whenever Grand-dad shot a rook I had to run and fetch it to him and he would tie it on to a thatching-rod and make me stick it into the ground some distance away. Here the unfortunate bird would swing from its gibbet as a grim reminder to those that got away.

That is where I first heard him sing:

> 'There was a crow sat on a tree,
> And he was as black as black could be.
> And he was as black as black could be . . .'[1]

By the time Jim was seventeen years old he had been made what was known as odd carter. He did not have a team of his own but did all manner of odd carting jobs with a team made up from the spare horses from other teams. Carting forage for the cows, water for the thatchers, and in very dry spells, to the sheep on the hills if the dew-ponds ran low or failed altogether. When there was a regular passage of waggons carting heavy loads on a journey which entailed climbing a steep hill, he would work the trace horse. This was an extra

[1] 'The Old Crow.'

horse which would be hitched on in front of the team pulling the waggon at the bottom of the hill to give additional power for pulling up it. Then at the top Dad would hook off and go again to wait for the next load.

Occasionally he was given the job, peculiar to this particular area, of digging out chalk from one of the various pits along the cliff and lining it up in heaps about twenty feet or so from the cliff edge. The heaps provided markers for the coastguards who patrolled the coastline night and day. On a moonless night, the white heaps of chalk gleamed in the light from their lanterns and by keeping them on the seaward side the coastguards knew there was no danger of walking over the edge.

Getting about from town to town gave the carters opportunities of picking up bargains and varieties of food unobtainable in the village. Sacks of apples from the Wealden orchards, herrings from Brighton beach, or at this time of year, scallops off the boats lying in Newhaven harbour. The fishermen there were always glad to fill a corn sack with them for half-a-crown, so there would still be enough for a good feed for all the family after selling five or six dozen at a halfpenny each to get your money back. The price, even allowing for changing valuation, may seem extraordinarily low, but as Jim said, that was before the 'gentry' found out how nice they were.

Beer played an important part in the life of the farm worker. This is not to say that they were all inebriates. Beer was regarded as a daily beverage and no one realized more than the old farmers the value of its restorative qualities in the hay or harvest field, and the stone beer jars, lying in the cool shade of the hawthorn hedge at the field's corner, were never allowed to run dry. After all, tea had been practically unknown to the working folk of only a generation or so before. There is nothing in the world that can quench an honest English thirst like honest English beer; when the load of hard, dirty repetitive work begins to weigh heavily on the shoulders, beer will strike new heart into a man and spur him on to fresh efforts.

One day when they were threshing out oats at Court Farm

at the back of the church, Jim was carting the sacks of grain from there to the granary across the other side of the village green. The sacks were being weighed off at two cwt each and he was carting ten sacks to the load in a two-wheeled tip-cart drawn by one horse. He had to load them into the cart and at the granary, carry them up two flights of wooden steps on to the second floor, tip them and take the ten empty sacks back to Court Farm to be checked in.

He was working single-handed and knew it was going to be thirsty work so he resorted to one of the little subterfuges that were commonplace in those days to raise a few 'perks', and to which the authorities usually turned a blind eye. On his first journey he sold one of the sacks of oats to the village carrier for his horse, which was stabled right next door to the granary, and that got him his beer money for the day. He had been sure to smuggle out an extra empty sack so that he could work it in with the other nine to be checked in back at the farm. On the journey back, instead of going across the green and up past Rudyard Kipling's house he took the longer road past the Plough and popped in there for a quick pint of beer. That first trip set the pattern he followed for the rest of the day's work—pubs were open all day then. By the time he hitched off at the end of the day he had made eleven trips, carried eleven tons of oats and drunk eleven pints of beer, and that would appear to be a good day's work by anyone's standards.

When Jim got home that evening Grand-dad said, 'Well, mairt, you've had a pretty stiff day up an' down them granary stairs. You'd better 'ave a glass of beer.' Then he went to the barrel under the stairs and drew him a pint. Jim did not dare say that he was not particularly thirsty, for the old man would have wondered where he had got his beer money. No wonder Jim could sing with such enthusiasm and conviction:

> 'It is of good ale to you I'll sing
> And to good ale I'll always cling.
> I like my glass filled to the brim
> And I'll drink all that you can bring.

O, good ale, you are my darling
You are my joy both night and morning.'[1]

March brought plenty of work in the way of spring cleaning, which was carried out just as ardently in the farm buildings as in the cottage homes. All the cowstalls and stables had
also to be sprayed white with lime-wash. If any of the boys
were engaged on this job Granny would get them to bring
home enough in a bucket to whitewash the scullery and
lavatory. The 'dunnick', as Jim called the lavatory, was down
at the end of the garden path and was built back to back and
all under one roof with that of the cottage next door. The
cross members of timber that carried the wooden, boxed-in
seats were all in one piece and passed through the dividing
wall. Over the years they had worked a little loose so that
when you sat down the seats went up and down like a see-
saw. When Jim was in residence, he said he could always tell
who went in from next door by their weight. He could
manage to outweigh either of the two daughters and by sitting heavily and using all his weight he could even keep the
old lady up in the air, but when the master of the house paid
a visit, Jim lost his supremacy and his seat was suddenly elevated by about two inches. He added that you had to be
careful not to have your fingers underneath if the old man got
up first or they would be pinched as the seat dropped down
again.

[1] 'O, Good Ale.'

# April

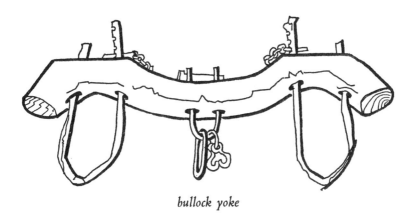

*bullock yoke*

*When Spring comes in the birds do sing*
*The lambs do skip and the bells do ring,*
*While we enjoy their glorious charm so noble and so gay*
*The primrose blooms and the cowslip too,*
*The violets in their sweet retire, the roses shining through the*
   *briar*
*And the daffy-down-dillys which we admire will die and*
   *fade away.*

'The Spring Glee'

April saw scenes of great activity in the cottage gardens. When work in the stable or farmyard was done for the day the cottagers, anxious to make full use of the extra hour or so of daylight, went straight on to the garden even before sitting down to their evening meal. Spades and forks gleamed in the last rays of sunlight and the air was sweet with the smell of newly-turned soil and rich, well-rotted stable manure. The evening would be quiet and still and blue tobacco smoke, spiralling up as the gardener paused to light a well-blackened clay, hung in wispy, horizontal layers under the lower branches of the budding sycamore, whilst cascading over all from the top-most twig came the liquid, piping notes of the blackbird's evening litany.

A well-ordered, freshly-sown kitchen garden proclaims an act of faith. The man that bends his back in April for the practical purposes of setting seeds in the drill is also bowing his head in a prayer of supplication and looking towards the fruits of July and the harvest he hopes to gather. When he stands erect and looks back over his work at the well-raked plot, drilled and trodden into neat straight lines, each one marked with a stick bearing an empty seed packet, he can see the burgeoning rows of broad beans and green peas that will soon appear and the long ropes of onions hanging on his cottage wall and ripening in the September sunshine. He has implicit faith that if he plays his part Providence, most surely, will not fail him. Seasons may vary. Dry spells are good to ripen fruit, wet ones good to swell the root, but a harvest of one sort or another he knows he will have.

Jim had little to say about this period between seedtime and haysel, but we read:

After seeding there is plenty of stirring fallow ready for rape and at Easter time there is corn-rolling on a Good Friday, which was a very funny day, some people going to Church, some going to sport and some on holiday.

The two bullock teams were used a lot for rolling, for it was held that they did as much good with their hooves as the roller did in breaking up the clods into a fine tilth. While Jim was still a carter boy, he was taken away from Bill Reid and his team, very much against his wishes, and put to work with old Luke Hillman, one of the two ox-men. He lived in a little cottage at Newlands, which was the middle of three farm outposts that stood up the Saltdean Valley, and it was the only one that boasted a cottage in addition to a large barn and cattle yard. Newlands had been farmed by our family many years before and Honest John, my great grandfather, was born there in 1817. The outbuildings included the bullock sheds which housed Luke's team of eight bullocks. Their names were Turk and Tiger, Lark and Linnet, Trot and Traveller and Buck and Benbow. When working, they were yoked up in pairs; the yokes were crude, hand-hewn affairs consisting of a heavy oak beam and two green ash bows to encircle the necks of the bullocks. They had not changed in pattern since Saxon days and those illustrated in the illuminations of the Luttrell Psalter of the fourteenth century are identical to those used in the eighteen-nineties.

Jim's first job in the morning was to 'muck out' the bullock stalls and stack the manure outside and, after giving them their first feed, yoke the team up ready for the day's work. They were always yoked up in the same pairs and in that way got used to working with each other. But Jim found that yoking up oxen was a very different job from harnessing horses. He got into trouble on the very first morning.

'No, no, boy!' shouted Luke, 'that 'ent the way t'do it. You've got 'em arse about face. You want Lark on the near side and Linnet on the awf—short name on the left, and long 'un on the right. Any fool knows that.'
'I caan't see no names wrote on 'em Maas Hillman.'
'Not s' much o' y' cheek boy, or I'll 'ave t' tel y' faather.'

When ploughing, Luke would be at the plough tail while Jim walked along beside the team with a goad, which was a long ash or hazel rod approximately nine feet long. A piece of wire or a length of horse-nail was driven into the end with the sharp tip protruding so that it looked like a sharpened lead pencil. It was not, apparently, very often necessary to use this and the animals, having once tasted the prodding on their flanks, would usually do what was required of them if the goad were merely laid across their backs and the words of command shouted at them.

To get the team to pull round to the left, you would shout to your leading nearside beast, 'Heigh, Turk, heigh!' or to his team mate, 'Cup, cup, Tiger,' to lead off to the right. Bullocks were very good workers, and with their strong, steady pull they could move tremendous loads, but unless they were hustled along all the while with encouraging calls of 'Git up wid ye', 'C'm arn then' and like expressions not always so delicately framed, they would gradually get slower and slower until they would eventually stop altogether.

Luke was a heavy, lethargic sort of man and his speed was well suited to that of his bullocks. Jim swore that sometimes Luke would follow behind them with one foot in the furrow, holding onto the plough handles, and drop off to sleep walking along. One day, when they were ploughing up at the Kompt, he was suffering a little from flatulence and relieved himself of gastric pressures with such violence that the sound, rattling across the morning air, prompted his team to pull up to a dead halt. 'Wal', said Jim when he was relating the incident, 'they thought he said, "Whoa", leastways, they made out they did.' The thought that the lowly oxen could be intelligent enough to conspire in such a clever intrigue did not appear at all unusual to Luke either. 'C'm on, git on wid ye,' he bellowed, 'I didn't say nawthen, I only got rid of a liddle wind. I dunno, you'll soon be cunning enough to be Almanack makers.'

Luke used to cut the goad to a length of 8′ 3″ so that he could measure and mark out the land for ploughing. The old single-furrow ploughs turned a furrow approximately nine inches wide so that in a 'went'—which was once up the field and back again—they would plough eighteen inches. Two wents covered a yard and eleven wents a rod—that is five and a half yards, which was twice the length of the goad. So if, for instance, your field was forty rod long you had to plough four rods wide to make up the acre and four rods could be measured by marking out eight goad-lengths. Every man had to plough an acre a day so that would mean, for example, forty-four wents on a field forty rod or 220 yards long. The ploughman, as Jim has told us, had to trudge over ten miles behind his plough every day.

The most interesting point about all this is that what was being done on the farm in the way of tillage in 1900 had not changed from a thousand years before in any detail of method, nor even in the amount which was expected to be done in one day. Compare a day's work by Luke and Jim with this extract from a dialogue of Aelfric, a Saxon abbot of the tenth century:

'What sayest thou, ploughman? How dost thou do thy work?'
'O, my lord, hard do I work. I go out at daybreak, driving the oxen to the field and I yoke them to the plough. Nor is it ever so hard winter that I dare loiter at home, for fear of my lord, but the oxen yoked, and the ploughshare and coulter fastened to the plough, every day must I plough a full acre, or more.'

'Hast thou any comrade?'
'I have a boy driving the oxen with an iron goad, who also is hoarse with cold and shouting.'
'What more dost thou in the day?'
'Verily then I do more. I must fill the bin of the oxen with hay, and water them, and carry out the dung. Ha! ha! hard work it is! because I am not free.'[1]

So for over a thousand years man and beast had teamed up in precisely the same manner to wrest a living from these self-same acres of Sussex downland soil. No one has captured this fascinating thought better than Mr Alfred Noyes, the poet, who lived in Rottingdean for some time. Jim remembered him well. He was a most imposing figure, dressed in a long, dark cloak and black, wide-brimmed felt hat. He could often be seen striding along over the downs at the back of the village or seated on the corner of Vicarage Laine on top of a steep bank above a chalk road. From this vantage point he could look right over the village in the valley across to the black windmill on the opposite hill and down southwards out to sea. He would, Jim said, sit there for hours and one thinks that that must be where he was inspired to write:

Crimson and black on the sky, a waggon of clover
Slowly goes rumbling, over the white chalk road;
And I lie in the golden grass there, wondering why
So little thing
As the jingle and ring of the harness
The hot creak of leather
The peace of the plodding
Should suddenly, stabbingly make it
Dreadful to die.

Only perhaps, in the same blue summer weather,
Hundreds of years ago, in this field where I lie,
Caedmon, the Saxon, was caught by the self-same thing;
The serf lying, black with the sun, on his beautiful wainload,
The jingle and clink of the harness,
The hot creak of leather,
The peace of the plodding;

[1] Quoted in *Our English Villages* by P. H. Ditchfield (1889).

98

And wondered, O terribly wondered,
That men must die.[1]

Jim's first job alone with the team was re-lining a dew pond at High Barn. Several cart-loads of clay had been dumped there before his arrival and after he had spread it evenly over the bed of the pond, which of course was dry, he had to drive the team of eight bullocks round and round to puddle it in with their hooves. To break the monotony of the job he would change direction with a figure-of-eight movement after every ten circuits and proceed to do ten more the opposite way round. In the normal run of events, bullocks were slow and peaceful enough in their movements, but if the prick-fly was about in the summer months that was entirely a different matter. They seemed to know by instinct when there was one within twenty yards of them. If it came any closer their tails would stick straight up in the air like broomsticks and their eyes would bulge with fear. Then without warning they would suddenly take fright and bolt away at top speed regardless of what they had hitched on behind. Jim had a team bolt with him once when he was ploughing at Vicarage Laine. The prick-fly came round and off they went, plough and all. They pulled the plough right up out of the furrow and galloped up over East Hill with young Jim hanging on to the handles for dear life. There is no telling where they would have ended up if the plough had not got stuck fast in a ditch and anchored them down.

The oxen used at Rottingdean were Welsh runts. They were black, heavy creatures and were fed chiefly on oat-straw and swedes, which was much cheaper than foraging horses, who had to have oats, hay and bran. The red Sussex oxen were used for draught purposes on some of the neighbouring farms but not at Rottingdean at that time. All the Rottingdean beasts were bought at Patcham and every year the oxman and his boy would drive four of their team, including the two oldest which were due to be cast, over there, a

[1] 'The Waggon' from *The Collected Poems of Alfred Noyes*, published by John Murray.

99

distance of about ten miles. There they would leave the two that were considered to be past their prime and too old for work, and drive the other two home again together with two new younger ones, about three years old. This method of droving was adopted because it was found that the two younger ones would travel much better when in the company of the older, more experienced animals. At Patcham the discarded pair would be fattened up and eventually appeared in the butchers' shops as appropriately graded beef. At the change-over they realized almost enough to cover the cost of the two new ones. By casting the two oldest every year from a team of eight, the ox-man kept each pair in his team for four consecutive years, by which time they were about seven years old.

These oxen, having a certain amount of road work to do, had to be shod and their cloven hooves needed two shoes, or 'cues' as they were called, on each. The method adopted was necessarily a little bit rough and certainly hazardous for those carrying it out. Oxen cannot be trained to lift their feet with the patience and discipline of a horse and so they were hobbled with a rope slung around their legs and thrown on to their sides before the operation began. It was usually carried out on the green in front of Challoners Farm and always attracted a little circle of onlookers. The smithy found that it was an advantage to grease the special nails before driving them into the hooves and sometimes this was done by sticking all the nails into a piece of fat pork so that the shoe-smith could take them out one by one, like taking pins from a pincushion, as he wanted them. Meat being a once-a-week luxury to the average farm worker, there was usually a scramble when the job was completed to see who could grab the piece of pork to take it home for mother's stock pot.

In those days a normal working week was six full days' work with a clear day on Sunday, except for the men who were in charge of stock. Shepherds, cowmen, carters and ox-men had to feed and clean their charges on Sunday the same as on any other day. The custom of having a Saturday after-

noon holiday had not been introduced at that date, but sometime during April the farmer would arrange for all general
farmwork to stop at 1 p.m. on a Saturday and the men would
spend the afternoon in planting their own potatoes on a piece
of farm land alloted for their use. Mr Brown, the farmer,
allowed each man eight rods and each boy four rods of
ground in which he could plant enough potatoes to keep his
family supplied throughout the winter. The men placed their
orders for seed potatoes with Grand-dad, who would send off
to Scotland for them to be delivered in bulk, and the money
was deducted from their wages. They were also allowed the
use of the horses and ploughs to turn the ground over and get
them planted. This was known as 'Spud-planting Saturday'.
When the time came round later in the year they were
allowed to use the horses and ploughs again to lift the potatoes and cart them round in sacks to their respective cottages.

On 'Spud-planting Saturday' there would be a well-atten-
ded gathering of men and boys down in the tap room of the
Black Horse to celebrate the evening on "tater beer'. The
slightest opportunity for a celebration was never missed, and
"Tater beer night' became a favourite annual event. Old
Uncle Tommy, the landlord, used to put an enamel bowl on
the counter so that every man, by mutual arrangement, made
a contribution towards the cost of the evening's refreshments.
Each man threw in a penny for every rod of potato ground
he had planted that afternoon; so a man with two boys living
at home would have to throw in one shilling and fourpence—
that is, eightpence for his own piece and fourpence for each
of the lads. In this manner there was soon enough in the bowl
to start the beer jugs going round.

Few things are quite so effective for releasing tongues as
good company and good beer, particularly tongues that spend
endless hours of inactivity whilst the owners are alone on the
hills with no other company than the birds of the air and the
beasts—horses, oxen or sheep—with whom their working
days are so closely linked. Although a song sung alone on the
hillside under the wide blue sky helps the day along, a song

with good companions in the hot smoky atmosphere of the tap-room is something altogether more cheery and satisfying. There is, for instance, plenty of support in the choruses and the long lingering harmonies, swelling under the low, heavy-timbered ceiling, send vibrations of joy through the whole room. There were plenty of songs appropriate to this time of year, like 'By the Green Grove'.

> 'All that you come here the small birds to hear
> I'll have you pay attention so pray all draw near
> And when you're growing old you will have this to say
> That you never heard so sweet, you never heard so sweet,
> You never heard so sweet as the birds on the spray.'[1]

Then there was all the range of love songs to choose from, which were never out of season. Uncle Tommy would sing

> 'Charming Molly, fair and fresh and gay
> Like nightingales in May,
> All round her eyelids
> Sweet Cupids play.'[2]

He could also put a diamond of grief into everybody's eye when he came to the last verse of 'The Veteran'.

> 'The old man's heart seemed broke, said he, "This is my own
> I hoped with friends to end my days", Alas that hope has gone,
> He clutched the moss-grown tomb, without welcome, Death, said he
> Forgotten now by all on Earth, Oh, God, remember me.'[3]

But all traces of sentimental sadness would be melted into wide grins by the broad humour of 'Wop She Hadity O'.

> 'They took me to the Doctor's and there I showed my case
> And didn't they do a grin when I showed 'em me Sunday face.
> They thought I was making a fool of them, but a fool of them, by gum,
> I thought they were making a fool of me when they turpentined me bum.

[1] 'By the Green Grove.' See Jim Copper's Song Book.
[2] 'Charming Molly.'
[3] 'The Veteran.'

'With my Wop she had it, I tell you I had it
I wop she hadity O,
Wop she had it, I tel you I had it
I wop she hadity O.'

Old Bandy Lloyd would be there with his friend the local
chemist, Mr Coe, for they both had a great love for the old
songs and went along to the bar, where normally they would
never be seen, just to listen to them. When the strains of a last
verse had died away and the unstinted applause and cries of
'Good ol' so and so' had ended, 'Keep those pots topped up,
Tommy,' he would call and the jugs would go round again,
foaming to the brim and filling everyone's heart with glad-
ness. Uncle Tommy would enter right into the spirit of the
evening and used to put a pint pot on the counter and fill it
up with new clay pipes of all shapes and sizes—negroes' heads,
acorns, wrinkled pattern or just plain. 'Help yourselves and
pick where you like,' he would say, then he would offer a pot
of beer to the man who could sing a complete song in the
shortest time. Jim used to try to get in quick with:

'Now all you lads that go a-courting
Mind which way you choose a wife,
For if you marry my wife's sister
You'll have the devil for the rest of your life.

20, 18, 16, 14,
12, 10, 8, 6 4, 2, none,
19, 17, 15, 13,
11, 9, 7, 5, 3, and one.'

That was the shortest song he knew, and usually resulted
in his winning a free pint, for he had developed a terrific speed
in singing the chorus.

"Tater Beer Night' was always one of the most convivial
evenings of the year.

# May

*hay-rake—'tumble-down-dick'*

*'Twas in the pleasant month of May in the springtime of the*
  *year,*
*And down by yonder meadow there runs a river clear,*
*See how the little fishes how they do sport and play*
*Causes many a lad and many a lass to go there a-making hay.*

'Pleasant Month of May'[1]

The 'merry month of May' has been the inspiration of poets and song writers since time out of mind and if you 'walk out one May morning' over these hills you will no longer wonder why. Dawn bursts across the line of the downs with all the exuberance of a leggy colt and in the early light the patchwork fields and hills, the sinuous flint-walls and the ribbons of white chalk road stand out in fresh, dazzling colours not seen at any other time of the year. As you reach the hill-crest a dozen skylarks, riding the morning breezes with a song, will hang poised in the air overhead or slowly fade upwards into the blue and disappear like small pebbles that spiral downwards into the limpid depths of a summer sea.

The air, heavy with brine, goes to your head like champagne and it is a time for expectation and optimism. The year is young but gaining strength and the sun climbs higher and higher in the sky, cutting the noonday shadows shorter each day. The sap, swelling up in all things rooted to the earth, splashes the gorse-patch with gold and dresses even the most gnarled and ancient tree-branch with a spray of green. Clouds of wild parsley cling to the lane-side hedgerow like froth on a beer drinker's whiskers. The grasses in the meadow grow tall

[1] See Jim Copper's Song Book.

and heavy and soon it will be time in the words of one of our songs, to call for

> '... the scytheman that meadow to mow down,
> With his old leathered bottle and the ale that runs so brown.
> There's many a stout and labouring man comes here his skill to try,
> He works, he mows, he sweats and blows and the grass cuts very dry.'[1]

When Jim was still a boy they still mowed some of their meadows by hand. By 6 a.m. the quiet of the field would be invaded by a gang of six or eight men arriving carrying their scythes across their shoulders and two or three boys with swop-hooks to cut round under the hedges and clean out the field corners. Most of the old men wore straw sun-hats which came out year after year at this season. Old 'Duster', from Piddinghoe, had one bought in Trafalgar Street, Brighton, for 2½d, which he considered had been money very well spent. It had already sheltered his ageing head from the sun for forty summers and, although a dark brown in colour from an application of varnish he had made with a view to preserving it, it was still in fine fettle and would easily outlast all the haysels he was likely to see.

The gang would strip off their jackets and waistcoats and leave them with their lunch-baskets tucked away in the cool shade of the deep grass under the hedgerow that marked the field's boundary. Then, after the usual preliminaries of 'sharpening up' and making one or two practice swipes with their blades through the nettles at the side of the field, like a golfer taking dummy swings at an imaginary ball before making his drive, they would roll up their shirt sleeves, spit into the palm of each hand and rub the two together, and start their processional progress across the meadow. The headman, who was to set the pace at which the gang would work, was out in front with the remainder following at regular intervals behind and one swathe's width over to the near side. If the grass were heavy and bowed with dew they would wait for a

[1] 'Pleasant Month of May.'

reasonable time for it to dry out, as a blade cuts sweeter when it is dry and they could draw a finer edge on it with the sandstone rubbers that each man carried to keep his blade in trim. But they would not wait too long, for every moment was precious and the more they could cut in the cool of the morning the better. Mowing can be very hot work by noon, even in May. Their braces thrown off their shoulders and hanging looped down from the waist, they would bend their backs to the task with a will, swinging their scythes with steady, rhythmic strokes and advancing across the field step by step leaving the tall grasses laid low in swathes behind them, while the sweet, sappy fragrance of fresh-cut 'green-meat' filled the air. As they worked they would stop at regular intervals to 'sharp up' and when the leading man eased up and straightened his back they would all follow suit, put the end of the sneath, or handle, on the ground with the blade uppermost and turned away from them and stroke their rubbers down the full length of the blade, first on one side and then on the other, all in time together. The sweeping sound of the sand-stones on the steel rang out clear across the morning, all the skylarks overhead seemed to be bursting their throats with song and, although the work was hard, some of the men would find breath enough for a snatch of song themselves:

'Now seedtime being over then haying draws near,
With our scythes, rakes and pitchforks those meadows to clear.
We will cut down their grass, boys, and carry it away,
We will first call it green grass and then call it hay.'[1]

Half-way through the morning the boys would be sent to the farmhouse to fetch the beer in two-gallon stone jars and when they got back everyone would have a welcome breather on the bank in the shade of the hawthorn. Hats would be pushed back or taken off altogether while sweating brows and pates were wiped with the ubiquitous red and white spotted handkerchieves. Then, as the beer jar went round from man

[1] 'The Ploughshare.'

to man, there would be a lot of puffing and blowing as each in turn raised it to his parched mouth and sucked in that nutty, life-giving juice to put back some of the moisture he had lost in sweat. 'A-agh!' old Fodge would say, 'I'm baggered if I warn't just about ready f' that.' Then he would smack his lips, wipe his whiskers with the back of his hand and let off a great sigh of satisfaction as he passed the jar of 'scythe-oil' on to the next waiting man. Then away they would go again with a near-mechanical precision of timing, slowly but surely laying the field down.

They were long, hard, hot days at mowing time but those old men could stand up to it day after day until the work was done. They were certainly not afraid of work, in fact they were pleased enough to have the chance of earning a little extra money. After twelve to fourteen hours in the field they were still in good heart and as the sun sank out of sight behind the Windmill Hill they still found spirit enough for a song and a joke as they made their way down the homeward tracks leading to the village. A good day's work had earned them 'a wet shirt and a dry shilling'.

Later, when Jim had become a young carter, they used machines. He wrote:

There was no hay-sweeps or side-delivery rakes or anything like that them days. We used to get our hay into rows with a 'tumble-down-dick'. It was like a comb with teeth both sides drawn by one horse. In the middle there was two handles; a lad walked behind the rake holding the handles which had cleats in it. With one cleat you could hold it down and with the other you could lift it up. When the rake was full you released the cleat on the offside and lifted with the cleat on the nearside and over she goes—then catch her with the right and off till she was full again, and by the time you had had a day clambering over them rows of hay behind 'dick' you was tired. The hay was carted by two-horse waggons and we always built our haystacks up against a barn-yard wall, which was shelter and feed for the sheep in the winter.

The haying day started at 6.30 a.m. till 7 p.m. In the old days they used to have beer sent out and tea and 'dowdles' at 5 o'clock. Dowdles was a sort of plain bun and I've heard my old Daddy say if they was more than a day old, one was enough. But that was before I started work and when it was stopped they paid 8d a day beer money instead, making a farm labourer's days pay 2/2d. Farm labourers pay then was 13/0d per week—2/2d a day.

Jim, of course, had his birthday in haying time and, although diligent and conscientious in the ordinary run of events, he was not averse on such a special occasion to taking the matter into his own hands and turning his back on work for the day. Furthermore, he was not beyond stooping to a little deception to explain his absence if by chance it was discovered.

On one such birthday he woke in the morning with, as he put it, 'the smell of the hops in my nostrils'. His orders for the day were to go along with John Goddens and another carter, and mow the ten-acre piece at Honeysocks. When he left the stable with his two horses he made a detour on the way to the field and pulled up outside the Black Horse in the High Street. His Uncle Tommy, having been a carter, was always up and about in good time and although it was not yet 6.30 a.m. the doors were open for business and Jim hitched his team outside and went in. They had a drink together by way of what he called a 'pipe-opener' and he got old Tommy to fill up a gallon jar with beer to take along with him to the hill. Then off he went, riding one of the horses and leading the other, with the beer jar slung over the hames alongside his jacket. The morning was wonderfully clear and the sun, already well up, gave every promise of a scorching day ahead. Clomping and jingling up the winding chalk road, Jim was as 'happy as all the little birds in the air' and he sang as he went, if not as sweetly, as lustily as they:

> 'The morn was bright the sky was clear
> No breath came over the sea,
> When Mary left her island cot
> And wandered forth with me.'[1]

He greeted his two mates, who were already at the field on his arrival, by inviting them to share the contents of his jar,

[1] 'Rose of Allendale.'

but they declined firmly as they thought it was a little early in the day. He did not share this view and promptly removed the cork and demonstrated his own opinion. John and Jim then set to mowing, their horses pulling with a will round and round the field with the machines whirring steadily while the square of standing green grew slowly smaller. Every time Jim completed a circuit and came again to the spot nearest last year's haystack, where the third man had set up his trestles to sharpen the knives, and Jim had left his beer with the lunch baskets, he hopped off the machine and ran across and took another pull at the jar. By about 9 a.m., however, he went in vain; he had drained the last drop. Without these visits to the jar on every turn Jim lost a bit of heart and the work began to pall. A discontented mind is fertile ground for the seeds of temptation and when, in his own words, 'John Barleycorn came sliding down a sunbeam, crooked his finger and said, "Come on, Jim",' he drove his machine off to the side of the field and hitched off. Then with a piece of cunning that would have deceived hardly anyone, least of all his father, the bailiff, he took the knife off the machine and hid it deep in the old stack and asked John to explain his absence, should the old man come along, by saying the knife had broken and he had taken it down to the forge to be mended. Then he tilted his cap over one eye as a gesture of defiance, stuck a marguerite in the buckle of his braces and in high spirits rode his horses over the hills to Piddinghoe. There at the Royal Oak he called for a pint and enquired after his old friend 'Shad' Attrill. 'He's doin' a bit of odd ship-shearin' up Rodmell,' said the landlord. 'Right,' said Jim, 'fill up my jar an' I'll go an' find him.' He found Shad busy in a barn at Rodmell with about 'half a hunderd' sheep to shear, but he took a spare pair of shears and between them they finished the job in record time. By this time the jar was empty once again and so they returned to the Royal Oak and spent the remainder of the day there in the company of a number of friends, all good old shearers and beer drinkers, reminiscing on past escapades, laughing at old jokes, singing the old songs. Eventually, he rode home over the hills by the light of the moon and as he turned his horses into the stable the church clock struck midnight.

Getting the hay in and stacked was a fairly big job on a farm of this size and had to be done quickly whenever a suitably fine spell of weather came along. For this reason a lot of casual labour was hired and several men from Brighton came along every year. One old fellow called John was a regular. A very rough character he was, a homeless individual who slept under the Palace Pier most of the year and went into the workhouse for a spell in the winter when the weather was too bad to sleep outside. He never carried a lunch basket and if he brought any food at all it was a crust or two of bread that he had picked from the dustbins at the back of the seafront hotels—any money he earned went on beer. But he played a sharp trick on Grand-dad one day. He had been working with a stack-building gang at Court Farm and when they stopped for dinner he sat down with the rest although he had nothing to eat. Presently he saw Grand-dad walking up through the farmyard so he picked up his prong and started hitting out at one of the farm cats that always appeared at mealtimes to pick up anything there was to be had in the way of scraps. He chased it, swiping madly at its bristling, furry hide until it jumped up and disappeared over the churchyard wall. 'Whoa, there! Hold on a bit,' came Brasser's resounding voice, 'don't hurt the cat, John.' 'Hurt'n, Mr Copper,' said John, 'I'll kill the bugger, 'e's ate all my dinner.' 'O damn,' sympathized Grand-dad, 'that's bad. You doddle up to the cottage and see Mrs Copper. She'll see you don't go hungry.' John went along and Granny gave him a lovely plate of hot meat pie and vegetables—and a pot of beer. It was probably the best meal he had had for years.

# June

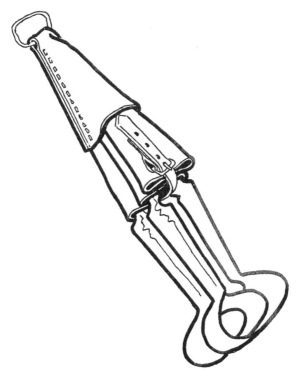

*sheep shears in pouch*

*Come all my jolly boys and we'll together go*
*Together with our masters to shear the lambs and ewes.*
*All in the month of June of all times in the year*
*It always comes in season the lambs and ewes to shear.*
*And then we will work hard my boys until our backs do break*
*Our Master he will bring us beer whenever we do lack.*

'Sheep-shearing Song'[1]

Rottingdean used to be right in the heart of the sheep
country. It was on these hills in the latter part of the eighteenth
century that John Ellman of Glynde, near Lewes, first started
to develop the Southdown breed of sheep which has since
become so famous. The main area extended from Beachy
Head in the east all along the range of the South Downs
westward to Steyning and this great, rolling area of open
downlands supported at one time, it is said, some 200,000
head of sheep. Wherever you walked on these hills you were
seldom out of earshot of the peculiarly toneless yet haunting
sound of a ring of sheep bells, and the sweet herbage that
clothed the chalk was cropped down close to the ground. In
order to escape the voracious jaws of the nibbling multitudes
the flora of the downs had evolved into diminutive counter-
parts of their more fortunate cousins in the lush, uncut water
meadows of the lower lands. But scabious, rampion, cowslip
and harebell, although dwarfed in size, went the way of all
greenstuff and, together with the wild thyme, the trefoils
and clovers and sweet downland turf, contributed very
largely to the succulence of those small-jointed Southdown

[1] See Jim Copper's Song Book.

lambs. Only the stemless plantains and ground thistles, whose leaves grow quite flat on the ground, avoided the fate of nourishing the flocks.

Round about Rottingdean the downland range is at its widest and some seven miles separate the cliff-edge on the coast from the steep northern escarpment overlooking the Weald. The long valley between Telscombe and Southease was so thickly stocked with sheep that it was referred to by the locals as 'Mutton Barracks'. The Rottingdean farm alone maintained a number of flocks amounting to about 3,000 sheep in all and from the surrounding hill country their plaintive bleating could be heard down in the village from dawn until dusk; the steep hillsides were ribbed with sheep tracks; sheep's wool clung to the hedgerows and wire fences; the smell of sheep was borne on the downland breeze and there were times when, if your street door was not kept closed, you would have had sheep in your very parlour.

When the shepherds were taking their flocks on to new grazing ground and had to pass through the village to get there, a flood of woolly-backed invaders would come pouring down, threatening to engulf the entire village. The transformation scene that took place would be as sudden as it was complete. The village street, which had been basking in the monasterial calm of a summer afternoon, the only signs of life the mongrels lying sprawled in the scanty shade and the wasps hovering around the fleed-cakes in the window of the baker's shop, would suddenly be flooded with all the animation and bustle of a fair-ground. The High Street would be so solid with sheep that you could have walked on their backs from wall to wall, and cottage and shop doors alike would be hastily slammed. The dogs, in fact, did jump up and run about on the backs of the sheep, urging those in the forward ranks to move along a little faster. With all the bleating and the clonging of sheep-bells, the shouts of the drovers, the barking of their dogs and the trample and scuffling of thousands of hooved feet, the drowsy peace was most effectively shattered. But then, as suddenly as it had come, like a wave that has spent its force on the shore, the upheaval receded, the barking and bleating, the shouting and bustling faded away into the distance and left the street as it had been before it all happened. No, perhaps it is wrong to say the same. The evidence that the sheep had passed that way was liberally strewn over the road-surface and pavements. But this was quickly removed by diligent housewives and children with shovels and buckets, not so much for the cleanliness and hygiene of the street in front of the cottages as for the good of the garden plots behind them.

June was one of the busiest months in the sheep farmer's year. It brought none of the anxieties of lambing time, but in terms of sheer hard work, it stood out from all the others. All the sheep had to be dipped or washed, and that in itself was a big job on a farm like that at Rottingdean, and after the dipping came the sheep-shearing, the biggest job of all. Shearing the wool off the back and belly of a sheep in such a manner as to finish up with a fleece of the maximum weight in one piece and in the minimum time was by no means a simple task. It was a skill that was developed over a number of years and, even then, really good shearers were few and far between. For this reason when it 'came in season the lambs and ewes to shear' a crew of expert shearers was formed to travel round from farm to farm in a given area and shear all the sheep at each farm in turn by piece-work. The crew from the Rottingdean area called themselves the Brookside Shearers, because the area they covered included all the 'brook farms' up the western side of the Ouse Valley from New-haven to Lewes in what was known as Brookside Country. A crew consisted of a captain, who wore two stars on his hat, a lieutenant, who wore one star, twelve to fourteen men, picked for their skill at shearing and willingness to work hard for long hours, a wool winder to roll and stack the shorn fleeces and a tar-boy whose job it was to go round as required and dab tar—or, in later years, powdered lime—on any accidental cuts in the sheep's hide to stop the bleeding and to prevent flies from entering.

Old Tommy Copper was one of the most celebrated captains of the Brookside crew. He was a good shearer and also well liked and respected by his men. On his shoulders fell the responsibility of organizing the entire tour, arranging the dates on which different farms should be visited, ascertaining the size of the flocks to be shorn, agreeing on the rate of pay and other important details like estimating the quantity of beer likely to be required, depending on the number of sheep and the duration of the crew's stay. In addition to this he was the crew's treasurer. He was a renowned shearer in the district and had once, with his lieutenant Fodge Goddens, walked from Rottingdean to a farm at Hamsey—a distance of about fourteen miles—sheared sixty-five tegs between them and then walked home again all in one day. It was also his proud boast as captain that when they started in the morning he would wait until every man in his crew had a sheep on the barn floor and had started shearing before he went to fetch his own and would still have the first shorn sheep of the day to his credit. There were a lot of keen competitive efforts made, particularly by the younger men of Jim's generation, but old Tommy was never known to fail. Jim was a member of the crew and that is how he first met 'Shad' Attrill from Rodmell, who once said to me, 'If you shear forty ship in a day you're doin' all right, but I 'ave shore fifty.' This was in the days before the automatic power-driven clippers had been introduced; the type of shears they used were operated manually, which required a great deal of effort from a very strong wrist, especially when used for long periods. Even these old experts used to feel the strain for the first few days of shearing and wore stout, leather wrist-straps round their right wrists.

When the time came round the crew would all meet by arrangement at the pub which they had adopted as their headquarters. For a number of years this was the Red, White and Blue Inn at Lewes. This initial meeting was known as White Ram Night and was a somewhat perfunctory affair, when the captain would read out the itinerary, 'Monday we sh'll make a start down Willet's, Newhaven. Tuesday, Northease up at

Mr Stacey's. We'n'sd'y Hudson's, Kingston . . .' and so on. 'Nobody took much notice,' said Jim. 'It was just a rigmarole. Some would be singing, some would be waiting till it was all over to go out to look for some young lady and some wasn't there at all.' Then the captain would read out the list of fines which every man agreed to pay towards the cost of a sheep-shearing supper to be held on the first Saturday following the completion of all the shearing. It was called Black Ram Night.

### List of Fines

| | | |
|---|---|---|
| For leaving wool on sheep size of shilling | Fine | 6d |
| For leaving fleece half unshorn at meal break | | 1. 0d |
| For letting sheep break loose in barn | | 6d |
| For helping another man to catch his sheep | | 6d |
| For calling a man a liar | | 6d |
| For calling him anything worse | | 1. 0d |

On a table in the corner of the room would be a pile of new shears and every man could fit himself out with a pair or two to suit his taste and pay for them when he drew his money at the final settlement at Black Ram. They varied a good deal in weight and length of shank and blade, but the price was the same for all at 3/9d a pair.

All the farms they visited were within a ten-mile radius and they walked from one to the other and quite often would have a four or five mile walk to the next farm after a long day's shearing, so as to be there ready to make an early start next morning. The arrival of the crew was always an important annual event on a farm and, although they expected no elaborate preparations to be made for their accommodation, the farmer would be sure to have one end of the barn littered with good, clean wheat straw for the men to sleep on—not oat straw, because it was too prone to harbouring tiny insects in the hollow stems—and to have a barrel of beer stolleged up in the corner. The men slept rough and removed only their boots before pulling a corn sack up over their legs for warmth. But their demands were small, and after a hard day in the shear barn 'once you got y' head down it din' sim long afore it wuz t'morrer.'

At night they would fold as many of the sheep as they could in the barn under cover so that they could make a good start in the morning, because you cannot shear wet wool, whether it is wet with rain or dew. As soon as the first glimmer of the day appeared in the sky the ewes began to stir and miss their lambs and would start bleating for their absent offspring. That was the crow's alarm clock and was usually at about 4 a.m. 'C'mon then. They be ready for ye,' Uncle Tom would shout and the men would stir themselves, put on their boots and with a certain amount of grumbling, yawning and stretching, they would have a quick sloosh in a horse trough or any other water that was available and 'leather right into it'.

They were a rough and ready gang of chaps but their general standards of personal cleanliness were, for that day and age, very good. There were, of course, notable exceptions and these were not very highly thought of by their workmates. The talk turned this way one night many years later down at the Abergavenny Arms at Rodmell. We were sitting on a form at the trestle table in the crowded long room and there were several old sheep-shearers in the company. Jim and his old pal Shad, Peter Dudeney, Jack Goddens and others. They were all in their seventies by then, slower, greyer, balder and more lined about the face, of course, than they had been when they all worked together, but still singing, laughing and talking about the old days. Under the low ceiling the atmosphere was hot and smoky and the scrubbed-top table was networked with a complicated sort of Olympic Games motif in wet beer rings.

'Ol' Charlie Putten up Kingston, now, 'e wuz a dirty ol' sod if y' like. Why 'e 'adn't washed 'is fit [feet] fer thirty years.'

'A-ah! But 'e used t' walk through the pond with 'is boots on sometimes though. Specially if we 'ad a 'ot summer.'

'Yeah. 'Twere a real shame 'e 'ad to wash one an 'em in the end.'

'Oh, 'ow wuz that then?'

'Wal, an ol' cart-'orse stepped back on 'im and broke two or three of 'is toes and 'e 'ad to clean 'er up a bit afore 'e went to the doctor's.'

But to get back to sheep-shearing: the captain and lieutenant would take up their positions, one on each side of the barn door, so that while they were doing their own shearing, they could cast an eye on every sheep that was shorn as it left the barn to see if the job was up to standard. Then it would not be long before the first fleeceless victims, voicing their protest and bewilderment in a number of different keys, would emerge into the grey light of early morning looking slightly absurd and as naked as freshly peeled oranges.

The crew would stop every two hours or so to sharpen their shears, light their pipes and sit down for a pot of beer. At dinner time they had an hour in which to eat their main meal and they sometimes played a game to determine who should be the next man to get up and draw the beer from the barrel and pass it round to the rest. They sat round cross-legged and tailor fashion on the floor in a rough circle and presently one of them would start the game by throwing his legs back over his head until the toe-caps of his boots touched the floor behind him, and at the same time chanting the first line of the verse below. Then the man on his left would do likewise and call the second line and so on until the man who chanted the fourth line had to get up, go to the barrel in the corner and replenish the empty pots.

> 'Here goes old Adamses Bells,
> Here goes old Tymothy Tuff,
> O, can you see my arse,
> O, yes, quite plain enough.'

At about 6 p.m. they would stop for 'bait' and then the local gardens or allotments used to suffer, if there was a chance of picking up a lettuce or two and a few radishes without being seen, to supplement the basic meal of 'Joe and 'Arry', or bread and cheese. Then they would work on again until sometimes as late as ten o'clock, shearing in a circle round a tallow candle set on an upturned bushel measure, so that they could finish off the sheep on that particular farm ready for the next move.

Before they turned in for the night they might "ave a blow' and relax for awhile sitting around on trusses of straw or piles of empty corn sacks with elbows propped on widespread knees and their chins cupped in their hands, or lolling back on the soft, billowing heap of rolled fleeces in the corner of the barn, which represented the sum of their day's efforts. One or two would light their pipes at the candle flame and then the sweet stench of sheep and the heavy, greasy smell of the shorn fleeces, with which they had lived practically night and day for the past two or three weeks, would be cut through with the pungent tang of strong, black-shag tobacco smoke. A final pint of beer for each man would be drawn from the barrel and as they sat, pots in hand or stretched out luxuriously on the huge woolly bed, easing backs that were ready to break in two from being bent double since dawn, all the sweating and the swearing and the stupid, stinking sheep would be forgotten and the calm and contentment that comes only to tired men at the end of a long day of hard work and achievement would begin to steal over them. Life wasn't so bad after all.

Someone would start to sing—

'Oh, the shepherd of the downs being weary of his port
He retired to the hills where he used to resort.
In want of refreshment he laid himself down,
He wanted no riches, nor wealth from the Crown,
He wanted no riches, nor wealth from the Crown.'[1]

One by one those that were capable or felt inclined joined in adding a harmony here and there or a good old bass run at the end of a line while the barn owl, squatting like a dim, grey ghost high up in the cobwebbed rafters, where the pale candlelight scarcely penetrated, blinked down on the scene and was puzzled, perhaps, at the unfamiliar sound.

[1] 'Shepherd of the Downs.'

On the very last day of the tour, work went along merrily enough. With all that work almost behind them and Black Ram Night and pay out not very far in front, they were all feeling 'as high as a magistrate on stilts' and in the very best of spirits. They always finished up on the Rottingdean farm because that had the largest flocks, and in the afternoon Uncle Tommy would send the tar-boy down to the village store for a bottle of gin, which in those days cost half-a-crown, and he would pour it into what was left in the beer barrel. As Jim said, 'That used t' make 'er run a bit thickish, but we didn't mind that.' They used to get up to all manner of capers. As a man went to get another sheep he would pass close behind another who was bent over shearing and try to push him over, because a man who let go of his sheep in the barn or called another man anything worse than a liar would be fined. The chances were that the man who was pushed over would commit both of these offences and that would mean another eighteenpence totted up in the captain's fine book for beer at Black Ram.

On the following Saturday evening they would all gather at the headquarters again and the captain would pay them out. The rate was 5/0d a score. Altogether they might have earned, say, £60, about half of which would have already been drawn out in wages. A shearer's wages was 18/0d a week. The remainder was divided equally between them and each man's fines would be deducted and handed over in bulk to the landlord against food and drink for the evening. This might amount to two or three pounds, which ensured a convivial evening with plenty to drink—beer was 1/4d a gallon, whisky 3/0d a bottle and rum 2/6d—and plenty of good food. Later the table would be laden with a big round of salt beef, a ham and bread and cheese and pickled onions, and with fare like this in front of you, a couple or three golden sovereigns in your money pouch to take home to mother, what else would a man want to do but sing? The songs came thick and fast, for the more they sang the more they drank—every song a drink was the rule—and the more they drank the more they sang. Frequently at the end of a song the whole company joined in this little chorus:

'A jolly good song and jolly well sung
And jolly good company every-one
And if you can beat it you're welcome to try
But always remember the singer is dry.

'Give the old bounder some beer
He's had some, he's had some,
Well give the old bounder some more.

'O, a half a pint of Burton
Won't hurt'n I'm certain
O, half a pint of Burton won't hurt'n I'm sure.
S U P!'

A favourite game at any of these social evenings, 'Tater Beer Night, sheep-shearing suppers, or Harvest Homes, was what was called 'Turn the Cup Over'. At Black Ram the captain would assume the role of chairman and sit at the head of the company with a felt hat, wide-brimmed and deep in the crown, which he would hand to each man as he came up to test his skill at the game. The object of the test was to hold the hat by the brim with the crown uppermost while a horn cup full of beer was placed on the top, then at a given signal to raise the whole until the beer could be drunk whilst still balanced on the crown. The company would then start to sing:

'I've been to London, boys, I've been to Dover
I've been a-travelling, boys, all the world over,
Over, over, over and over.
Drink up your liquor and turn the cup over.'

When the ale was all consumed the contestant was required to throw the empty cup into the air, twist the hat over and catch the cup in the inverted crown. If he failed to complete his little performance successfully by the time the chorus was finished he was made to try again. This could lead to further complications as the more ale the unfortunate man drank the less likely he was to accomplish the trick successfully, but he was expected to keep up the attempts until he managed it or the chairman used his discretion and called for the next contender.

Though the evening was a rather roisterous and noisy affair, there was never any trouble or rowdyism. When a singer was called upon for a song he was accorded the utmost attention and there was absolute silence until the whole company were invited to join in the chorus. Then a great wave of sound from a score of lusty throats would rise up and nearly burst the walls of the small room in an effort to ring out across the sky and tell the world that Sussex sheep-shearers could play just as hard as they could work. Their lives were the richer because of this.

Jim started shearing about the turn of the century and it is interesting to see how little the procedure had changed over the preceding seventy years or so by studying a document recording an agreement drawn up by John Ellman at a meeting held in 1828 at the Swan Inn, Falmer, only three miles over the hill. The work was hard and the farmers obviously knew the importance of keeping up their men's morale with plenty of fortification in the way of food and drink. At the meeting, it was unanimously agreed that they should have 'Cold Meat or Meat Pies for their Breakfast and One Quart of Ale each man.' Twice during the forenoon they were to be allowed time for a smoke, with a further pint of ale on each occasion. For dinner they were to have 'Boiled Meat, Meat Puddings or Pies, what small beer they like and a $\frac{1}{2}$ a pint of strong Beer each Man after Dinner.' Two more stops during the afternoon to 'light up' gave the men a chance to quench their thirsts again with 'a pint of Mixed Beer, half ale and half strong, the first time and at the other a Pint of Ale each man.' Supper consisted of 'Cold Meat and bread and cheese' and 'one Quart of Ale each man with one Pint of Strong Beer a Man after Supper.' They were allowed 'one Hour and a half for Supper and to drink their beer and that no Smoking or Singing be allowed.'

The pay was agreed at the rate of '10d per score for Ewes, Lambs and Tags' and '20d per score for a Wether Flock.'

The charge for wool-winding was one shilling per hundred fleeces plus threepence towards Black Ram Night with two shillings and sixpence per day extra for the captain and one penny for the tar-boy.

Apart from the fact that there had been a pretty steep rise in prices and the rules regarding smoking and singing had been relaxed a little, there was really hardly any change. It was still very hard and, of course, very thirsty work.

# July

*sheep bell*

*As I was a-walking one fine summer's morning*
*The fields and the meadows they looked so green and gay,*
*And the birds they were singing so pleasantly adorning,*
*So early in the morning at the break of day.*

'Sweet Lemeney'[1]

With all the flocks shorn it was time to start thinking about
the sheep sales which were held at various places around the
district on the same day each year. Farmers, shepherds and
drovers from all over the area, and many from other coun-
ties as well, would accompany the flocks, so that these events
had developed into important and keenly anticipated social
occasions. Being held on fixed dates they had become familiar
milestones in the year and were as firmly embedded in the
minds of the sheep-farming fraternity as the religious fasts and
feasts are in the thoughts of a church congregation. When
referring to a certain date they would say, 'Let me see, that
was a couple of wiks before St John's,' which would mean
St John's Fair, held near Burgess Hill on 5 July every year.

Uncle John went to all the sheep fairs around Sussex for
many years and he told me a good deal about them. He had
been a shepherd on the Rottingdean farm for over thirty
years, and a lifetime of work up on the hills seemed to have
left an indelible mark on his character. Knowing him, one
was inclined to wonder just how much a man's make-up can
be influenced by the nature of his work and daily surroundings. He was quiet, unhurried and methodical and, although
because he came from a long line of downland shepherds and

[1] See Jim Copper's Song Book.

farm-workers certain of these qualities were doubtless inherent in him, his many long years of tending the flocks up on the open hills must have developed what was already there. The downland itself can be a great moral educator. There is something about the prospect of wide expanses of hills, sea and sky that helps to put life in perspective. A shepherd's work breeds patience in a man. The yearly rote of lambing, lambing, shearing and sales runs on, one season following another as surely as night follows day, and will not be changed by any amount of fretting or undue haste.

John, then, if ever a one there was, could be regarded as a typical downland shepherd. His crook and his dog were his constant companions and he had developed that mode of walking peculiar to men who are used to covering long distances alone and often in bad weather. He strode forward from the hips, thrusting his heavy-booted feet over the ground in long raking strides which carried him along at a surprising speed with little apparent effort. He was above average height, broad-shouldered, though slightly stooped, with large capable hands, but the thing I remember above all else was the aura of calm that surrounded him. His actions, speech and thought were all geared down in speed and proclaimed an inner peace that made his presence as soothing and reassuring as the slow, quiet ticking of a grandfather clock. He had a fund of tales and experiences which he loved to narrate with his short-stemmed briar pipe held rigidly in position by one, strong, isolated, off-white upper incisor. His anecdotes were often protracted and included long repetitions of dialogue liberally punctuated with, 'he sez t' me' and, 'so I sez t' 'im.' As the humour of a remembered situation reclaimed him his eyes would twinkle through lids that gave the impression of closing upwards like a pigeon's, and his words came through a grin that widened as the story unfolded. His voice would gradually climb higher and higher in pitch until he became almost, if not quite, unintelligible. But so infectious was his mood that, although the theme had been lost, everyone ended up laughing as merrily as he.

'I slept in a goose coop, one night, over St John's,' he said, opening a story that at once appeared to have Chaucerian potentialities. 'We used to set off from Rott'n'dean three days before a sale t'give us plentys of time on the road so as not to tire th' ship out too much and allow us one day for pitching 'em out into the various lots. On the road, the same as when we got there, we used to doss down wherever we could, y'see. Wal, we was sleeping rough in a barn there and that ol' heap o' straw we wuz laying in was just alive wid rats. Rats? I've never known so many rats in m' life. They wuz swarming about like ants on a ant heap, my boy, and kept runnin' all over us. I'm jiggered if I could sleep no how. Presen'ly I sees this ol' goose coop over in the corner so I crawls inside and shuts the door. That kept 'em off all right and I sleeps like a top.' Here his voice started to soar. 'Nex' mornin' I'm damned if t'other cheps could find me anywheres. They looked all over th' place. Then drackly they sees me fast asleep in this 'ere coop. "C'mon," they 'ollers, "look lively, John, you'll hatch out if y' lays in there any longer." '

At St John's it was usually the poorer quality ewes which were put up for sale. In those days they would be sold for about ten to fifteen shillings each. 'They used t' be a pretty rubbishy ol' lot,' John said, 'some of 'em would only jest about fetch the price of a pound of cherries.' But to Lindfield Fair, which was held on 8 August, all the best wethers were sent; good prime sheep that could command anything from twenty-five to thirty shillings apiece. Lewes, which was the last fair of the year in this immediate vicinity, was held on 21 September. In the evenings they all got together swopping yarns and singing songs—shepherds and drovers from Kent, the shires and even further afield, and that accounts, in some measure, for how the songs travelled around so freely before the days of radio. There was a little rhyme which was a long way from home on the South Downs of Sussex and which, no doubt, came into the area by these means:

'Malvern Hills are very high, sometimes wet and sometimes dry,
Down in the valley the sheep are feeding

Under their tails the maggots are breeding
Eating the flesh and spoiling the fleece.
O, brother Lazaras, come down and look upon this.'

If John was tardy in many other things, he was very quick to pick up a new song. He had only to hear it two or three times and he had 'captured it'. Then on his return home, 'How d'you like this one, ol' brother?' he would ask Jim:

'There was a young shepherd attending of his sheep,
Attending of his sheep on a fine summer's day,
When a charming young maiden by chance should come that
way
And on this young shepherd she fixed her bright eye.'[1]

All cattle and sheep had to be driven everywhere on foot and there was a great demand for drovers. At every market and fair, dozens of these men could be seen, some with dogs but all with hazel switches or sticks, waiting to be hired. They had a great knowledge of the roads between the market towns, the old droves and ridgeways along the crest of the downland range and the rivers and ponds where the flocks could be watered. Some of the old ridgeways were of Roman origin, or even older, and had been used by generations of drovers. Mr Brown, the Rottingdean farmer, preferred to use his own men for this purpose and Jim had done his share. Once he had to fetch some lambs from West Dean, near Eastbourne. Let him tell his story in his own words:

When I was first married 1907 I lived next door to my old Daddy, and if ever he wanted me for anything he would knock on the wall with a poker. If I was at home I would go in and see him, if not my wife would knock back.

One evening along the end of September time I was sitting there after having a cup of tea when there was a rat tat tat. I went in and he says, Well Me'att I want you to have a day in the country tomorrow. I said, That'll be a change. Yes, he said, the Guvnor's bin here he's just got back from Westdean, he's bin over to the Duke of Devonshire's Farm Sale and bought 30 lambs and he wants you to go tomorrow and get them home. I said, Righto. He said do you know where Westdean is. I said I dunno as I do justly. Well,

[1] 'The Shepherd's Song.'

he said it's pritnear to Eastbourne, do you know Exceat. I said I know
Exceat Bridge. Oh well, he says, you want to go over the bridge
and across to that farm at the bottom of the hill tother side of Cuck-
mere Valley, when you get there turn left handed and take the road
leading to Litlington and Milton Court, but you don't want to go
up as far as that. When you get up there a tidy way you'll see a sign
post at a right hand turning and Westdean lays just round under the
hill, and I should get away middlin' time if I was you its going to be
a long day for you. I said about how far do you reckon it is then.
Well, he says, Eastbourne's 26 mile I should reckon roughly its between 16 and 17 mile so you've got somewhere between 30 and 40
mile. I said, I reckon my boots will ache by the time I get back. He
said, Yes. Well, don't leave it too late 'cos you won't be able to hurry
um too much, they be only 6 months old, and that how we left it.

So next morning I got up at half past four as I wanted to get back
before dark (and that was before they started playing with the sun
and poking the clocks about) so I made a pot of tea and cut off a bit
of grub and started off. It was a lovely autumn morning but rather
dreary walk from Rottingdean to Newhaven, there was nothing
only Saltdean and Portobello Coast Guard Cottages and the old
Hoddern Pay Gate between them and there was no earthly chance
of a lift in them days, the only vehicle I saw was a fishmonger's cart
and he was going the wrong way. He was off to Brighton market
with fish from Newhaven.

However, I plodded on and on and eventually I got to Westdean
after passing through Newhaven, Seaford, Sutton, and Exceat and
what a walk, it was now quarter to eleven and I had done half of my
so called day in the country.

I found the Bailiff and he took me to the lambs and after a little
yarn with him about the sale, weather and things in general I said,
Well, how about a drink. Ho, Ho, he says, you're in the right place
for that, there's nothing here. I said, None left over from yesterday
then. Left over, he says, there wasn't half enough to go round and
the nearest place you'll get one will be Seaford or Eastbourne, de-
pends which way you are going. I said I'm bound for Rottingdean
so it means Seaford, another 6 or 7 miles. What about the lambs, I
said is there anywhere I can water them. I expect they've been shut
up for 24 hours. He says, there's a pond round the back of the barn
you can take um round there on your way out if you like. I wished
him good day got my lambs and started off again and I can tell you
for the first three or four miles I had the devil's own job to get them
along. It was a country road with a grass bank on either side and of
course they were very hungry and sometimes they were on one

bank and when I turned them off over they went to the other side. What I wanted was a good dog. I was like a postman, I had business both sides of the street. I must have walked miles until I got to Sutton which is a suburb of Seaford. Then I had a pavement and garden walls each side so I was able to make a bit of headway, even then they had to find their way in the gateways on to somebody's lawn. But I hustled them along until I got to Seaford and there was a pub there with a nice little corner off the road and I had got everything planned but there was a policeman standing outside, so I asked him if I could let the lambs stand in the corner while I went in for a drink. He replied, You get them damned things out of here as soon as ever you can. All cattle should be out of town by 9 o'clock a.m. so you'd better get moving.

Well my next hope was the Buckle. The Buckle is a little old inn standing right on the foreshore with one straight bar with a door at each end. I should think it had been an old Smuggler's Tavern in the old days, and in the winter when we get the south west gales and high seas, if the landlord wanted to keep his socks dry he had to go upstairs while it was high tide, the sea dashes right over it, and even today the Seaford and Eastbourne buses have to make a detour through East Blatchington when the tide's in. Well, I arrived and I knew I should be safe here for a little while if only to give the lambs a blow. There was a nice walled in corner with only a garden gate so I made sure that was safely shut and in I went. In the old days if 2 or 3 of us went to a pub we didn't call for pints we used to have quarts, a jug with a handle and you would get 2 glasses and drink out of them and fill the quart up when it came to your turn. I wished the landlord a good day and called for a quart, he looked me up and down a bit which they always did a stranger in the country pubs. He drawed me a quart and set down a couple of glasses and I gave him half-a-crown. I up with the old quart and while he was at the till I said take for another. He looked at me and out the window and put down the change 1/10d, and said, Han't ye got a me'aat then. I said, I shall have when I got that other quart into me. Lumme, he says, you was pretty dry. I said, Yes I reckon you would be if you had walked from Rottingdean to Westdean and back here without a drink. Rottingdean he says, that were you got to go? I said, Yes and I've got 30 lambs outside and I've got to get them there. Goor, he says, them little lambs will be tired I know. What about me then, I says, I shall have done it twice.

I finished my quart and went out and got my flock, feeling much better. Most of them was laying down but I stirred them up and got them on the road again. They seemed a bit stiff when I started but they walked it off which pleased me rather as I was not half way home yet.

My next call was the Newfield Inn, Newhaven. Here again I had grass banks each side of the road but I think the lambs were getting too tired to feed so I rattled along fairly well. I wondered if I should get held up at Newhaven Bridge with shipping passing through, but she was all clear (there wasn't many ships went through the bridge that time of day. They was all sailing craft, schooners, brigs and windjammers) so we soon got through the town and up to the Newfield which is the last pub out of Newhaven and you won't find another until you get to the Hole in the Wall at Rottingdean. The Newfield then had only just been built and stood quite on its own. On the opposite side of the road it was rough grass lands and beyond that some allotments I found out later, which I could not see from the road. So I turned them on the grass with 2 chances, rest or feed, and feeling pretty safe I went in for a sit down and a pint. It was rather a big bar and over in the far corner sat some old chap nearly asleep. We didn't speak, I ordered a pint and had a good drink and sat down for a few minutes. When I'd finished my drink I felt as if one more would about get me home so I called up again. I had just taken the top off when the door opened and a chap come in and said to the old fellow in the corner, Have you got any allotments over the way? Yes, he says, but it's right down the other end. Oh well he says, there's a flock of lambs out there in somebody's sprouts. I thought, Yes, and I know whose they are. So I scoffed up my pint and out of it without a word, and was they enjoying themselves. I had quite a job to get them away but I did and off we went again.

I had now got about five mile to go and it took me a long time to do it. Not running from side to side but just dragging along straight ahead. I thought when I got to Blackie's hut at Portobello that I should have to carry one. In fact there was two getting pretty groggy but we toddled gently on and when I got to the top of Saltdean Cutting, I whipped them across East Hill into the big field up Whiteway Road and I come down the road into the Plough. That was about half past seven, so I'd had about 15 hours walking nearly all the time.

When I got in the pub I sat down with two or three of the old regulars who wanted to know all about my day and did I see so and so and was old who-is-it still there. But whether I was tired or what it was, I didn't get home soon enough to see my Old Daddy that night. And next morning when I went for orders at 6.30 a.m. he said, Well, Me'aat, got round then? I thought you had lost your way or something had happened. I reckon you was pretty tired. Did ye get yer lambs home alright? I said Yes, and put them in the big field. Well, he says, you'd better run out and see if theyre alright. Which I did, and there they was just inside the gate where I had left them and there was only one standing up but they was all alive, so I rousted them up and walked them about a bit. Some of them went a bit stiff, but after I'd got them across the other side of the field they started feeding and seemed none the worse. I come back and told the Old Man they was alright. He said, Yes that's a pretty long way for um. Did they travel middlin'? I said, Yes, and told him I was a bit doubtful about 2 of them but they was alright now. I also told him how I had been fixed for a drink, and he seemed to think it had worked out a bit hard for me. But he says, don't get going down the Plough today to make up for it. You'd better go and have a good breakfast and then you can go up on Wheelers Gallops, there's a few little docks up there. Cut um off with yer pen-knife and chuck um in High Barn wheel-ruts. That'll be a little easy for ye.

So I went up there and got in behind Big Ben our old bullock roller, and had 3 or 4 hours well away. When I came down to dinner, the Old Man said you'd better have a little rest saafnoon, so I didn't go back.

Well the lambs prospered after they'd got used to their new surroundings, but I shall always say it was too far for them to walk.

# August

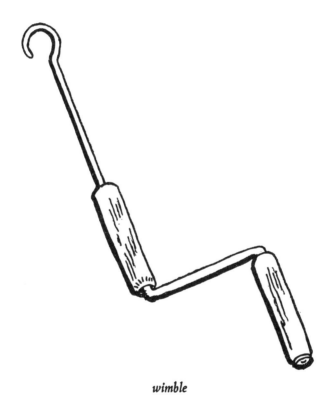

*wimble*

*There is April, there is May, there is June and July*
*What a pleasure it is for to see the corn grow.*
*In August we will reap it, we will cut, sheaf and bind it*
*And go down with our scythes for to mow.*

'Two Young Brethren'[1]

By the time August arrives the fierce, early brilliance of the
year has grown into a more subdued maturity. The piercing
greens of the springtime meadowland have softened into the
browns and greys of fully-blown pastures, and each step
taken by the grazing herd sends up a little dusty cloud of
pollen and flushes small butterflies—the chalk hill blues and
marbled whites—through the deep tangled grasses where they
shine like untethered flowers. The vigorous tide of early
growth has slackened, some of the glory fades, the petals fall
and the seed is scattered wide. Cabbage whites chase flecks of
thistledown across the still summer air, both fulfilling their
separate, yet identical destinies—to fly abroad and propagate
their species—and the birds of the air, the full-throated frenzy
of the mating season over, nourish their progeny in silence
and the woods are quiet.

This is the time of fruition—the month on the farm that all
the other seasons of planning, ploughing, sowing and nurtur-
ing have been leading up to. The bearded barley hangs its
head, the wheat-fields stand tall, baked to a deep shade of
copper and bronze, and the delicate antennae of ripened oat-
sprays tremble in the gentlest breeze. Now is the time, just
before the seed shucks burst and throw the seeds to the
ground, for the farmer to apply the sharp blade of harvest, to

[1] See Jim Copper's Song Book.

gather in the wealth of the year and transform these rippling acres into fields of bristling stubble.

In Jim's younger days quite a lot of the corn was still being cut by hand.

When the hay was all cleared it was soon time to think about harvest. But in between came mangle and cabbage hoeing. This also was done piece work £1.0.0 per acre to flat hoe twice over, then flat hoe again and set out. We used to grow a good quantity of mangle and cabbage for the cow's winter feed. About 20 acres of mangle and 12–15 acres of cabbage so this kept the men busy until it was time to think of harvest.

In them days we had to cut a lot of our corn by hand. Self-binders were just coming in, but we had three reaping machines and we had to get 'swoppers' from Kent. The reapers were a machine drawn by three horses—2 in the shafts and a trace-horse in front with a boy riding to guide it round the corners. It had a table to hold the corn as it was cut and 5 rakes went round and round to lay corn on to the table and you could adjust it to make one of the rakes slide it off the table in a wad. We used to throw out at every third rake which was about the size of a binder sheaf. If the straw was a good length you could put two wads in one sheaf, but it made hard work for the boys loading—also for the feeder when threshing. These machines would cut about 6 acres a day. The first binder ever I saw was a big wooden box arrangement, made by Hornsby's, and took four horses to pull it in double tandem fashion and a boy rode on one of the front two to get them round the corners. As with reaping, it was not a very big success at first—too big and cumbersome. It would tie one sheaf and miss two. But they soon made an improvement and turned out a nice little all steel framed binder with a much more reliable knitter and a 5' 6" cut.

These swoppers from Kent used to come every year regular. There was old George Reed who used to bring the whole family— mother, three sons and a daughter and make it their holiday . . .

Of the daughter Nell, Jim said, 'She was a nice little gal and just the right age for me—about sixteen or twenty.'

. . . Two of the boys, Bill and Arthur, were big enough to use a swop hook and tie their own sheaves and for the rest old George used to mow with a scythe and Nell would make bonds. Ted would rake up and lay the corn on the bonds and mother came along behind and tied them up. So with the scythe and two hooks they used to knock down a tidy bit and about 7 p.m. Bill and Arthur stopped cutting and shocked the day's work up.

They used to make the Granary their home while they were here and sometime if the hops were not quite ready they would stay and help us with the harvest. But as soon as the hops were fit to gather off they would go. Old George would shake hands with my old Daddy and say, 'Well, goodbye, Foreman and thank you very much. We'll see you again next year if the Lord spares us and I'm pritnear sure he will.'

Then there was old Jack Hick and his two sons, all swoppers and Harry Ashdown. He had two sons and used to bring a good hefty lad with him—all four of them could swop. We used to put these swoppers in where the corn was laid flat and the machine could not take or on a side hill where it was bad travelling. There was also always a few 'roadsters' came along to give us a hand.

We used to run five binders each taking three horses and three men. The horses were driven abreast by the Carter and two labourers jobs was to 'open out'. This was mow round the field to be cut and tie it up to give the machine a clear road round the field. When the binder had been four times round the field the two men would follow round behind it setting up the sheaves into shocks (or stooks). This again was done piece-work we were paid 2/6d an acre and used to average eight or nine acres a day. We were satisfied with eight acres which meant a pound between three of us—6/8d a day, but we liked to get a bit in hand to make up for a 'dewy morning' or a shower of rain which would hold us up for a few hours. I have cut eleven acres in a day but to keep on at that rate would be too much for the horses.

We used to grow between four and five hundred acres of corn so it was ten days or a fortnight's job for all the machines then four would be knocked off for carting the corn into stacks and one left on to finish the late sown crops.

The key to a good harvest is, of course, good weather and depending for a livelihood on the vicissitudes of a climate such as ours can be hazardous. Even during the high summer a breeze off the sea of pleasant, refreshing proportions in early morning can become a raging gale by nightfall, with the sea that started off the day as a piece of rippled glass a brown, boiling cauldron. Then the wind will come screaming up the funnel of the High Street, prematurely snatching the green leaves from the trees and flinging them down into the streets where they will line the gutters and block the drains a good two months ahead of time. Out on the hills at the back of the village the crops will be laid flat by the lashing weight of rain and the buffeting of the salt-sea gale and present a sorry sight to the farmer and his men who, perforce, must stay indoors and kick their heels while there is yet so much work to be done. After about forty-eight hours or so it will usually blow itself out and the next morning, with the wind diminished to a gentle zephyr, the sun will rise and beam down benignly on the widespread damage, appearing to dismiss the whole thing as a little joke—a mere whim of the weather gods who cannot concern themselves with the petty affairs of men and their harvests.

But, given fair weather, the long, sweltering days of sunshine would see acre after acre of corn laid flat by the scythe and the reaper instead of by the wind and the rain. The men, with their faces and forearms burnt to a deep shade of mahogany by the sun, toiled as hard as their horses who, sweating until flecks of white foam dripped from their muzzles and edged the black straps of their harness, strained round and round the field, dragging the reaping machines that reduced the standing corn in broad roads towards the centre. As the last few rounds came nearer the rabbits and other wild things within the corn found their island refuge shrinking until it no longer afforded sufficient cover. Then, one by one, they made a frantic bolt across the wide stubble margin towards the safety of the next field. Quite a number would be successful but as many were stopped by a shot from a gun or a clout from a bat and finished up as twitching, furry bundles on the sun-baked ground, with no other prospects than becoming the filling for next Sunday's rabbit pie.

For harvest, as for haying, the men were paid beer money instead of having the beer, but if they happened to be working up the Saltdean Valley near where old Luke Hillman the oxman lived, they could always buy home-brewed beer at his cottage. Luke was a very prudent man, or perhaps he was as Jim more colourfully described him, 'a tight-fisted ol' bugger'.

He used to brew his beer from a herbal mixture for which he used to send away by post and which was called 'Botanic Beer Mixture'. What it lacked in strength it made up for in thirst-quenching qualities and at haying and harvest times he would brew extra quantities and sell it to his parched workmates. If the harvesters were working anywhere within reasonable distance of his cottage, Grand-dad would send one of the boys along with the beer jug, 'Take this up t'old Luke's and fetch a couple of gallons of Boe-tanic, will ye, bwoy?' Then at dinner time they would sit round, leaning against the shocks of corn, and wash their meal down with Luke's beer. Later in the afternoon the wives and children of some of the men and the sweethearts of others would go out into the fields with tea and cake and juicy apples and for a brief half hour the toiling would cease. The horses would stand with their heads down in an attitude that spoke of utter weariness while they munched the contents of their nose-bags. The wet-shirted men sat around with their womenfolk, enjoying a brief respite while they had their 'bait' and the children laughed and played in the sunshine, gathering bright coloured nosegays of cornflowers and poppies at the edge of the still standing corn or trying to catch with their sun hats the baby field mice that had been ousted from their nests. All too soon the break would be over and the plodding of the horses and the whir-ring of the reapers began again. They went on through the evening until not a single stalk of corn was left standing and the golden ears had all been laid low like the banners of a defeated army. Then, when at last the sun was dipping and a welcome coolness crept over the fields, the horses were un-hitched and ridden slowly home to their stables in the village. The men with heavy feet dispersed and took their various roads to home, tired but content that they had earned another good day's 'harvest money'. Luke, of course, had the addi-tional comfort of counting up the pennies he had taken in return for his 'Boe-tanic'.

Luke's self-imposed frugality played back on him in a rather unkind manner on one occasion. He was never in normal circumstances to be seen in the village pubs, presumably on the very sensible economic grounds that he was not willing to pay good, hard-earned cash over the counter for beer when he had plenty at home. But one Sunday evening, having heard that the landlord at the Plough was to celebrate some local occasion by supplying free beer to the locals, he dressed himself up in his best clothes and walked the two miles into Rottingdean to avail himself of this kind offer. Just as he reached the Plough and was about to enter, Bob Cowley, who was blessed with a quick wit and a good turn of humour, came out of the door and, seeing Luke, showed some surprise and said, 'What cheer, Luke, fancy seeing you down here tonight, I should've thought you would've left it till next Sunday when the beer'll be free.' Luke stood nonplussed for a moment and, thirsty though he must have been, his rigid economic principles prevented him from going through the door. He waited until Bob had disappeared out of sight, then turned about and walked home again. Poor Luke had missed his opportunity of enjoying a free drink by the narrowest of margins. It had been the right night, of course, and Bob had only been joking, having no idea that it would be so effective. Luke remained unaware that he had been the victim of a joke until the following Sunday evening when he dressed himself up and walked down again. He ordered a pint and stood amazed when the landlord said, 'Thank'ee, Luke, that'll be tuppence. Pity you 'adn' bin down here laast Sunday, the beer was free then.'

# September

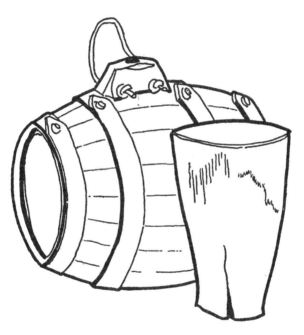

*harvest keg and drinking horn*

*And in the time of harvest how cheerfully we go*
*Some with hooks and some with crooks and some with*
*scythes to mow,*
*And when our corn is free from harm*
*We have not far to roam,*
*We'll all away to celebrate the welcome Harvest Home.*

'Brisk and Bonny Lad'[1]

Carting the corn to safety for the winter, either into the capacious high-hipped barns in and around the village or to the stacks which were to be built in the corner of the stubbles, was in those days still done by waggon and horses. Any spell of fine weather presented an opportunity of which full advantage had to be taken, for to clear five hundred acres of corn-fields before the weather broke was a considerable job.

Every man, boy, horse and waggon was pressed into service. A full harvesting gang moving off in the morning from a farm of this size was a brave sight indeed. By 6 a.m. the carters at the various stables, all within two hundred yards of the village green, would have their teams fed, brushed and harnessed ready for the long day's work ahead. The great, lumbering shire horses would be led out of the stables, their heavy-shod hooves stomping and skidding down the cobble-stoned slopes into the yard. After deep, slobbering draughts of water from the moss-grown troughs built against the stable walls they would be led across to the cart-lodges and hitched to the blue-and-red painted waggons that would be their burden for the day. Out from the various farmyards they filed on to the road and, in a long procession, passed the

1 See Jim Copper's Song Book.

church while the morning air was yet as cool and as clear as well-water and where, on the pond opposite, several white ducks with their heads tucked underneath their wings drowsed and drifted like May petals on a laneside puddle.

Down through the village the jingling, creaking cavalcade would make its way. The dozen waggons and tip-carts with upwards of thirty horses and half a hundred men and boys extended the entire length of the High Street, where most of the bedroom curtains were still drawn close and the sleeping tradespeople—the 'down-streeters'—buried their heads beneath the covers in an effort to shut out the noise. Up on the coast road, which at places ran within a few feet of the cliff edge, the voices of the men in the lobster boats half a mile off shore would come clear across the water as they lifted the pots and gathered their own harvest from the sea-bed.

'How pleasant and delightful on a bright summer's morn
When the fields and the valleys are covered with corn,
When the blackbirds and the thrushes sing on every green spray
And the lark sings so melodious at the break of the day.'[1]

The long day had begun and not until the sun had run its full, wide arc across the sky to drop behind the ridge of hill and the windmill in the west, and the great orange lantern of the harvest moon was climbing steadily up out of the evening mists in the east, did the work-weary company return homeward up the street again. Through the open windows of the little chapel in Park Place came the enthusiastic voices of a Band of Hope meeting raised in singing, most appropriately for this time of year, 'Bringing in the Sheaves', and as the teams were unhitched and stabled in the ancient flint buildings behind the church the deep diapason of the organ, leading the choir at practice for the coming Sunday's Harvest Thanksgiving, boomed out through the gathering dusk and inspired at least one or two carters to join the muted hymn of the choir voices,

'... all is safely gathered in
Ere the winter storms begin ...'

[1] 'How Pleasant and Delightful.'

The cycle of the farming year was nearing completion.
In Jim's book we read,

Now for getting the harvest in we used to run four gangs which each took 6 horses, 3 waggons, 3 carters, 2 boys, one pitcher and one stand-fasting, that is leading the front horse from shock to shock, and if the empty waggon got in the field before the other one was loaded the boy would go to it and start loading the bottoms. Then there was the stack-builders and two men on the stack and the carter would pitch off his own load and back for another. That was 7 men and 3 boys in each gang and we always reckoned to build a stack a day which took 20 waggon load. We never built them bigger than that because we had to get them home in the winter to the barns for threshing. 20 load was just about right for getting in by daylight and it was just about the right amount to get in the barn in the dry. That was the first thing we done when we started harvest, get 2 of our home barns filled with wheat sheaves so that if the corn was too wet to carry or if it rained we would have a job threshing in the dry.

We always built our stacks on the field or on a bit of turf or droveway if near but always on high ground so that they would come down hill in bad weather.

We built our wheat stacks round-shaped 7 yards across and the oat stacks square 8 yards by 5 yards and as aforesaid 20 load in a stack. To do this you built up straight or a little on the run outwards for 13 load and with the 14th you put a ring. 'Laying on the ring' is building out about 6 inches farther to carry the thatch making sort of 'eave', then fill in the middle well and build the roof with the other six load.

For the harvest we were paid as for haying beer money instead of beer. The hours were 6 a.m. till 8 p.m. with ½ hour lunch at 10 to 10-30 a.m. one hour for dinner 1 to 2 p.m. and ½ hour 'bate' or tea at 5 to 5-30 p.m. and for that 12 hour working day we were paid 1/8d. beer money per day on top of the days pay 2/4d. making 4/– per day. We only picked up our day's pay through the harvest, the beer money was left and we settled up when the job was done and we used to pick up 2 to 3 pounds for just the harvest season. But if you had been with the binder and had the harvest you would get from 5 to 6 pounds.

On the last day of harvest when all the barns were full and the rest of the corn was safely stacked they used to celebrate by having the 'Hollerin' Pot' or 'Last Load'. The very last waggon would carry only a token load of just two layers of sheaves on the floor and it would be decorated with flags and bunting slung between the corner poles. Jim would sit up 'for'ard', like Grand-dad had in the old days when he had been bailiff, and the waggon would be drawn by a team harnessed up in tandem fashion with the best horse from each of the four gangs, with each carter leading his own horse and a boy riding on each of the three trace horses. All the rest of the company, sometimes as many as forty or more, would clamber into the waggon ready to make the last triumphant and ceremonial journey down into the village with the remainder of the waggons, carts and horses following on behind. When they reached the cross-roads at the lower end of the High Street they would turn down towards the sea, right on to the cliff edge, and pull up in front of the old White Horse. Jim would holler:

> 'We've ploughed, we've sowed,
> We've ripped,[1] we've mowed,
> We've carr'd our last load
> And aren't over-throwed.
>
> Hip, hip, hip . . .'

and then a great Sussex cheer from fifty thirsty throats would rattle round the valley proclaiming the completion of a job well and truly done. The landlord would come out with members of his staff carrying enough beer to go all round and lubricate the cheering. His health would be drunk and various toasts followed such as, 'God speed the plough' and 'May the ploughshare never rust', and almost invariably someone would break into song with the 'Brisk and Bonny Lad' or another favourite that made reference to the harvest.

When the villagers in the street heard the singing they knew at once what it signified and would stand at their open doorways and await the procession, falling in behind as it passed and swelling the cheering, which grew progressively louder the further up the village they went. Halts were called outside each of the public houses, the Royal Oak, the Black

[1] reaped.

Horse and the Plough, where the rhyme and the mighty cheering brought out the landlords with the same show of hospitality with which they had been met at their first call. After perambulating the village round by the pond and into the High Street again they would finish up in the yard of Challenors where the farmer lived. He would come out to greet them with his wife and daughters and everyone would give them a 'good old holler'. Then, after the horses had been stabled, the whole company would adjourn to Challenors Cart Lodge, where there was an eighteen-gallon barrel of beer stolleged up for the men and crates of lemonade and ginger beer for the boys. Jim would tap the barrel, clear the tap and taste the first pot out and if it met with his approval, which can be taken for granted, he would raise the pot aloft and cry, 'Cocks and hens upon the midden and, by crites, she's a good 'un.' Then the drinks went round and the harvest would be rounded off with robust celebrations that would not end until the very last tawny drop had dribbled from the tap of that rotund, eighteen-gallon cask or 'kilderkin'.

'And after we've reaped it off every sheaf
And gathered up every ear,
With a drop of good beer, boys, and our hearts full of cheer
We will wish them another good year.'[1]

Jim continues,

When all the corn was cleared we had a holiday the first Saturday after and the Guvnor would let any of the men have 2 or 3 horses and a waggon to get in his winter coal. We always paid on Friday nights so when we got our harvest pay we were off next morning at 2.30 a.m. or 3 a.m. into Kemptown Station for our coal. We could get as much as we liked for 17/– per ton and if you took 2 or 3 empty sacks with you in case of a shower you could always get them filled with coke for a quart of beer—4d. And we always reckoned to be home and unloaded, put away and unharnessed by 6.30 a.m. Then for the old 'rasher waggon' full of beef steak and fried onions.

After this was over we were all dressed and ready for Brighton shopping by 10 a.m. If you was not ready by 10 or 10.30 a.m. you had to walk, as they were the only two buses in the morning, the

[1] 'Two Young Brethren.'

next was 2 p.m. We always had our regular shops for getting our winter clobber. We could get shirts at from 1/11d to 2/6d; vest 1/6d; pants 1/od; cord trousers 3/11; cord sleeve waistcoat 5/11d; cord jacket 7/– to 10/–; hob-nailed boots 4/11d; braces 6d; collars 6d; ties 4½d to 6d; and overcoat 12/6d. So your harvest money got you coal £1.14.0d, outfit about £2.5.0d, so if you picked up £4.10.0d there was still enough for mother to have a new hat after having a good blow out for dinner at Barber's Restaurant, Church Street.

By that time you would begin to feel a bit tired but there was no pictures where you could go and sit down. It was either on the pier or in the Aquarium for a rest and put your parcels down for a bit, till 5.30 p.m. when the bus left and you had to be there as all the farm people from Rottingdean was in Brighton that day and there was only one bus after that which was 6 p.m. But that was only a two-horse bus that we called the 'rabbit hutch'. After returning we would put the old fry-pan on again and have a feed of meal-fed pork chops to end a very tiring day—but we was all set up for the winter.

So much for the men, the boys would gang up and have a trip on the *Princess May*, Brighton's Pleasure Steamer, to Eastbourne or Worthing or sometimes mid-Channel. Some would go to the pleasure grounds at Devil's Dyke.

# October

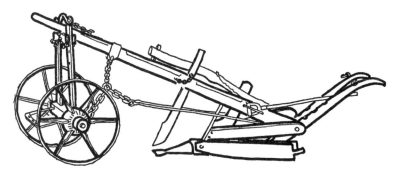

*Sussex turn-wrist plough*

*Sportsmen arouse the morning is clear*
*The larks are singing all in the air.*
*Go and tell your sweet lover the hounds are out,*
*Go and tell your sweet lover the hounds are out,*
*Saddle your horses your saddles prepare*
*We'll away to some cover to seek for a hare.*

'Sportsmen Arouse'[1]


October bears the unmistakable hall-marks of autumn. The deep greens of high summer give place to the russets and gold of a falling year and as the migrant swallows, congregating in their hundreds, write their impossible musical scores on the telephone wires, one is aware that they are the early out-riders of winter. The sun may still strike warm on the back of the ploughman as he bends to his task but it is really nothing more than an affectionate pat of farewell carrying the reassurance that it will return again next spring.

However, these veiled threats of approaching winter held no special fears for the prudent cottage household. There was fuel enough for firing in the coal and wood sheds, potatoes and carrots were clamped down safe from frost in the garden, onions were hanging in long strings from the outhouse rafters and plenty of 'green stuff' was coming along in the cabbage patch. Everyone was also well fitted out with warm clothing, was dry-shod and, what was far more important, there was enough work on the farm to ensure that a regular, if meagre, wage would be coming in even during the darkest and shortest days to come.

[1] See Jim Copper's Song Book.

Jim wrote,

Well, after harvest it began to feel a bit like autumn. With the fields all bare but there was still plenty of work to be done. All our cornland was raked so there was a waggon, horse and man going round picking up rakings which were stacked and threshed separately to be ground for pigs. The thatchers they had to be moved from one stack to another they also had to have water taken out to them and when it was all got in and covered up it was then coming the time for topping, pulling, carting and pieing, or clamping, the mangle. This was done day-work. 6 men would get their orders at 6.30 a.m. and go off pulling and topping till eleven o'clock which was lunch time. After lunch the horses and carts arrived 3, 4, or 6. I have known 8 it depended how far the field was from the main road. We always pied them near a hard road so they could be got to the cowstalls with one horse. 4 men stayed in the field filling and 2 men tipped the carts and pied them and the boys drove to and from the field and we had to pie what was pulled each day on account of frost.

This was the month that marked the beginning of the hunting season in the area and the Brookside Harriers were kennelled at Rottingdean in those days with Mr Steyning Beard as Master. It was a celebrated Hunt and very well followed, being supported sometimes by a field of as many as sixty horses. The village boasted a hunting butcher, Mr William Hilder, and a hunting parson, both of whom rode regularly to the hounds. It was said that old Parson Thomas would often stand in the pulpit and deliver his sermon with his cassock and surplice worn over his riding boots and breeches. Either he had returned from the chase too late to change properly before the service began or he wanted to make an early getaway into the field after it was over. 'We had some good hares around this way then,' said Jim, 'some that would give 'em a good two-hour gallop without a check on a bright, frosty morning.'

'All along the green turf she pants for breath
Our huntsman he shouts out for death.
Relope, relope, retiring hare,
Relope, relope, retiring hare.

Follow, follow the musical horn,
Sing follow, hark forward the innocent hare.'[1]

However, while the 'gentlemen of high renown' in their immaculate riding habits were taking their stirrup cup, riding to their hounds and enjoying all the brave pleasures of the chase on horseback, a rather less colourful character was pursuing the sports of nature, at times somewhat furtively, on a much humbler plane. Jim always kept a good dog and had several red-eyed ferrets in the small, dark hutches round by the chicken house. He was passionately fond of the downland and had an extensive and intimate knowledge of the ways and habits of the wild creatures that made it their home. Few badger sets or partridge nests within walking distance of the village escaped his keen eye. He knew the patches of thistles that had gone to seed and had become the favourite feeding places of the goldfinches, and the dew ponds where the flights of linnets drank and dabbled. Fox earths and rabbit runs alike were listed in his store of knowledge. Though he loved the local country as his life, his view was not clouded with any sentiment towards the animal kingdom. His attitude was gentle but practical and an empty pot on the cooking stove at home was often filled with something pulled from the capacious pocket on the inside of his jacket with all the aplomb of a magician producing a rabbit from his top hat—only Jim's rabbit would be paunched and ham-strung. He was a keen rabbiter and dedicated bird-catcher and loved nothing more than an hour or two spent on the hills in pursuit of, or sometimes merely observing, 'flick or feather'.

Here are three tales by Jim about his field pursuits, exactly as he wrote them.

### The Luck and Sport of Ferreting

We'll take the luck first. One morning I went to Court Farm and got my ferrets, nets, spade and bar, to have a day's ferreting in Loos bushes and the routine was to go to the Plough, get half a gallon of beer in a stone jar to take with me (pubs was open all day then 6 a.m.

[1] 'Sportsmen Arouse.'

till 11 p.m.) which I did but I didn't used to pay for it, the Landlord and I always agreed that the first rabbit I got that day paid for the beer 8d. So I put the jar in my net bag and tied that and my bag of ferrets together and slung them over my shoulder with the nets at my back. Off I goes up Whiteway Road and when I got up to the Parson's top garden joining the big fields the cord either broke or come undone and down went my bag of nets and beer. I heard the old bottle go crack, but I hung on to my ferrets and looking around there was my beer running down the road, what hadn't soaked into the nets. I took the broken pieces out and flung them over in the field. I hadn't got far I was only about 400 yards from the Plough but I wouldn't go back. I said, No you go without beer today old boy. So I had a fresh tie up and started off again.

Loos was a rather tricky place for ferreting there was 10 or 12 little burrows and one very big one over in Slonks corner. When I got there I thought I would do all the little ones first. I thought I might get what rabbits I wanted without touching the big burrow, that day. So I started I put nets down and picked nets up, went further on and put nets down and picked nets up and I done the whole of them small burrows without seeing or hearing the sign of a rabbit. I know it wasn't the smell of the beer on the nets that kept them from bolting there was none there to bolt my ferrets told me that. Now I knew I should have to go to the big place which took about 70 nets. I got all fixed up and turned in a couple of ferrets hoping for a busy afternoon. Well I listened and watched for pretty well half hour I expect and not a movement anywhere so I thinks I'll have a bit of dinner. I had a lovely loin chop of roast pork and a crust of bread which I was just about to enjoy. I'd had about one mouthful when swish over on my left. Down goes my pork, bread and knife and off I went and got there just soon enough to see a little white tail go scampering off through the bushes. The net had caught in the roots of an elder tree and didn't shut properly so he got out. I cleared the roots and put the net up again and I got back to my dinner, just in time to see one of the ferrets dragging my pork into a hole. That put the lid on. I knew then that my day was ended so I picked up my knife and put the bread in my bag and promised them they should have that for their supper when I did get them home again for fat pork was rather rich for a biscuit fed ferret. Anyway I stopped there till 4 o'clock trying all the tricks I knew to get them out, but no, and I knew when the other ferret found the pork they would lay there for perhaps a week or ten days so I left an empty bag in one of the holes. Sometimes they will curl up in that if they come across it but I went over three days running but no luck.

My brother Charlie came over from Brighton on the Friday and sometimes when he came we would have a afternoons sport. This day I said to him if you want to go ferreting you'll have to go to Loos to get a ferret, he said I'll have a run over if you like and see if I can get them and off he went. He was a real Copper he loved a walk over the downs. I told him where to go and as luck should have it he went straight to the hole where I had left the bag and believe me one of the ferrets was in it so he got something for his trouble. Old Jack Reed picked the other one up when he was coming home from Telscombe two nights afterwards and they was as fat as moles. I had some lovely ferrets, two small white bitches hardly big enough to hold a rabbit so they seldom laid up but roast pork was a Christmas dinner to them. Then I had a white dog ferret which I used as a liner if the little bitches did happen to lay up sometimes, they would corner a rabbit so that he couldn't get out. I'd put the old dog in on a line and after he had found them he would fix the rabbit and if I pulled on my line gradually he would drag the rabbit right out which saved a lot of digging. I always found the moon made a lot of difference about rabbits bolting when she is making they generally come out pretty well but when waning they won't budge as a rule. I used to breed my own ferrets and one year I sent 40 to France at 3/6d a time.

Well, that's the luck of ferreting. No beer. No pork. No rabbits. No ferrets, not even a rabbit for the landlord, I didn't have the beer anyway.

### That Was the Luck, Now we'll Have the Sport

It was 2 days before Christmas and I was feeding the Steam Threshing machine in Court Farm barn, Billy Snudden was bon cutting and we had just started after lunch 10.30 a.m. when I see my old Daddy coming up the ladder, he says to me the Guvnor's just gone into Brighton do you know where you can get a brace of rabbits pretty quick, I said I dunno I might get a couple out of the Links bank, he said well let Snuddy feed and I'll send a boy up to cut a few bons and you slip off and see what you can do only you must be back by dinner time whether you get any or not, I said Righto so I went down to the cart lodge and got my ferrets and gear and off.

Now the Links bank is just above Newlands Barn and at the Loos end there is a very big burrow and half way along towards Saltdean there is a small burrow. The big one has anything from 80 to 100 holes and the small one 10 to 12 holes so on my way over I thought I would do what I had intended to do lots of times, that was net the small burrow and put the ferrets in the big one. So when I arrived I put my nets down at the far end of the big place. I hung my coat on the bar and an empty bag on the spade to frighten them down into the small place and then in went 2 ferrets and I went back to where the nets were and was just going to hide myself a bit in the grass when I saw a rabbit coming and in he goes but not far—you see I was trapping them going in instead of coming out. I was taking him out of the net and I saw 2 more coming my way, thinks I it looks as if I'm going to be busy and they kept coming along nearly as fast as I could get my nets back in position they didn't seem to mind me a bit. I was taking one out when I heard someone coming on horseback I looked around and it was the Old Man. He rode up and said, Well me'aat have ye got a couple, there's one coming there now look, I said yes stand still if I can get him in here that will be 16. He thought that would be enough. He said where's your ferret up tother end? Pick him up as soon as you can and get off home Old Bill Avis has brought Turpin home with the gripes and he's pretty bad. I give him a drink before I came away you give him another one as soon as you get back they're in my cupboard in the store room give him one of them No. 2's and then keep him on the move till I get back. I took one of the rabbits and went along to get the ferrets and just as I got there out comes another one the ferrets following so I put my rabbit down to them they both grabbed it and I lifted them out and put them in the bag and started off back but I can tell you I didn't like leaving the place I'll bet I should have got 40 or 50 rabbits if I'd had the time. I got home at 12.30, that's walk over to the Links get all fixed up bag 16 rabbits and back in under 2 hours.

Well Turpin was better when Daddy got back just before 1 o'clock so I had my dinner and went back to Steam Threshing. After tea that evening I went in to see the Old Man and he said what are ye goin' to do with yer rabbits Me'aat. I dunno I said how many do you want, Well he says 2 will do us just for a pie Christmas night. I dunno as there's anyone else. Everybody's got plenty of grub at Christmastime. I said how about the Guvnor would he like a brace, Hell a bit no he says don't you go takin' any over to him, Dam' it all I don't want him to know you've been an' got um, Righto I said I daresay I can find a home for them. So I put them in a big bag and took them down to the Plough and laid them out on the tap room floor, where you like for 8d. a time. The Landlord had 2 for a start and 2 or 3 more went then they begun to hang a bit so I knocked them down to a tanner that got rid of 2 or 3 more. Then it got to 10 o'clock. Thinks I there won't be many more come in for the last hour so down we go to 4d. Then I had three left at 11 o'clock so I said to the crowd that was left you'd better pick them rabbits up and take them home, Im not going to take them back. Ah, Ah it seemed that was the price they had been waiting for whoever got there first had um and I could have done with another 2 or 3 brace.

These 2 little tales will just show that you never know what you are up against when you go for a day ferreting its a case of 'hap I shall and 'hap I shant. Well I didn't show much profit on my 2 hours sport but I just did have a nice drink of beer.

### Now a Day of Luck and Sport Combined

I went one day to ferret Long Down hedgerow, that is the parting of Northease Farm and our own running from the top of Longdown down to Slonks hovel it meant a very big day and when I had a day like that I could always get old Ted Bartholomew (Batts) to give me a hand. He worked for Brighton Sewer Board but he always seemed to find it convenient to get a day off if there was any rabbits to be had. So we took my gear and away to the top of the hedgerow where we made a start and we worked them down till we got about about half way and we didn't see a bit of flick big enough to cover a mouse. Then to our surprise we found out why, there was a deuce of a scuffle all at once and just inside one of the holes there was the 2 ferrets fighting a stoat. Well we soon finished him off, picked up our nets and went further down to try again. Then when we got nearly to the bottom we picked up a stray ferret left behind by poachers who had left in a hurry perhaps. Anyway I put her in my bag and brought her home and she turned out to be quite a good little thing in fact and I bred from her later on. We knew then why we had got no rabbits but we finished the few burrows that were left, but it was a blank. It was then 5 o'clock and getting dark so we picked up and started for home not feeling too happy about things. As we were coming along under Loos bushes where the waterworks is now the moon was just coming up over Tenant Hill Pond and when we got to the pit near the barn we saw 2 or 3 rabbits run in there. Ted says how 'bout it I said well I dont like goin' home empty handed lets have a go. There is about 20 holes in the pit so we slapped our nets down and turned in 2 ferrets and out they come as fast as we could pick um up I said get the ferrets as soon as you get a chance. I got one and he got the other and we picked up our nets and had a count up and we'd got 22 rabbits in 40 minutes. That made the remainder of our journey home a bit more cheerful. When we had put our tackel away I took half a dozen and Ted said he didn't want any but he had a pal or two in Brighton who he would like to give a brace to so we arranged to meet at 8 o'clock. We met and off up to Steyning Beard's stable. Old Joe Brooker had a pony there, we didn't see Joe but we put the old pony in a trap, went to Court Farm, got the rabbits and off. We went to a little Pub in George Street. Ted stuck the old pony in somewhere and then we went in and had some free of charge and there seemed to be no closing time. We left just after 12 o'clock. Ted didn't drive home no more did I but the old pony landed us outside Down House stables alright. So we started with the luck and finished with the sport of ferreting.

Jim, over the many years he spent on the farm, had a succession of dogs each of which in his day was both an inseparable companion and indispensable help in field pursuits. 'Raffles' must have been his favourite for he is the only one mentioned in his writings.

I had a little fox terrier once and he *was* a real good dog. He was a good dog with ferrets. I could put them all in one bag together and he has helped me out of many problems. If the ferrets happened to kill a rabbit or get the rabbit in a dead end with no bolt holes for escape I would say, 'Where have they got to?' and he would point directly over them and shew me where to dig and I don't remember him telling me a lie which saved me a lot of time.

His name was Raffles but there were times when I had to call him by other names, for instance. I was out in the hayfield one day and in the afternoon it came out very hot so I took my jacket off and laid it down. After a time I had occasion to go to the haystack being built about a mile away and getting towards 7 o'clock, knocking-off time, I began to miss my jacket. So I sent a boy up into the field to collect it. He came back crying saying Raffles would not let him have it, which meant I had to go back to the field, get my jacket and walk over the hill home instead of riding in one of the waggons. He didn't get a lot of meat on his bones for supper that night.

On one occasion the relationship between Jim and Raffles suffered an even greater strain. Raffles, probably hearing a fox on the prowl in the garden, woke the entire household in the middle of the night with his incessant barking. Jim shouted several times to quieten him from the cosy depths of his feather bed but to no purpose. At last, grumbling to himself, he climbed out, lit the candle and staggered sleepily down the narrow stairs. 'Get in your box!' he ordered in his sternest and most authoritative manner. There was no response; this sort of behaviour in such a well-trained dog was most unexpected and quite inexcusable. 'Box!' hollered Jim and pointed towards the scullery where the dog usually slept. Poor Raffles was puzzled. The voice was so familiar but this strange, candlelit figure clad in a short shirt on two white spindly legs was quite alien and bore no resemblance whatever to his master, the usual owner of the voice. He growled his distrust. 'Go to your box,' shouted Jim rather less confidently. But Raffles advanced snarling angrily with his lips curled back to expose his teeth. He meant business. 'Bloody dog,' cried Jim, as he scrambled on to the kitchen table. 'It's me. Get in your box.' But Raffles, faithful, as he thought, to his master snoring in bed, barked and jumped at this weird-looking intruder and kept him dancing on the table-top first on one foot and then on the other to avoid the snapping jaws. Until 'Mother. Throw me down my trousers,' Jim called. With his trousers his dignity and authority returned and peace was at last restored. Raffles slunk shamefacedly into his box.

'He's a good dog—damn him,' said Jim.

Some years after this Raffles met an untimely end.

I used to do the threshing on the farm and Raffles loved the thresher as we usually found a few rats when finishing a stack. Any number from 20 to 100 in one stack and when we had done and I was ready for home he would always look round, pick out the biggest rat he could find and carry it home and lay it on the mat outside my backdoor. When my wife knew I was threshing she would not venture outside the backdoor after 4 o'clock.

I threshed a stack at Saltdean once and we got about 70 rats and when I packed up for home he went his round and picked out a big one and off we go. We had to pass a patch of gorse bush on our way and suddenly I saw him scratching a hole so I waited a bit. He made the hole, buried the rat then off he went over to the gorse. I took no notice as he was always dashing into bushes and I hoped he was going to bring mother home a nice rabbit instead of a rat. Well that was the last I ever saw of him.

Jim searched the clump of bushes and several neighbouring clumps, whistling and calling over a wide area. He listened and looked for a couple of hours or so and went back on successive days. But neither Raffles nor any evidence to explain his disappearance ever turned up.

It was rather a mystery, but I think he must have crawled in a rabbit or fox hole and when trying to get back out a tree root got under his collar and held him.

This was a very sad end for the little dog, particularly as Jim would normally always remove a dog's collar before allowing him to hunt in the bushes, for this very reason.

# November

*flail*

*Now harvest being over bad weather comes on,*
*We will send for the thresher to thresh out our corn.*
*His hand-staff he'll handle, his swingel he'll swing,*
*Till the very next harvest we'll all meet again.*

'The Ploughshare'[1]

In the grey, shrinking days of November when the Channel gales drive flocks of sea birds up inland in search of food and the endless rain slants in from the south-west, the village seemed empty and lifeless and appeared almost to have entered a state of hibernation. The High Street, strewn with shingle and small pieces of seaweed that had been thrown high in the air by mountainous waves as they thundered against the old sea walls, would be practically deserted. Only those that had to be were abroad, clasping their coats close about their shoulders, leaning into the wind and shouting as they passed, 'Tidy ol' blow!' Even the village pond, sheltered as it was from the full fury of the storm, was corrugated into wavelets that lapped against its grassy banks where small boys, impervious to weather, paused on their way home from school and risked wet feet and parental scolding by reaching out into the flotsam for fallen 'conkers'. The pulse of the farm, too, had slowed right down. Nearly all signs of outdoor activity had disappeared and only the steady thump-thump of the flail from the threshing barns told of the continuity of work within and that the heart of the farm was still beating.

A flail thresher would be sent to the same barn every year and he would remain there for the better part of the winter with an extra man to help him from time to time. Conse-

[1] See Jim Copper's Song Book.

quently a barn was often known by the name of the man who threshed in it; Home Barn at Challenors, opposite where the bowling green now is, is still referred to by some of the few remaining old-timers as 'Drummer's Barn', although it has been converted into a dwelling-house for some years now. The threshers used to make their own flails, usually a nice straight cut of hazel for the hand-staff and a piece of holly for the swingle. The swivel caps were usually cut out of a piece of green ash and steamed over a kettle before being bent into the right shape, and knit-bands, which lashed the swingle to the swivel cap, were thongs of leather or sometimes a dried eel-skin.

Flail threshing was a very dusty and back-breaking job and most of the men wore skull caps or sort of tam o'shanters to keep the dust off their heads. Flails were also ticklish tools to handle. Their behaviour was unpredictable and if the knit-band broke or the swivel got stuck there was a very good chance of giving yourself a knock on the head. 'If the 'nidbun broke in two sunders,' Jim said, 'you'd fetch y'self sech a swipe acrawss the back of the bleddy 'ead with the swinjul.'

Boys worked along with the thresher bond-winding and wimming. When bond-winding the boy used a wimble, which was a cranked handle, rather like the starting handle of a car, with a hook at the end. The man would make a loop of the loose straw on the barn floor and the boy would put the hook through it and walk away backwards, at the same time winding the handle of the wimble round and round so as to twist the straw into a rope or bond, while the man paid the straw out through his hands. Wimming, or winnowing, was done by shovelling the threshed-out grain into a patent hand-operated machine with a large wooden barn scoop, while inside the machine a system of sieves and fans separated the chaff and cavings from the grain. Before they had these machines a more primitive method was used. The large barn doors, which were always opposite each other, would be flung wide open to allow the wind to blow right through, and across the door on the lee side wooden boards would be placed about three feet high, taking care to leave a gap at the bottom of about six inches to allow the draught to blow underneath. Then the grain would be thrown across the doorway at floor level allowing the draught to carry the chaff and cavings out under the boards while the grain itself, being heavier, was held by the door-sill. The fact that the 'thresh' was held in this manner might account for the fact that a door-sill is referred to as the 'threshold'.

Although at that time the primitive flail was still being used for threshing oats the bulk of the grain harvest, wheat and barley, was threshed by machines driven by either steam power or horses. A steam-driven machine was at Court Farm.

Jim writes:

> As I have mentioned we always had a barn full for threshing in wet weather. We had two barns for this job one was a steam thresher and the other was a machine driven by four horses. When a steam threshing we used to do a stack a day which took six trussers—Avis, Whale, Fodge, Drummer, Shirty and Bill Hearn. They worked piece-work ½d a truss and sometimes they would tie up to 120 trusses in a day 5/–d. The other work was done day work. Three men on the mow, one man carrying straw away, one man taking off sacks, one man feeding, one bond cutting, a boy clearing chaff and cavings and the engine driver—thirteen men and two lads.

The 'feeder', whose job it was to work on top of the machine and take each sheaf after the bond had been cut and pay it evenly over his arm across the table and into the drums, would take a great pride in keeping a steady flow of corn going into the machine and not to drop in a whole sheaf at a time. This would maintain the high-pitched droning of the machine on a level note. If the load for the drums were suddenly increased by a whole sheaf being fed in, the speed would drop and the humming note would be lowered by a tone or two. Hence it was said that 'you could pritnear play a tune on that ol' 'chine.'

At Challenors Farm there was a horse-driven machine. There was an apparatus outside the back of the barn consisting of wooden cross-beams about twenty-five feet across—like the sails of a windmill only lying horizontal—and four horses were harnessed up, one to the end of each. Over the centre of the hub was a box for the carter in charge who, standing like the ringmaster in a circus, kept his team walking round at a steady pace with a long whip. This drove a gear, and a long spindle carried the power through a hole in the barn wall to drive the threshing machine inside. This, of course, was much slower work than the steam-driven method.

The horse machine would take two days to thresh a stack and sometimes more. Here we had four trussers who worked piece-work again ½d a truss and the day's work was 80 trusses each—3/4d for the day. The rest was day-work 2 men on the mow, 1 man carrying straw away, 1 man caven up, a feeder and a carter and a boy to cut bons—10 men and a boy.

The horse-driven thresher was one of the earliest invented and there is nothing to suggest that its introduction on to the farm many years before had met with anything but resignation. There had been none of the machine-breaking riots of the eighteen-thirties which were so rife in other parts of the country, when labouring men, fearing that their winter-long jobs of threshing in the barns were in jeopardy, went about in gangs smashing the machines that they thought were a threat to their livelihoods. On the other hand, a song still being sung a lot at that time by the sons and grandsons of men who had seen the first machine arrive was clearly written in praise of rather than in protest against it.

It's all very well to have a machine
To thresh your wheat and your barley clean,
To thresh it and wim it all fit for sale,
And go off to market all brisk and well,

Singing rumble-dum-dairy flare up Mary
And make her old table shine.

The man who made her he made her so well,
He made every cog and wheel to tell.
While the big wheel runs and the little one hums,
And the feeder he sits above the drums,

Singing rumble-dum-dairy flare up Mary
And make her old table shine.

There's old Father Howard the sheaves to put,
While old Mother Howard she does make up.
And Mary she sits and feeds all day,
While Johnny he carries the straw away,

Singing rumble-dum-dairy flare up Mary
And make her old table shine.[1]

Threshing, then, in spite of being mechanized, still provided work for a large proportion of the farm hands practically all through the winter.

Another big-scale job at this time of year, when there was
no frost, was ploughing. Just over a thousand acres of arable
land had to be turned over sometime before the following
springtime, to do which they had sixteen ploughs. They were
old, wooden, Sussex turn-wrist ploughs which turned but a
single furrow at a time and each one was capable, as Jim has
told us, of ploughing only one acre in a day, so this was a
mammoth task. He remembered having seen a full muster of
all sixteen of them at work at one time up the Saltdean Valley.
Fourteen of them pulled by two- or three-horse teams and the
other two by teams of bullocks, eight bullocks in each team.
He told me, too, about his own first day at plough as a boy.
He was fourteen years old at the time and had to take Prince
and Swallow up to the Watch-house piece, a twenty-six-acre
laine behind the Coastguard Cottages at Saltdean. He could
see all the other teams at work up the valley and felt pleased
and proud to be doing a man's work at last.

The morning was bright with a stiffish wind coming in off
the sea and by about nine o'clock the 'messengers' started
coming in out of the west. That is what they called the small,
white, fluffy clouds that sometimes came running in before
the wind heralding a rainy period to follow. Sure enough, by
midday the grey clouds had gathered until they closed the sky
right in and the rain came sweeping in off the sea. One by one
the other carters hitched off and made for home but Jim

[1] 'Old Threshing Song.'

stayed on determined at all costs to plough his acre. He stayed on all alone and finished his day's work, by which time he was soaked to the skin. When he got home Grand-dad shouted at him and called him a fool but he took no account of that. He had ploughed his first acre and the pride of achievement kept his spirits high. 'Never mind, boy,' said Grand-dad, concealing very effectively the admiration he must have had for the boy's tenacity, 'you'll learn.'

Inspired, perhaps, by the traditional and whole-hearted celebrations of the occasion in the nearby county town of Lewes, the 5 November was always 'remembered' with great enthusiasm. A long procession, consisting mostly of the younger element, would march all round the village carrying aloft flaring naphthalene torches. Singing, shouting, banging on doors and ringing bells the merry gang would make their way, tearing the soft, black velvet of the night into shreds with brilliant flashes and violent explosions from squibs, chinese crackers and especially 'Lewes Rousers' which were renowned locally for the violence of their detonations. As they proceeded they would from time to time chant out in unison:

'Remember, remember the fifth of November
The Gunpowder Treason and Plot,
I see no reason why Gunpowder Treason
Should ever be forgot.
Guy Fawkes it was his intent
To blow up the King and his Parliament,
With four-score barrels of powder below
To blow old England overthrow.

'But by God's Providence he was catched
With a dark lantern and burning match.
Holler, boys, holler, boys, make the bells ring,
Holler, boys, holler, boys, God save the King.

'A tuppeny loaf to feed old Pope
And a penn'orth of cheese to choke him,
A pint of beer to rinse it down
And a faggot of bush to burn him,

Burn his body right off his head
And then we'll say old Bogey's dead.

'Hip, hip, hip ... Hooray!'

The village street that night was no place for the timorous.
A large bonfire would have previously been built in the
middle of the cross-roads where the lower end of the High
Street was intersected by the main coast road. It was to this
centre that the noisy throng finally made their way to light
the fire with their flaring torches; then they danced round the
blaze in the flickering flame-light, still mechanically repeating
their anti-papist chant, with a total lack of religious conviction.

Jim related how on one particular occasion they had built
a large fire with drift-wood picked up on the foreshore,
including the keel and bottom planks, all covered with tar,
of a wrecked dinghy. This made a wonderful blaze and the
local policeman, P.C. Wills, had assumed the role of chief
stoker. When later in the evening the fuel began to run low
he urged the lads to go and search for more. 'We want more
firing, me lucky lads. Get about and pick up what you can
where you can.' Off they went in different directions, picking
up anything combustible that they could lay their hands on,
and when they got to his garden they saw his runner-bean
rods all tied up in a bundle and stacked against his shed ready
for next year. They humped them down to the fire with the
rest of the stuff and poor P.C. Wills, failing to recognize
them in the excitement of the moment, threw them on the
fire himself. 'Come along, me bonny boys,' he hollered,
'Keep her burning. The more the merrier.'

# December

*hand-bells*

*Our barns they are full, our fields they are clear,*
*Good luck to our master and friends.*
*We'll make no more to do but we'll plough and we'll sow*
*And prepare for the very next year.*

'Two Young Brethren'[1]

As we got further into winter especially if it was frosty there was the yards to be cleared of dung. We had five sheep yards and our home nine stables and the cowstalls to clear of dung, and I have seen over 200 cartload in Court Farm Yard outside the cowstalls where Tudor Close lawn and sundial is now. And then there was the dung from Brighton which was always taken straight from Brighton to the field where it was going to be used and unloaded in a lump which we called the 'mixen'. This was taken out with 3 horses and carts— sometimes if a big laine,—3 fillers, carter to shelve, or unload, and boys to drive to and fro till 2.30 p.m. The fillers would take their dinner with them and when the horses had gone home they had to stop and spread 40 load to fill in their day.

Well this dunging made off with a good bit of our time in the winter and it covered a good many acres with beautiful stuff.

Some dung-spreading was done piece-work. One day Jim was in the store-room filing up with the other chaps to Grand-dad's office to collect what was due to him in the way of wages. He had done some overtime but when it came to his turn he was handed his exact weekly wage. He stood for a while looking at it and Grand-dad said, 'Get on there, mairt, what are y' 'anging about for?'

'We done a bit of overtime this wik, Dad, dung-spreading up Man and Mare.'

[1] See Jim Copper's Song Book.

'You ben't goin' t' charge me f' that, be ye?'

'Well, we've bin thinkin' of it over,' said Jim,' and we reckon that bein' 'eavy it's worth three shillings an acre.'

'You come an' see me agin after the wik-end,' said the old man.

On Monday morning he called Jim over. 'I've bin up Man an' Mare and 'ad a look at that 'ere dung you wuz supposed to spread,' he said, 'an' I've bin thinkin' of it over, too. If you go an' spread it agin, I'll pay y' 2/9 an acre'.

After telling me this tale Jim observed thoughtfully, 'You 'ad a job to git one over on my ol' Daddy.'

By this time it was beginning to feel a bit like Christmas. The puddings had been boiled in the copper in the corner of the scullery some weeks before and the boys had started hand-bell ringing and practising the 'Mummer's Play' in the evenings down at the Black Horse. During the week before Christmas they used to visit all the big houses in the village in turn with the bells and the Mummers and were welcomed with plenty of Christmas fare in the way of wine, beer and cake. One night, they were on their way up the High Street making for 'Hillside' where Colonel Phillips and his family and friends were awaiting their arrival. They were all fairly talkative, having spent a considerable time around the punch-bowl at the previous call, and by the time they reached Reading Room Corner Father Christmas and Black Jack were having a heated argument. A few yards further on Father Christmas gave Black Jack a swipe round the head with his holly bush and Jack, forgetting for a moment the 'peace and goodwill' part of the Christmas message, retaliated with his birch broom. They 'leathered into each other like a couple of tom-cats' but after a short while were separated and prevailed upon to proceed in an orderly fashion. On being admitted to Colonel Phillips's parlour, however, Father Christmas, who had still not quite regained his composure, stepped through the door and blurted out with an air of defiance, 'In come I ol' Faather Chris'mus, be I walcum or be I bain't?' Then in the lighted interior of the room they could see that his cotton-wool beard was all askew and hanging from one ear, and his holly bush, which was his badge of office, had been broken and stripped of all but one or two leaves. Black Jack, too, showed signs of battle. He had had a slight nose-bleed and there were only two or three twigs of birch left on his broom. The company of players, however, made a brave recovery and the audience accepted these little discrepancies in the spirit of the occasion. After the beer jugs and wine decanter had gone the rounds the play ran its course and with wishes all round for a merry holiday they all parted on the best of terms.

It was under the tiny roof of Grand-dad's cottage at Northgate that the whole family met at Christmas time, the one and sometimes only occasion in the year when they all got together at the same time, in spite of the fact that most of them lived in the village. There was, however, one exception. Jim had an uncle that lived just off the High Street who was not of a very sociable disposition. He was happier spending his evenings sitting on the settle in the corner of the Black Horse tap-room in the company of his beer pot and clay pipe. He was, it seems, a 'queer ol' cove' who habitually wore a smock, 'Lord above knows what he wore underneath', comments Jim, 'rags I shouldn't wonder.' He was also an inveterate tobacco-chewer, as were many of his contemporaries. 'He didn't like comin' to our place,' said Jim, "cos he wouldn't be allowed to spit in the fire. Anyway,' he added scornfully, "e couldn't sing.'

Grand-dad, being foreman on the farm and a man of some substance in the village, kept a good table all through the year but at Christmas time it creaked beneath the weight of extra drink and foodstuffs. There was always a huge turkey of about twenty-five lbs or more so that you 'could cut an' come agin' and the farmer every year gave him a sixteen-lb round of local beef as a seasonable gift. These two items alone were far too large for the cottage oven and so the boys had to take them down to Allwork's the bakers, who always lit the ovens specially for the Christmas morning roastings.

By about midday that small cottage was fairly bulging with people. There were aunts and uncles, cousins and second-cousins, aunts' brothers and uncles' sisters and all the motley gang of various ages that were connected, by whatever tenuous relationships, to the family home. Long trails of star-leafed ivy festooned the dresser and sprigs of holly sprouted from behind the pictures on the wall. To mark the occasion Grand-dad would be wearing his fancy waistcoat, the one with the knitted panels in red and green, bisected vertically by a curving line of small round buttons like cat's eyes, and horizontally by a gold 'Albert' watch-chain which looped away in opposite directions from one of the central buttons to disappear into two pockets on either side of his sturdy frontage. There would be a lively exchange of family and village trivialities going on while glasses of sherry or 'hot toddy' were sipped in a log-blazing cigar-filled atmosphere.

About one o'clock, the lads went down to the bakehouse to see if the bird was fit for the table. Being such a giant of a bird the turkey was very often the last one out of the oven and, as the bakehouse was so conveniently close to the Black Horse—the back door of which was almost within arm's reach—they would wait in the tap-room until the baker gave them a shout. By the time this happened they had probably consumed two or three glasses of Uncle Tommy's strong Christmas Ale. That was a powerful good beer, and as Jim said, 'Carrying the beef and turkey home after a couple of glasses of that was a bit of a dido. You 'ad to take middlin' short steps sometimes to keep from spillin' the drippin'.'

Grand-dad was fortunate in that he had learnt how to turn water—and pond water at that—if not into wine, at least into beer. In return for allowing the various breweries on their weekly visits to the village to fill up their steam-driven drays with water at the farm ponds he was rewarded in kind. From one he had a regular supply throughout the year of mild beer in casks, which were stolleged up in the cupboard under the stairs, and at Christmas time this was supplemented with a cask of XXXX Ale, and a further cask of double stout for the ladies. From another brewer he received a cask of specially brewed Christmas Ale. 'Dan'l that would make your ol' eyes strike fire,' said Jim, 'That was like rhubub wine—lovely.'

Grand-dad, with his deep booming delivery, said grace much slower than usual which, together with the sight of the laden table, added weight and significance to his words,

'For what we are about to receive may the Lord make us *truly* thankful.'

There was always something rather odd about tea-time on Christmas Day. It seemed more of a ceremony than a meal. Whereas no one could imagine Christmas Day without its lavish display of a huge iced cake, sweet and savoury sandwiches, chocolate biscuits and cream confections and homemade mince pies, neither could they raise the slightest enthusiasm for it. They just were not hungry.

While teacups were drained in quick succession, the mountains of foodstuffs remained practically untouched. The Christmas cake was pecked and nibbled at as a sort of ritual but the mince pies remained a problem. Each mince pie eaten, it used to be said, ensured one happy month in the ensuing year and although from January until about April or May could be accounted for fairly comfortably, the fate of high summer would be in the balance until finally after August or September, despite the loosening of belts and the unfastening of top trouser buttons, the struggle would have to be abandoned and the remainder of the year reluctantly left to chance.

After tea and after the beer jugs had been passed round to 'wet their whistles', Grand-dad seated in his armchair on one side of the fire would nod gravely to Uncle Tom on the other and with no more ado would launch into the first carol. All the company of uncles and aunts, brothers, sisters and cousins would join in with their home-spun harmonies and variations until the little cottage fairly shook with sound. Christmas hymns followed carols one after another and the natural, unsophisticated voices raised in simple worship expressed the pleasure and gratitude of everyone for being all together on yet another Christmas night.

'Shepherds arise, be not afraid with hasty steps prepare
To David's city, sin on earth,
With our blest Infant—with our blest Infant there,
With our blest Infant there, with our blest Infant there.
Sing, sing, all earth, sing, sing, all earth eternal praises sing
To our Redeemer, to our Redeemer and our Heavenly King.'[1]

Thus the earlier part of the evening was spent in singing
sacred music and as Jim said, 'If you was fed up with beer by
nine o'clock you'd have to sit and wait for anything stronger.
For my old Daddy wouldn't allow any wines or spirits on the
table until half-past nine.' By that time the repertoire of
Christmas music was about exhausted and the 'old songs'
would follow, while passers-by paused and stood for a while
outside to listen. Brasser and his family were keeping up
Christmas in the traditional way once again.

At eleven o'clock they would shut down for supper. The
first thing to be put on the table was a 12 lb ham which was
an annual present from the farmer's wife to Granny. Then the
round of beef and, what was probably the favourite of all, a
great, cold, boned-rabbit pie all set in thick jelly with flank of
bacon and hard-boiled eggs. If Granny had not got a pie dish
large enough she would bake two. Grand-dad would carve
the ham and beef and when everybody had got a plateful, he
would sit down to his own and then start singing,

'O, don't you remember a long time ago
Those two little babies their names I don't know,
They strayed away one fine summer's day,
Those two little babies got lost on their way.
Pretty babes in the wood, pretty babes in the wood,
O, don't you remember those babes in the wood.'[2]

This song was always sung during supper on Christmas
night and by an ingenious method of alternating the singing
and eating, the continuity of both the song and the supper was
maintained. The song would swing from one side of the table
to the other like a shuttlecock. Roughly one half of the singers,

[1] 'Shepherds Arise.'          [2] 'Babes in the Wood.'

with food-laden forks poised in front of them, taking the first
two lines of a verse while the other half hastily devoured a
mouthful of rabbit pie in time to take the last two, on the
completion of which all had to be clear for the whole company to join in the chorus. One cannot help thinking that in
the interests of everyone's digestion it was a good thing the
song had only three verses.

On Boxing Day in the morning the Brookside Harriers
always met on the Green opposite Down House where Mr
Steyning Beard, the Master, lived. At 11 a.m. sharp Grand-
dad would pour himself a strong hot gin, light a cigar in his
meerschaum and amber holder and 'doddle off down to the
meet'. After the stirrup cup had gone round to the gentlemen
and the jugs of beer had been handed out the hunt would
move off to draw their first cover. They could always rely
on one of the shepherds, who were well acquainted with the
wild life on the downs, to tell them where they would be
likely to find a hare and they would pay him four shillings
for his information.

The hunt usually returned at about 4 p.m. and after they
had had time to have dinner, Grand-dad, Uncle Tommy,
John and Jim would go to Down House and stand on the lawn
and start singing carols. Jim said, 'We usually started off on
something pretty easy as we had all had a bit of a stinger the
night before and usually felt a little bit ornery.' By the time
they had got to about the third verse, Mr Steyning Beard
would open the door and say, 'Come inside, Jim, come in,
Tommy—all of you, and let's have some decent hunting
songs. We can hear those other things when we go to church
on Sunday mornings.' When they got inside there would be
a big log-fire flaring away on the hearth with the gentlemen
all sitting round still in their hunting gear and on the table
would be a 'damn gurt bowl of punch', piping hot. The
master would ladle some out and say, 'Come on, you must
have some punch before you start. You can't sing on an
empty stomach y'know.' And so they would sing all the old
hunting songs and many others well on into the evening.

'You gentlemen of high renown come listen unto me
Who take delight in fox and hounds of every high degree.
A story true to you I'll tell concerning of a fox,
In Oxford town in Oxfordshire there lived some mighty hounds.'[1]

The wheel of the year had run round another full circle—
from lambing-time to the long, hot sheep-shearing days of
June along through haying and harvest and on to the dark,
dung-spreading days of December. Each season bringing its
own particular tasks and long, hard days of labour. O, yes,
there was plenty of work and worry but there was also a song
for every season and always a stout heart and a lusty voice
to sing it.

[1] 'Gentlemen of High Renown.'

# Epilogue

Grand-dad had died in 1924 but not before the spirit of singing the old songs, already adopted so faithfully by Jim and Uncle John, had been passed on to our generation. My cousin Ron and I sang together whenever the opportunity arose and also in a foursome with our fathers. Ron took on the bass line with Jim while I modelled my style on and sang with Uncle John. Right up until the nineteen-thirties the Black Horse was still the place for a sing-song on a Saturday night and, although their ranks were rapidly thinning, one or two of the old-timers were still to be seen and heard there. Long before I had reached the proper age to visit licensed premises I did in fact make many surreptitious visits into the Bottle and Jug department of the 'Black 'un' to try my hand at drinking beer and to listen to the old men singing. Sometimes, if I was spotted, I would be called through into the public bar, 'Come round 'ere, young Copper, and let's 'ave a song, boy.' The 'every song a drink' rule still held and so I had a good early schooling in how to sink a pint.

These men were the last of the old school and they clung on to the singing of the old songs as one of the few things that remained constant in a rapidly changing world. With what affection and enthusiasm did they join in the old familiar choruses of songs like 'Twanky Dillo'.

'Here's a health to the jolly blacksmith the best of all fellows
Who works at his anvil while the boy blows the bellows,
Which makes his bright hammer to rise and to fall.
There's the old Cole and the young Cole and the old Cole of all,
Twanky Dillo, Twanky Dillo, Twanky Dillo, dillo, dillo, dillo,
And a roaring pair of bagpipes made from the green willow.'[1]

[1] See Jim Copper's Song Book.

'Well done, young 'en,' said old Bill Hilder one night, 'ol'
Jimmy Copper'll never be dead all the time you're alive.' I
was never really certain whether he meant my father or
grandfather but in either case I accepted it as a compliment.

In that jam-packed room where the atmosphere was near
curdled with strong shag tobacco and even stronger language
someone would call for a 'bit of hush' and the glass-chinking
would stop and the voices die away as some old fellow, bowed
nearly double with years of work and weather, got up to sing.
He would take a sooted-up clay pipe from his mouth with a
hand like a clump of blackthorn, clear his throat, spit approximately in the direction of the spittoon, then, raising his eyes
to heaven as if listening for a cue from some celestial promp-
ter, would sing naturally and tenderly a song like 'Sweet
Lemeney'.

> 'Oh hark, oh hark, how the nightingale is singing
> The lark she is taking her flight all in the air.
> On yonder green bower the turtle dove is building
> The sun is just a-glimmering, arise my dear.'[1]

The choice of song and the way in which it was sung
revealed a chink in that tough exterior and something of the
tenderness of the man himself showed through.

It is difficult now to realize just how much these songs
meant to the old people. In most cases, particularly to the non-
churchgoers who were in the majority, in the circles in which
I moved, they were the one and only source of cultural
nourishment. In their songs they found their music, their
poetry, their drama and their humour and singing them was
their main escape from the heavy yoke of repetitious, mind-
dulling toil.

But these men were the last of a dying race of old-time
countrymen and outside of their ranks the appreciation of
such songs was practically non-existent. Among our contemporaries Ron and I found that far from being appreciated
the songs even met with a good deal of antipathy. They were

[1] See Jim Copper's Song Book.

old-fashioned and out of date and not nearly so exciting as the American importations that came though the horn loud-speakers in the corner of almost everyone's living-room. This only strengthened our resolve to keep them alive. When out walking on the hills as we often were, Ron and I would sing to our hearts' content with no one to offend but the larks in the sky or the rabbits in the gorse patches.

One day in 1950 Jim came to me and said, 'They sung one of our songs on the wireless last week in a programme called Country Magazine.' 'Oh,' said I, 'what kind of a job did they make of it?' 'Bloody awful,' he said, 'they had some chap tinkling away on a jo-anna all the time t'other 'en was singing. Anyway they didn't know it properly.' However, I persuaded him to write to the B.B.C. and say how pleased he had been to hear on the air one of the many old songs that we still sang. On receipt of Jim's letter, Mr Francis Collinson, the musical director of the programme, came at once to Rotting-dean and in the front room of the cottage at Northgate noted down the words and music of about forty songs as Jim and I sang them. On subsequent visits he collected twenty or so more.

Soon after this Jim and I were asked to sing a song, 'Claudy Banks', in a Country Magazine programme which took place, live, in the garden of the Eight Bells Inn at Jevington, Sussex on Sunday 20 August 1950. The Rottingdean songs were, for the first time, sung to a nation-wide audience instead of to a handful of friends in the tap-room of the Black Horse.

Our very first radio broadcast took place in conditions and surroundings that might have been purposely designed to set at ease two inexperienced country singers to whom the world of broadcasting was more than a little frightening. The garden was in all its late summer glory and we stood on the lawn looking down to the high, bare ridge of the South Downs in the heart of that part of Sussex to which we all—both songs and singers—belonged.

"Twas on one summer's evening all in the month of May
Down by a flowery garden where Betsy did stray.

I overheard a damsel in sorry to complain,
All for her absent lover that ploughs the raging main.'[1]

In the calm, avuncular presence of Ralph Wightman we were made to feel at home. But Frank Collinson was our counsellor and guide. I often wonder what he must have thought about being responsible for two tap-room songsters going out on a live broadcast to such a huge audience. He must have had terrible misgivings but he was ever charming, courteous and complimentary about our efforts. As we were singing at rehearsal he moved around us, as attentive as a hen with a brood of chicks, inclining his head from side to side, beating time with his arms or closing his eyes and cupping an ear to listen intently first to Jim and then to me. For my part I found it pretty disconcerting to have a professional and critical ear poised within inches of my mouth while singing and Jim felt a trifle uneasy too. We were in full song once and Frank's ear was nearly inside Jim's mouth as he listened to those deep, rolling bass runs. He was beaming with satisfaction and muttered, half to himself I fancy, 'Just listen to those diminishing fifths.' Jim stopped singing abruptly. 'What the 'ell d'you mean—"diminishing fifths"—'ave we gone wrong or summat? That's the way we always 'ave sung 'er.' Frank tried to explain what he meant, without much success, I fear, but at least he assured us that all was well and we were doing all right. The broadcast was well received and many people expressed their appreciation of a 'country song sung by country people'.

Later a programme entitled 'The Life of James Copper' was transmitted on the B.B.C. Home Service, and Jim appeared on the front page of the *Radio Times*. Recordings followed for inclusion in the B.B.C. Permanent Library of Music and upwards of sixty tracks were added to the slender ranks of what remained of the English folk-singing tradition. Two songs were taken to Washington, U.S.A. by Mr Alan Lomax to be included in the World Library of Folk Music there. Inspired and heartened by this comparative mine of

[1] 'Claudy Banks.'

songs from one source in a country where it was thought traditional folk music had gone the way of the dodo, the B.B.C. instigated a country-wide search for the remnants of traditional singing to make field recordings and preserve them for posterity. It proved to be an excellent follow-up to the splendid spade work done by those pioneers of the eighteen-nineties, like Mrs Kate Lee, who were, of course, restricted merely to noting down the words and music of the songs. This time, thanks to tape recorders, the actual voices of the singers could be recorded and this conveyed precisely the intricate and often delicate styles adopted by the older singers, which had proved practically impossible for the earlier collectors to transcribe faithfully on to paper. These efforts resulted in an excellent and representative collection of songs from practically every county in the British Isles being added to the B.B.C. Library. It also marked the beginning of the folk music revival.

In January 1952 we were invited to sing at a two-day folk music festival at the Royal Albert Hall, London, sponsored by the English Folk Dance and Song Society.

'Albert 'all?' said Jim, 'there'll be a tidy ol' few people up there, wun't there?'

'About six or eight thousand, I shouldn't wonder,' volunteered John.

'Yeah. Wal,' Jim looked ponderous, 'we wanna pick out a couple o' songs and work into 'em until we can rattle 'em off word perfect. Then it's up to you, Bob, to pitch 'er right fust time. There wun't be no going back once we've started up there.'

I was acutely aware that the success, or otherwise, of this our first major public appearance would hinge on my ability to pluck the correct note on which to start singing out of the highly charged atmosphere of a concert platform in front of a huge audience. The two songs we chose were 'Twanky Dillo' and 'Brisk and Bonny Lad' and with the latter there was absolutely no margin for error in pitching. One note and one note alone enabled us to sing it correctly.

Knowing only too well my own musical shortcomings I decided that this was too important a thing to be left to chance and bought a tuning fork in 'C'. Not that the key made any difference. I only wanted a note to work from. When we sang at home I often used an old sheep bell but it was not so convenient to carry. Through trial and error I found that by 'dinging' my new musical aid, dropping an octave and singing the first three notes of a popular song of the 'Twenties called 'Memories', I could get on the note that was required.

This gave us confidence but we nevertheless arranged to meet at my place on the afternoon before we were due to appear in order to run through the two songs together. We stood in a semicircle near the boiler for warmth and Jim propped a broom, head uppermost, against a chair. 'Make out that's a microphone,' he said. We were creating, as nearly as possible, the excitement and taut atmosphere that we would be bound to experience on the following day when our big moment arrived. I dinged the fork, singing mentally, 'Mem-or-ies'. That was it. I leant across and hummed the note lightly to the others and was just about to give a 'one-two' beat with my forefinger to signal the off when—

"Old 'ard a minute,' said Jim. He sniffed mightily, cleared his throat with a great deal of hawking, opened the boiler door and spat. 'Ah, that's better,' he said as he clanged the heavy door shut on the sizzling embers, 'catarrh, dun't ye know.'

'You'd best remember to see to all that before we get up there on that stage tomorrow,' said John, 'I don't suppose they've got a boiler up there.'

After this shattering interruption we resumed and the songs went along merrily enough. When we had finished John returned his pipe to his mouth and lit up. 'Wal, there 'tis. If they don't like it that's their fault. They shouldn't 'ave ast us —'cos we can't sing it no bloody better.' This neat shift of the onus of responsibility appealed to us all immensely and we approached the occasion in high spirits.

At the Albert Hall next day I looked at a programme and noticed that we were due to go on after the interval. I asked Peter Kennedy, who was in charge, at about what time he thought we would be expected on stage. He estimated that it would be about 9.45 to 10 p.m. 'Then you had better do something about that,' I told him, 'I shall never keep us all sober until then.' He wondered if I was serious. 'I've never been more serious in my life,' I said, 'This is a day out for us and on a day out we always enjoy ourselves and reckon to have a "tidy ol' wet"—Albert Hall or no.' We replaced four friendly Burmese dancers in the first half who kindly consented to go on in our spot in the second.

All went well and next morning, Preston Benson, the music critic in the *Star*, had this to say,

> Surprise of the Folk Dance Festival at the Albert Hall was the traditional folk song singing by four of a Rottingdean family. John Copper, 73; his brother James, 70; and their respective sons Ronald, 40 and Robert, 36.
> It was the first stage appearance of these Sussex characters from the B.B.C.'s 'Country Magazine'. They came on in their work-a-day clothes and spurning a microphone sang 'Brisk and Bonny Lad' and 'Twanky Dillo' naturally and sweetly. Their words, unlike those of many professional singers, were clear and comprehensible.

'Bugger,' said Ron, 'we'd all got our Sunday suits on, too.'
On the second day the lapels of our Sunday suits were adorned with the plaited-sword emblem of the English Folk Dance and Song Society badge and another link in the chain had been forged. Over half a century after Grand-dad and Uncle Tom had shared the privilege we too had been made honorary members of the Society.

There followed a number of radio broadcasts and television appearances from Alexandra Palace and, with the help and encouragement of various producers devoted to the cause, we did our damndest to bridge the gap between the tap-room and the concert platform. The pallid ghost of the old singing tradition was living on only in the artificial world of folk song recitals where, to the accompaniment of piano and 'cello, elegantly-gowned sopranos with flourishing chiffon handker-chieves, or moustachioed baritones in evening dress, made brave attempts at resuscitation. Their efforts were, in my view, unavailing for in the rarefied air of the concert hall some subtle yet essential element was missing. If we contri-buted in any measure to breathing a little life back into a dying art then we shall count it a great privilege to have had the opportunity. We certainly enjoyed trying.

On 12 May 1952 we had arranged to give a concert of songs at Cecil Sharp House, the headquarters of the E.F.D.S.S., in London, but early in the morning of that very day Uncle John was suddenly taken ill and died. I trav-elled up alone to make a token appearance and give the sad reason for our non-appearance as a family. I felt little like singing but was prevailed upon to sing just one item and I chose the song that Uncle John would have sung as a solo if he had been there, 'The Week before Easter'. The last verse ran like this:

> 'So dig me a grave both long wide and deep
> And strew it all over with roses so sweet,
> That I might lay down there and take a long sleep
> And that's the right way to forget her.'[1]

A few days later at a simple service in the little flint church John was laid to rest in that patch of Sussex earth to which so many of our family had been returned. I sent no wreath but threw on to his coffin as it lay in its last resting place a spray of roses and a card inscribed: '—and strew it all over with roses so sweet . . .'

To Jim the loss of his brother and lifelong friend was a bitter blow but so far as the singing went he was happy to know that Ron and I were determined and able to keep the tradition alive and made every effort to encourage us to do so.

Two years later in 1954 Jim, too, died. He had previously expressed in his own inimitable way a specific preference for

[1] See Jim Copper's Song Book.

cremation. 'When I die, boy,' he said to me one day, 'have me burnt and then you take my cinders up on the hill and shake 'em round that ol' boundstone near Blind Pit.' This was a favourite spot of his which he had known and loved ever since he had been a shepherd boy and in later years he would frequently visit it just to sit quietly and smoke a contemplative pipe looking down the valley between the interfolding hills and out to sea with no other company than the 'flick or feather' he had so often plundered in earlier life.

On a grey afternoon in steady rain I trudged up the hill from Saltdean Valley, where my family were waiting in a car, to the spot I knew so well and which Jim had delineated in a pencil-drawn map. I opened the plain cardboard box containing his last mortal remains and scattered them reverently around the boundary stone which had probably been there since Saxon days and now stands as Jim's unwritten epitaph. With the last handful of dust, amongst the young and tender blades of a crop of winter-sown barley close by, I traced a cross pointing towards the east. Jim's last request had been carried out. I waved my arm down to the waiting car and stood for a moment with bared head in the drenching rain. As I walked down the hill my head was ringing with snatches of many of the songs we had sung together and loved so much.

In 1958 there was the diamond jubilee of the English Folk Dance and Song Society. At a concert held to mark the occasion we were invited along to sing and were honoured to be in the company of such eminent stalwarts of English folk music as Dr Ralph Vaughan Williams, Mr Clive Carey and Percy Grainger. A cake which had been baked for the occasion bore the inscription in icing sugar 'English Folk Dance and Song Society 1898–1958' and in musical notation the opening bars of 'Claudy Banks', which Mrs. Kate Lee had noted down from Grand-dad and Uncle Tom over sixty years before—the first song collected on behalf of the Society. Ron and I sang the song, while Dr Vaughan Williams cut the cake.

We are singing to this day but a significant step forward was taken on 4 June 1965, when my son John sang with me on his sixteenth birthday at the Royal Festival Hall in a concert called the 'Sound of Folk'. By doing so he had become the fourth generation of bass singers in my lifetime and the third that I had had the pleasure of singing with in public. More recently my daughter Jill has joined us and it seems that the songs are in no immediate danger of dying.

Down in 'Copper's Corner' in the village churchyard, near the shed where the sexton keeps his tools, there is an air of calm and contentment and a total absence of gloom. I think all the old folk would be glad if they knew that something of those distant days in eighteenth- and nineteenth-century rural England lives on in their songs.

# Jim Copper's
# Song Book

Musical transcriptions of Copper family songs
by Soundpost Publications.

Music artwork by David Kettlewell.

'Come Write Me Down' copyright © 1969 E.F.D.S. Publications Ltd.
Reprinted by permission.

Four LP records of the complete Copper family songs
are now available on the Leader label.

# Contents

## Turn o' the Year

## 'Tater Beer Night

# Turn o' the Year

O don't you re-mem-ber a long time a-go Those
two lit-tle bab-ies their names I don't know They
strayed a-way one bright sum-mer's day Those
two lit-tle bab-ies got lost on their way Pret-ty
babes in the wood pretty babes in the wood O
don't you re-mem-ber those babes in the wood.

## Babes in the Wood

O, don't you remember a long time ago
Those two little babies their names I don't know,
They strayed away one bright summer's day,
Those two little babies got lost on their way.
Pretty babes in the wood, pretty babes in the wood,
O, don't you remember those babes in the wood?

Now the day being done and the night coming on
Those two little babies sat under a stone.
They sobbed and they sighed they sat there and cried,
Those two little babies they lay down and died.
Pretty babes in the wood, pretty babes in the wood,
O, don't you remember those babes in the wood?

Now the robins so red how swiftly they sped,
They put out their wide wings and over them spread.
And all the day long in the branches they throng,
They sweetly did whistle and this was their song,
Pretty babes in the wood, pretty babes in the wood,
O, don't you remember those babes in the wood?

'Twas of a brisk young plough-boy come lis-ten to this re-frain and
join with me in chor-us and sing the plough-boy's praise My
song is of the plough-boy's praise and un-to you I'll re-late the same. He
whist-les and sings and drives his plough, the brave plough-boy

(This song used to have the following rhythm:—)

# Brisk Young Ploughboy

'Twas of a brisk young ploughboy, come listen to this refrain
And join with me in chorus and sing the ploughboy's praise.
My song is of the ploughboy's praise and unto you I'll relate the same,
He whistles and sings and drives his plough, the brave ploughboy.

So early in the morning the ploughboy he is seen
All hastening to the stable his horses for to clean.
Their manes and tails he does comb straight, with chaff and corn he
    will them bate
And he'll endeavour to plough straight, the brave ploughboy.

When he goes out in the morning to harrow plough or sow
And with a gentle cast, my boys, he'll give his corn a throw.
All this I'll have you understand is just to fill the reaper's hand,
Likewise I'll have you understand, it comes from the ploughboy.

Now seedtime being over the fields look fresh and gay
There's merry lads to mow the grass while damsels make the hay.
The small birds sing on every tree, the cuckoo joins sweet harmony,
All welcome here as you may see, the brave ploughboy.

Then haying being over and harvest does draw near,
Our Master he does welcome us with plenty of beef and beer.
We all sit round to drink our beer while Peace and Plenty fill the
    year
And we'll be happy while we are here and drink to the ploughboy.

Now harvest being over we start the plough once more,
Our Master has invited us unlocks his cellar door.
With cake and ale we have our fill because we've done our work so
    well
And there's no one can despise the skill of the brave ploughboy.

The Trees are all bare not a leaf to be seen And the

mead-ows their beau-ty have lost Now win-ter has

come and 'tis cold for man and beast and the streams they are

and the streams they are all fast bound down with frost

## Christmas Song

The trees are all bare not a leaf to be seen
And the meadows their beauty have lost.
Now winter has come and 'tis cold for man and beast,
And the streams they are,
And the streams they are all fast bound down with frost.

'Twas down in the farmyard where the oxen feed on straw,
They send forth their breath like the steam.
Sweet Betsy the milkmaid now quickly she must go,
For flakes of ice she finds,
For flakes of ice she finds a-floating on her cream.

'Tis now all the small birds to the barn-door fly for food
And gently they rest on the spray.
A-down the plantation the hares do search for food,
And lift their footsteps sure,
Lift their footsteps sure for fear they do betray.

Now Christmas is come and our song is almost done
For we soon shall have the turn of the year.
So fill up your glasses and let your health go round,
For I wish you all,
For I wish you all a joyful New Year.

Come all broth-er trades-men that trav-el a-lone  O pray come and tell me where the trade is all gone  Long time I have trav-elled and can-not find none  And it's O, the hard times of old Eng-land— — In old Eng-e-land ver-y hard times

# Hard Times of Old England

Come all brother tradesmen that travel alone,
O, pray come and tell me where the trade is all gone,
Long time I have travelled and cannot find none,
And it's O, the hard times of old England,
In old England very hard times.

Provisions you buy at the shop it is true,
But if you've no money there's none there for you.
So what's a poor man and his family to do?
And it's O, the hard times of old England,
In old England very hard times.

If you go to a shop and you ask for a job
They will answer you there with a shake and a nod.
That's enough to make a poor man to turn out and rob,
And it's O, the hard times of old England,
In old England very hard times.

You will see the poor tradesmen a-walking the street
From morning till night for employment to seek.
And scarcely they have any shoes to their feet,
And it's O, the hard times of old England,
In old England very hard times.

Our soldiers and sailors have just come from war,
Been fighting for their King and their country sure,
Come home to be starved better have stayed where they were,
And it's O, the hard times of old England,
In old England very hard times.

So now to conclude and to finish my song
Let us hope that these hard times they will not last long,
And I may soon have occasion to alter my song,
And sing O, the good times of old England,
In old England very good times.

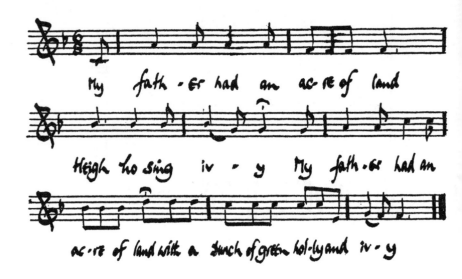

My fath-er had an ac-re of land

Heigh ho sing iv - y My fath-er had an

ac-re of land with a bunch of green hol-ly and iv - y

# Heigh-ho, Sing Ivy

My father had an acre of land, heigh-ho, sing ivy,
My father had an acre of land, with a bunch of green holly and ivy.

He ploughed it with a team of rats, heigh-ho, sing ivy,
He ploughed it with a team of rats, with a bunch of green holly
    and ivy.

He sowed it with a pepper-box, *etc.*

He harrowed it with a small tooth comb, *etc.*

He rolled it with a rolling-pin, *etc.*

He reaped it with the blade of his knife, *etc.*

He wheeled it home in a wheelbarrow, *etc.*

He threshed it with a hazel twig, *etc.*

He wimmed it on the tail of his shirt, *etc.*

He measured it up with a walnut shell, *etc.*

He sent it to market on a hedgehog's back, *etc.*

He sold the lot for eighteenpence, *etc.*

And now the poor old man is dead, *etc.*

We buried him with his team of rats, heigh-ho, sing ivy,
And all his tools lay by his side, with a bunch of green holly and ivy.

*The Ploughshare*

The sun has gone down and the sky it looks red
Down on my soft pillow where I lay my head,
When I open my eyes for to see the stars shine
Then the thoughts of my true love run into my mind.

The sap has gone down and the leaves they do fall,
To hedging and ditching our farmers they'll call.
We will trim up their hedges we will cut down their wood
And the farmers they'll all say our faggots run good.

Now hedging being over then sawing draws near
We will send for the sawyer the woods for to clear.
And after he has sawed them and tumbled them down
Then there he will flaw them all on the cold ground.

When sawing is over then seedtime comes round,
See our teams they are already preparing the ground,
Then the man with his seed-lip he'll scatter the corn
Then the harrows they will bury it to keep it from harm.

Now seedtime being over then haying draws near,
With our scythes, rakes, and pitch-forks those meadows to clear.
We will cut down their grass, boys, and carry it away,
We will first call it green grass and then call it hay.

When haying is over then harvest draws near
We will send to our Brewer to brew us strong beer,
And in brewing strong beer, boys, we will cut down their corn
And we'll take it to the barn, boys, to keep it from harm.

Now harvest being over bad weather comes on,
We will send for the thresher to thresh out our corn.
His hand-staff he'll handle, his swingel he'll swing,
Till the very next harvest we'll all meet again.

Now since we have brought this so cheerfully around
We will send for the jolly ploughman to plough up the ground.
See the boy with his whip and the man to his plough
Here's a health to the jolly ploughmen that plough up the ground.

*Toast:* Here's success to the bright ploughshare and may it never rust.

*Company:* May the ploughshare never rust.

*Seamen Bold*

You seamen bold that plough the ocean know dangers landsmen
  never know,
The sun goes down with an equal motion no tongue can tell what
  you undergo.
In dreadful storm, in dread of battle there are no back doors to
  run away
While thund'ring cannon loudly rattle, mark well what happened
  the other day.

A merchant ship a long time had sail-ed, long time being captive
out at sea.
The weather proved so unsettled which brought them to extremity.
Nothing on board, poor souls, to cherish nor could step one foot
on freedom's shore,
Poor fellows they were almost starving, there was nothing left but
skin and bone.

Their cats and dogs how they did eat them their hunger being so
very severe,
Captain and men in one position, Captain and men went equal
share.
But still at last a hitch came on them, a hitch came on them right
speedily,
Captain and men stood in a totter casting out lots to know who
should die.

The lot it fell on one poor sailor his family being so very great.
Those very words did he grieve sorrow those very words did he
regret,
I'm willing to die my brother mess-mates if you to the top-mast
will haste away,
And perhaps you might some sail discover while I unto our dear
Lord do pray.

Those very words did he grieve sorrow those very words did he
regret,
When a merchant ship there came a-sailing there came a-sailing to
their delight.
May God protect all jolly sailors who boldly venture on the main
And keep them free from all such trials never to hear the likes
again.

Shep-herds a-rise be not— a-fraid— with

has— sty steps pre-pare To Dav-id's

ci—ty sin— on earth with our blest in-fant

there— with our blest in-fant there, with our blest

in—fant there Sing sing all earth sing sing all earth e-

-ter—— nal prais-es sing To

our Re-deem-er, to our Re-deem-er and our heaven-ly King

## Shepherds Arise

Shepherds arise, be not afraid, with hasty steps prepare
To David's city, sin on earth,
With our blest Infant—with our blest Infant there,
With our blest Infant there, with our blest Infant there.
Sing, sing, all earth, sing, sing, all earth eternal praises sing
To our Redeemer, to our Redeemer and our heavenly King.

Laid in a manger viewed a Child, humility Divine,
Sweet innocence sounds meek and mild.
Grace in his features—grace in his features shine,
Grace in his features shine, grace in his features shine.
Sing, sing, all earth, *etc.*

For us the Saviour came on earth, for us his life he gave,
To save us from eternal death
And to raise us from—and to raise us from the grave
To raise us from the grave and to raise us from the grave
Sing, sing, all earth, sing, sing, all earth eternal praises sing
To our Redeemer, to our Redeemer and our heavenly King.

Come all jol-ly plough-men and help me to
sing I will sing in the praise of you
all If a man he don't lab-our how can he get
bread? I will sing and make mer-ry with-al

## Two Young Brethren

Come all jolly ploughmen and help me to sing,
I will sing in the praise of you all,
If a man he don't labour how can he get bread?
I will sing and make merry withal.

It was of two young brethren, two young brethren born,
It was of two young brethren born,
One he was a shepherd and a tender of sheep
The other a planter of corn.

We will rile it, we will tile it through mud and through clay,
We will plough it up deeper and low,
Then after comes the seedsman his corn for to sow
And the harrows to rake it in rows.

There is April, there is May, there is June and July
What a pleasure it is for to see the corn grow.
In August we will reap it, we will cut, sheaf and bind it
And go down with our scythes for to mow.

And after we've reaped it off every sheaf
And have gathered up every ear,
With a drop of good beer, boys, and our hearts full of cheer
We will wish them another good year.

Our barns they are full, our fields they are clear,
Good health to our master and friends.
We will make no more to do but we'll plough and we'll sow
And prepare for the very next year.

## The Shepherd's Song

There was a young shepherd a-tending of his sheep,
He's a-tending of his sheep on a fine summer's day
When a charming young lady by chance should come that way
And on this young shepherd she fixed her bright eye.

He drew forth his pipes and so prettily did play,
But this maid turned her head then so modestly away,
But so sweet and melodious the shepherd played his tune
She pleaded with this swain to go all on their honeymoon.

Then said this young shepherd of very low degree,
I know a young shepherd far richer than me.
Don't talk about riches or any sort of clothes
Take off your shepherding garments and I'll dress you in robes.

So straight to the church this young couple they did steer
And were married by asking as you shall quickly hear.
They have servants to wait on them, attendants by their side
So who could be more happy than that shepherd and his bride.

# 'Tater Beer Night

As I walked out one mid-sum-mer morn-ing For to view the fields and to take the air Down by the banks of the sweet prim-er-os-es there I be-held a most love-ly* fair

*pronounced "love-lie"]

## Banks of the Sweet Primroses

As I walked out one midsummer morning
For to view the fields and to take the air,
Down by the banks of the sweet prim-e-roses
There I beheld a most lovely fair.

Three long steps I stepp-ed up to her,
Not knowing her as she passed me by,
I stepp-ed up to her thinking for to view her,
She appeared to me like some virtuous bride.

I said, Fair maid, where are you going,
And what's the occasion for all your grief?
I will make you as happy as any Lady
If you will grant me once more a leave.

She said, Stand off, you are deceitful,
You are deceitful and a false young man,
It is you that's caused my poor heart for to wander,
And to give me comfort lies all in vain.

I'll go down in some lonesome valley
Where no man on earth shall e'er me find,
Where the pretty little small birds do change their voices,
And every moment blows blusterous winds.

Come all young men that go a-courting,
Pray pay attention to what I say.
There is many a dark and a cloudy morning
Turns out to be a sun-shiny day.

It's of a brisk and lively lad come out of Glouces-ter-shire And all his full in-ten-tion was to court some la-dy fair Her eyes shone bright like the morn-ing dew that dees on the li-ly lie she has grace all in her face all mixed with mod-es-tie

## Brisk and Lively Lad

It's of a brisk and lively lad come out of Gloucestershire,
And all his full intention was to court some lady fair,
Her eyes shone bright like the morning dew that does on the lily
    lie,
She has grace all in her face all mixed with modestie.

As these two lovers were walking they knew each other well
When someone heard them talking and did her father tell,
And when he came for to hear the same and to understand the
    thing,
Then said he, 'Twill never be, I will part them in the spring.

It was in the springtime of the year there was a press begun
And all their full intention was to press that farmer's son,
'Twas to press him and to send him far over the raging sea,
Where I'm sure he will no more keep my daughter's company.

On the twenty-first of August there was a fight begun
And foremost in the battle did they place this farmer's son,
There he received a dreadful wound in the hollow of his thigh,
Every vein was filled with pain he got wounded dreadfully.

She went straight to the Captain as Captain's handy mate
And everything he said to her she agreed to undertake,
So tenderly she dressed his wounds which so bitterly did smart
Then said he, A one like thee once was mistress of my heart.

She went straight to the Commander and offered very fair,
Forty or fifty guineas shall buy my love quite clear,
No money shall be wanted no longer tarry here,
Since 'tis so pray let us go, to old England we will steer.

She went up to her father's gate and stood there for a while,
He said, Lord in heaven bless me, there's my dear and only child.
She said, Father, I have found him and brought him safe on shore
We will spend our days in England, never roam abroad no more.

one May morning early I chanced for to roam And
strolled through the field by the side of the grove I was
there I did hear the harm-less birds sing and you
nev-er heard so sweet And you nev-er heard so sweet You
nev-er heard so sweet as the birds in the Spring

## By the Green Grove

One May morning early I chanced for to roam
And strolled through the field by the side of the grove.
It was there I did hear the harmless birds sing,
And you never heard so sweet, and you never heard so sweet,
You never heard so sweet as the birds in the spring.

At the end of the grove I sat myself down
And the song of the nightingale echoed all round,
Their song was so charming their notes were so clear
No music no songster, no music no songster,
No music no songster can with them compare.

All you that come here the small birds to hear,
I'll have you pay attention so pray all draw near.
And when you're growing old you will have this to say,
That you never heard so sweet, you never heard so sweet,
You never heard so sweet as the birds on the spray.

## Dame Durden

Dame Durden kept five servant maids to carry the milking pail
She also kept five labouring men to use the spade and flail.

'Twas Moll and Bet and Doll and Kit and Dolly to drag her tail
It was Tom and Dick and Joe and Jack and Humphrey with his flail.
Then Tom kissed Molly and Dick kissed Betty
And Joe kissed Dolly and Jack kissed Kitty
And Humphrey with his flail
And Kitty she was the charming girl to carry the milking pail.

Dame Durden in the morn so soon she did begin to call
To rouse her servants maids and men she did begin to bawl.

'Twas Moll and Bet, *etc.*

'Twas on the morn of Valentine when birds began to prate
Dame Durden and her maids and men they altogether meet.

There was Moll and Bet, *etc.*

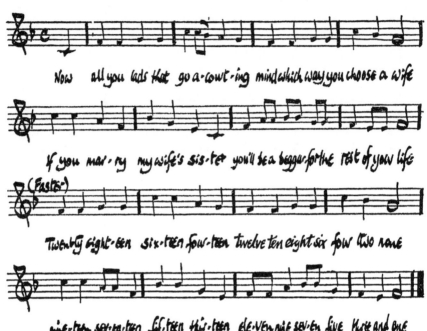

*Now All You Lads*

Now all you lads that go a-courting
Mind which way you choose a wife,
For if you marry my wife's sister
You'll be a beggar for the rest of your life.

Twenty, eighteen, sixteen, fourteen,
Twelve, ten, eight, six, four, two, none,
Nineteen, seventeen, fifteen, thirteen,
Eleven, nine, seven, five, three, and one.

There was a crow sat on a tree And he was as black as black could be and he was as black as black could be And he was as black as black could be

*Two Old Crows*

There was a crow sat on a tree
And he was as black as black could be.
And he was as black as black could be.
And he was as black as black could be.

Now this old crow said to his mate,
Let us go and find something to eat
Let us go and find, *etc.*

They flew across the wide, wild plain,
To where a farmer had sown some grain
To where a farmer, *etc.*

Up came the farmer with his gun,
And he shot them both excepting one,
He shot them both, *etc.*

The one that escaped flew back to the tree
And he said, You old —— farmer you can't shoot me
He said you old, *etc.*

'Twas in the plea-sant month of May in the Spring-time of the year And down by yon-der mead-ow there runs a riv-er clear see how the lit-tle fish-es how they do sport and play caus-ing man-y a lad and man-y a lass to go there a-mak-ing hay

## Pleasant Month of May

'Twas in the pleasant month of May in the springtime of the year,
And down by yonder meadow there runs a river clear,
See how the little fishes how they do sport and play
Causing many a lad and many a lass to go there a-making hay.

Then in comes the scytheman that meadow to mow down,
With his old leathered bottle and the ale that runs so brown.
There's many a stout and labouring man comes here his skill to try,
He works, he mows, he sweats and blows and the grass cuts very
    dry.

Then in comes both Tom and Dick with their pitch-forks and
    their rakes
And likewise black-eyed Susan the hay all for to make.
There's a sweet, sweet, sweet and a jug, jug, jug, how the harmless
    birds did sing,
From the morning till the evening as we were a-haymaking.

It was just at one evening as the sun was a-going down,
We saw the jolly piper come a-strolling through the town.
There he pulled out his tapering pipes and he made the valley ring,
So we all put down our rakes and forks and left off haymaking.

We call-ed for a dance and we tripp-ed it along,
We danced all round the haycocks till the rising of the sun.
When the sun did shine such a glorious light and the harmless birds
    did sing,
Each lad he took his lass in hand and went back to his haymaking.

These words were com-pos-ed by Spen-cer the Rov-er who

trav-elled Great Brit-ain and most parts of Wales He had

seen so re-duc-ed which caused great con-fus-ion And

that was the reas-on he went on the roam

## Spencer the Rover

These words were composed by Spencer the Rover,
Who had travelled Great Britain and most parts of Wales,
He had been so reduc-ed which caused great confusion
And that was the reason he went on the roam.

In Yorkshire near Rotherham he had been on his rambles,
Being weary of travelling he sat down to rest.
At the foot of yonder mountain there runs a clear fountain,
With bread and cold water he himself did refresh.

It tasted more sweeter than the gold he had wasted,
More sweeter than honey and gave more content,
But the thoughts of his babies lamenting their father
Brought tears in his eyes which made him lament.

The night fast approaching to the woods he resorted,
With woodbine and ivy his bed for to make.
There he dreamt about sighing lamenting and crying,
Go home to your family and rambling forsake.

On the fifth of November I've a reason to remember
When first he arrived home to his family and wife,
They stood so surprised when first he arrived
To behold such a stranger once more in their sight.

His children came around him with their prittle-prattling stories,
With their prittle-prattling stories to drive care away.
Now they are united like birds of one feather,
Like bees in one hive contented they'll be.

So now he is a-living in his cottage contented
With woodbine and roses growing all around the door,
He's as happy as those that's got thousands of riches,
Contented he'll stay and go rambling no more.

One morn-ing in the month of May As from my cott I strayed Just at the dawn-ing of the day I met with a charm-ing maid Just at the dawn-ing of the day I met with a charm-ing maid

N.B. Some verses begin :-

etc

## Spotted Cow

One morning in the month of May as from my cott I strayed
Just at the dawning of the day I met with a charming maid
Just at the dawning of the day I met with a charming maid.

Good morning, fair maid, fair weather, said I, and early tell me now,
The maid replied, Kind Sir, she said, I've lost my spotted cow.
   (*Repeat*)

No longer weep, no longer mourn, your cow's not lost, my dear,
I saw her down in yonder grove, come love and I'll show you
   where. (*Repeat*)

Then in the grove we spent our time and thought it passed too soon,
At night we homeward made our way when brightly shone the
   moon. (*Repeat*)

Next day we went to view the plough across the flowery dale,
We loved and kissed each other there and love was all our tale.
   (*Repeat*)

If I should cross the flowery dale all for to view the plough,
She comes, she calls me, Gentle swain, I've found my spotted cow
She comes, she calls me, Gentle swain, I've found my spotted cow.

'Twas on one Sab-bath morn the bells did chime for Church The

young and gay were gath-'ring there a - round that rus-tic porch There

came an age-d man in sol-diers garb was he And

gazing on that group he cried: You all re-mem-ber me

## The Veteran

'Twas on one Sabbath morn the bells did chime for Church,
The young and gay were gathering there around that rustic porch.
There came an ag-ed man in soldier's garb was he,
And gazing on that group he cried, You all remember me.

The Veteran forgot, his friends were past and gone
The manly forms around him there as children he had known.
He pointed to a spot where his dwelling used to be,
And turning round and smiling said, You now remember me.

Alas none knew him there. He pointed to a stone
On which a name he breathed was traced, a name to them unknown.
And then the old man wept, I'm friendless now, said he,
Where I had many a friend in youth not one remembers me.

The old man's heart seemed broke, said he, This is my own.
I hoped with friends to end my days. Alas, that hope has gone.
He clutched the moss-grown tomb, Without welcome, death, said he,
Forgotten now by all on earth, Oh, God, remember me.

Now a week be-fore East-er the morn bright and clear The
sun it shone bright-ly and keen blew the air I went
up in the for-est to ga-ther fine flow-ers But the
for-est won't yield me no ros-es

## A Week Before Easter

Now a week before Easter the morn bright and clear,
The sun it shone brightly and keen blew the air.
I went up in the forest to gather fine flowers,
But the forest won't yield me no roses.

The roses are red the leaves they are green,
The bushes and briars are pleasant to be seen,
Where the small birds are singing and changing their notes
Down among the wild beasts in the forest.

Now the first time I saw my love she was dressed all in white,
Made my eyes run and water quite dazzled my sight,
When I thought to myself that I might have been that man
But she's left me and gone with another.

Now the next time I saw my love she was in the church stand
With a ring on her finger and a glove in her hand.
So now she's gone from me and showed me false play,
She's gone and got tied to some other.

So dig me a grave both long, wide and deep
And strew it all over with roses so sweet,
That I might lay down there and take a long sleep
And that's the right way to forget her.

## When Spring Comes In

When Spring comes in the birds do sing,
The lambs do skip and the bells do ring
While we enjoy their glorious charm so noble and so gay.
The primrose blooms and the cowslip too,
The violets in their sweet retire, the roses shining through the briar,
And the daffadown-dillies which we admire will die and fade away.

Young men and maidens will be seen
On mountains high and meadows green,
They will talk of love and sport and play
While these young lambs do skip away,
At night they homeward wend their way
When evening stars appear.
The primrose blooms and the cowslip too, *etc.*

The dairymaid to milking goes her blooming cheeks as red as a rose,
She carries her pail all on her arm so cheerful and so gay,
She milks she sings and the valleys ring,
The small birds on the branches there
Sit listening to this lovely fair.
She is her master's trust and care
She is the ploughman's joy,
The primrose blooms and the cowslip too,
The violets in their sweet retire, the roses shining through the briar
And the daffadown-dillies which we admire will die and fade away.

# Wop She 'Ad It—io

Now once I courted a pretty girl I courted her quite well,
Her name was Kitty-mariga Maria and mine was Bobby Wells,
One night when I was courting Kit when her father was at home,
He said, If I catch you here again I'll tickle your bot-tum.

With a wop she 'ad it I tell you I 'ad it O wop she 'ad it—io
O wop she 'ad it I tell you I 'ad it O wop she 'ad it—io.

Now Kit and I we did agree a ladder for to bring,
We placed it under the window and by gum, it was just the thing.
We laughed and chattered and chattered and talked when all at once,
   by gum,
My foot slipped through the ladder and I fell and cut my bot-tum.

With a wop she 'ad it, *etc.*

They wheeled me home in a wheelbarrow they wheeled me home
   with care,
And when I got to the farmyard gate, oh, didn't the old folks stare.
My brother Joe came running out and said what have you done,
I've been a-courting Kit, said I, and fell and cut my bot-tum.

With, *etc.*

They took me to the doctor's and there I showed my case
And didn't they do a grin when I showed 'em my Sunday face.
They thought I was making a fool of them, but a fool of them, by
   gum,
I thought they were making a fool of me when they turpentined my
   bum.

With, *etc.*

Now Kit and I we did agree for to get wed,
She made me a sling to put my bum in and through it I cocked my
   leg.
As we were walking down the street the kids did shout, by gum,
There goes the man with his bum in a sling that fell and cut his bot-
   tum.

With, *etc.*

*Charming Molly*

Charming Molly, fair, brisk and gay like nightingales in May,
All round her eyelids young Cupids play,
She has eyes so bright they shine
Black as any berry, cheeks like any cherry.
Charming Molly with sparkling eyes.

See how the swain do admire and desire a pretty little girl,
To hold her hand it burns like sparkling fire,
In her face these things are seen,
Violets, roses, lilies and daffadown-dillies,
Charming Molly she is all divine.

Surely there's no one loves a pretty woman if she be not common,
Surely such beauty most men admire,
Surely there's no one can them despise
Because they are so pretty and they talk so witty,
Charming Molly with spark-ling eyes.

# Black Ram

Here's a-dieu sweet love-ly Nan-cy ten thou-sand times a-dieu I'm a

going a-round the o-cean love to seek for some-thing new Come

change your ring with me dear girl come change your ring with me For it

might sea tok-en of true love while I am on the sea

## Adieu Sweet Lovely Nancy

Here's adieu, sweet lovely Nancy, ten thousand times adieu,
I'm a-going around the ocean, love, to seek for something new.
Come change your ring with me, dear girl,
Come change your ring with me,
For it might be a token of true love while I am on the sea.

When I am far upon the sea you know not where I am,
Kind letters I will write to you from every foreign land.
The secrets of your heart, dear girl,
Are the best of my good will,
So let your body be where it might my heart shall be with you still.

There's a heavy storm a-rising see how it gathers round
While we poor souls on the ocean wide are fighting for the Crown.
There is nothing to protect us, love,
Or to keep us from the cold,
On the ocean wide where we must bide like jolly seamen bold.

There are tinkers, tailors and shoemakers lie snoring fast asleep
While we poor souls on the ocean wide are ploughing through the
    deep.
Our officers commanding us
And them we must obey
Expecting every moment for to get cast away.

But when the wars are all over there'll be peace on every shore,
We'll return to our wives and families and the girls that we adore.
We will call for liquor merrily,
We will spend our money free,
And when our money it is all gone we'll boldly go to sea.

As I walked out one May morning down by a river side I
gazed all around me when an Irish girl I spied So
red and rosy were her cheeks and coal black was her hair and
costly was the robe of gold this Irish girl did wear

## As I Walked Out

As I walked out one May morning down by a riverside
I gaz-ed all a-round me when an Irish girl I spied.
So red and rosy were her cheeks and coal-black was her hair
And costly was the robe of gold this Irish girl did wear.

Her shoes were made of Spanish leather all sprinkled o'er with dew,
She wrung her hands she tore her hair crying, Oh, what shall I do?
I'm a-going home, I'm a-going home, I'm a-going home, said she,
How can I go a-roving and slight my own Johnny?

I wish I was a butterfly, I would fly to my love's breast,
And if I were a linnet I would sing my love to rest,
And if I was a nightingale I would sing till the morning clear,
I'd sit and sing to you, Polly, for once I loved you dear.

I wish I was a red rose bud that in the garden grew
And if I was that gardener to my love I would prove true.
There is not one month throughout the year of what my love I
    would renew,
With flowers three I would garnish thee, sweet william, thyme and
    rue.

I wish I was in Dublin town a-romping on the grass
With a bottle of whiskey in my hand and on my knee a lass.
I would call for liquor merrily I would spend my money free,
With a rant and a roar all along the shore let the winds blow high or
    low.

One night as I lay on my bed so sick and bad was I
I call-ed for a napikin all around my head to tie.
But there's many a man as bad as me so why should I complain,
For love it is a funny thing, did you ever feel the pain?

'Twas on one summer's eve-ning all in the month of May. Down
by a flow-ry gar-den where Bet-sy did stray I—
ov-er-heard a dam-sel in sor-row to com-plain All—
for her ab-sent lov- er that ploughs the ra-ging main

## Claudy Banks

'Twas on one summer's evening all in the month of May
Down by a flow'ry garden where Betsy did stray.
I overheard a damsel in sorrow to complain,
All for her absent lover that ploughs the raging main.

I stepped up to this fair maid and put her in surprise,
She owned she did not know me, I being all in disguise.
I said, My charming creature, my joy and heart's delight,
How far have you to travel this dark and rainy night?

Away, kind sir, to the Claudy banks if you will please to show,
Pity a poor girl distracted for there I have to go.
I am in search of a young man and Johnny is his name,
And on the banks of Claudy I'm told he does remain.

If Johnny he was here this night he would keep me from all harm
He's a-cruising the wide ocean in tempest and in storm,
He's a-cruising the wide ocean for honour or for gain,
But I'm told his ship got wreck-ed all on the coast of Spain.

When Betsy heard this dreadful news she fell into despair,
In a-wringing of her hands and a-tearing of her hair.
Since Johnny has gone and left me no man on earth I'll take,
Down in some lonesome valley I'll wander for his sake.

Young Johnny hearing her say so he could no longer stand,
He fell into her arms crying, Betsy, I'm the man,
I am that faithful young man and whom you thought was slain,
And since we met on Claudy banks we'll never part again.

Come all you bold Brit-ons where ever you may dwell Come

list-en un-to me while a stor-y I will tell Great

crops of corn our Lord doth send where there is one farm there might better and

then more cows there might be kept in old Eng - land

## Come All Bold Britons

Come all you bold Britons wherever you may dwell,
Come listen unto me while a story I will tell,
Great crops of corn our Lord does send,
Where there is one farm there might be ten
And then more cows there might be kept—in old England.

Come all you bold statesmen that are of high renown,
Before the times get better rates and taxes must go down,
Let every farmer hear my thrive and to the poor some milk might
    give,
And that's the way we ought to live—in old England.

Oh, yonder shines Phoebe see how she shines so clear,
She will nobly rise and set, my boys, each day throughout the year,
And shiny nights they are so gay, both rents and taxes we must pay,
Or else find out some better ways—in old England.

Now some they do say we are made of mortal clay,
While others they do say we were born but yesterday.
But look into old Adam and Eve and in the scriptures you will read
That·we are all one flesh and blood—in old England.

Come all you bold heroes and God speed the plough,
I hope we shall see better times soon in old England now,
And in due time when mercy call all for the riches great and small
That death will come and seize us all—in old England.

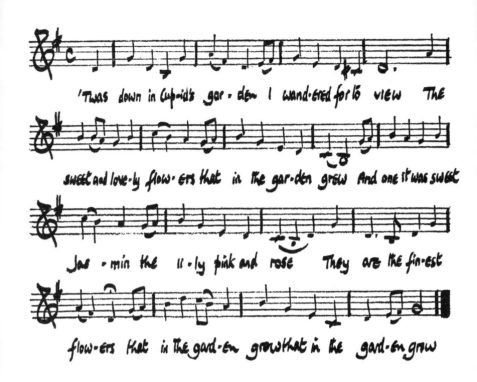

'Twas down in Cupid's gar-den I wand-ered for to view The
sweet and love-ly flow-ers that in the gar-den grew And one it was sweet
Jas-min the li-ly pink and rose They are the fin-est
flow-ers that in the gard-en grow that in the gard-en grow

# Cupid's Garden

'Twas down in Cupid's Garden I wandered for to view
The sweet and lovely flowers that in the garden grew
And one it was sweet jasmin, the lily, pink and rose,
They are the finest flowers that in the garden grow,
That in the garden grow.

I had not been in the garden but scarcely half an hour
When I beheld two maidens sat under a shady bower,
And one was lovely Nancy so beautiful and fair
The other was a virgin and did the laurels wear,
And did the laurels wear.

I boldly stepp-ed up to them and unto them did say,
Are you engaged to any young man, come tell to me, I pray,
No, I'm not engaged to any young man I solemnly declare
I mean to stay a virgin and still the laurels wear,
And still the laurels wear.

So hand in hand together this loving couple went,
To view the secrets of her heart was the sailor's full intent,
Or whether she would slight him while he to the wars did go.
Her answer was, Not I, my love, for I love a sailor bold,
I love a sailor bold.

It's down in Portsmouth harbour there's a ship lies waiting there,
Tomorrow to the seas I go, let the wind blow high or fair,
And if I should live to return again how happy I shall be
With you, my love, my own true-love, sitting smiling on my knee,
Sit smiling on my knee.

As I walked out one May morn-ing down by a riv- - er

side There I be-held a bold fish-er man come

(1)
+8ve
row-ing with the tide Come row-ing with the tide There

+8ve
I be-held a bold fish-er man come row-ing with the tide

254

## The Fisherman

As I walked out one May morning down by a riverside,
There I beheld a bold fisherman come rowing with the tide,
Come rowing with the tide.
There I beheld a bold fisherman come rowing with the tide.

Good morning to you, bold fisherman, how came you fishing here?
I came here a-fishing for your sweet sake all on this river clear,
All on this river clear.
I came here a-fishing for your sweet sake all on this river clear.

He lashed his boat unto a stake and to this maid he went,
He took her by the lily-white hand which was his full intent,
Which was his full intent.
He took her by the lily-white hand which was his full intent.

He then unfolded his morning gown and so gently laid it down,
There she beheld three chains of gold hang a-dangling three times
     round,
Hang a-dangling three times round.
There she beheld three chains of gold hang a-dangling three times
     round.

She then fell on her bending knees and so loud for mercy called,
In calling you a bold fisherman I fear you are some Lord,
I fear you are some Lord.
In calling you a bold fisherman I fear you are some Lord.

Rise up, rise up, rise up, said he, from off your bending knees,
There is not one word that you have said that has offended me,
That has offended me.
There is not one word that you have said that has offended me.

I will take you to my father's house and married you shall be,
Then you will have a bold fisherman to row you on the sea,
To row you on the sea.
Then you will have a bold fisherman to row you on the sea.

Come all my jol-ly boys and we'll to-geth-er go To-

-geth-er with our mas-ters to shear the lambs and yowes All

in the month of June of all times in the year It

al-ways comes in sea-son the lambs and yowes to shear And

then we will work hard my boys un-til our backs do break Our

mas-ter he will bring us beer when-ev-er we do lack

## Sheep-shearing Song

Come all my jolly boys and we'll together go,
Together with our masters to shear the lambs and 'yowes'.
All in the month of June of all times in the year
It always comes in season the lambs and 'yowes' to shear.
And then we will work hard, my boys, until our backs do break,
Our Master he will bring us beer whenever we do lack.

Our Master he comes round to see our work's done well,
And he says, Shear them close, my boys, for there is but little wool,
O, yes, good Master, we reply, we'll do well as we can.
Our Captain cries, Shear close, my lads, to each and every man,
And at some places still we have this story all day long,
Bend your backs and shear them well, and this is all their song.

And then our noble Captain doth to the Master say,
Come let us have one bucket of your good ale, I pray,
He turns unto our Captain and makes him this reply,
You shall have the best of beer, I promise, presently.
Then with the foaming bucket pretty Betsy she doth come
And Master says, Maid, mind and see that every man has some.

This is some of our pastime while we the sheep do shear,
And though we are such merry boys, we work hard, I declare,
And when 'tis night and we are done our Master is more free
And stores us well with good strong beer and pipes of tobaccee,
And there we sit a-drinking we smoke and sing and roar,
Till we become far merrier than e'er we were before.

When all our work is done and all the sheep are shorn
Then home with our Captain to drink the ale that's strong.
It's a barrel then of hum-cap which we will call Black Ram,
And we do sit and swagger and we swear that we are men.
And yet before the night is through I'll bet you half-a-crown,
That if you ha'n't a special care that Ram will knock you down.

A shep-herd of the downs be-ing wear-y of his
sort Re-tired to the hills where he used to resort In want of re-fresh-ment he laid him-self
down He want-ed no ri-ches nor wealth from the
crown He want-ed no ri-ches nor wealth from the crown

## Shepherd of the Downs

A shepherd of the downs being weary of his port
Retired to the hills where he used to resort.
In want of refreshment he laid himself down,
He wanted no riches, nor wealth from the Crown,
He wanted no riches, nor wealth from the Crown.

He drank of the cold brook, he ate of the tree,
Himself he did enjoy from all sorrow was free,
He valued no girl be she ever so fair,
No pride nor ambition he valued no care,
No pride nor ambition he valued no care.

As he was a-walking one evening so clear
A heavenly sweet voice sounded soft in his ear.
He stood like a post not one step could he move,
He knew not what hailed him but thought it was love,
He knew not what hailed him but thought it was love.

He beheld a young damsel a fair modest bride
She had something amiss and disguised in her face.
Disguised in her face she unto him did say,
How now, Master Shepherd, how came you this way?
How now, Master Shepherd, how came you this way?

The shepherd he replied and modestly said,
I never was surprised before at a maid.
When first you beheld me from sorrow I was free,
But now you have stolen my poor heart from me,
But now you have stolen my poor heart from me.

He took her by the hand and thus he did say
We will get married pretty Betsy today.
So to church they did go and were married we hear,
And now he'll enjoy pretty Betsy his dear,
And now he'll enjoy pretty Betsy his dear.

*Note.* At the end of this song Brasser added, 'My Grandfathers used
to sing this song'.

As I was a-walk-ing one fine sum-mer's morn-ing The fields and the mead-ows they looked so green and gay And the birds they were sing-ing so pleas-ant-ly a-dorn-ing So ear-ly in the morn-ing at the break of the day

## Sweet Lemeney

As I was a-walking one fine summer's morning
The fields and the meadows they looked so green and gay,
And the birds they were singing so pleasantly adorning,
So early in the morning at the break of the day.

Oh hark, oh hark, how the nightingale is singing
The lark she is taking her flight all in the air.
On yonder green bower the turtle doves are building
The sun is just a-glimmering. Arise my dear.

Arise, oh, arise and get your humble posies,
For they are the finest flowers that grow in yonder grove.
And I will pluck them all sweet lily, pink and roses,
All for Sweet Lemeney, the girl that I love.

Oh, Lemeney, oh, Lemeney, you are the fairest creature,
You are the fairest creature that ever my eyes did see.
And then she played it over all on the pipes of ivory,
So early in the morning at the break of the day.

Oh, how could my true-love, how could she vanish from me?
Oh, how could she go and I never shall see her more.
But it was her cruel parents that looked so slightly on me,
All for the white robe that I once used to wear.

Here's a health to the jol-ly black-smith the best of all fel-lows who
works at his an-vil while the boy blows the bel-lows which
makes his bright ham-mer to rise and to fall There's the
Old Cole and the young Cole and the Old Cole of all Twan-ky
dil-lo Twank-y dil-lo Twan-ky dil-lo, dil-lo, dil-lo, dil-lo And the
roar-ing fair of bag-pipes made of the green wil-low

# Twanky Dillo

Here's a health to the jolly blacksmith the best of all fellows
Who works at his anvil while the boy blows the bellows,
Which makes his bright hammer to rise and to fall.
There's the old Cole and the young Cole and the old Cole of all,
Twanky dillo, twanky dillo, twanky dillo, dillo, dillo, dillo,
And the roaring pair of bagpipes made of the green willow.

If a gentleman calls with his horse to be shoed
He will make no denial to one pot or two
Which makes his bright hammer to rise and to fall.
There's the old Cole and the young Cole and the old Cole of all,
Twanky dillo, twanky dillo, etc.

Here's a health to that pretty girl the one I love best
Who kindles her fire all in her own breast,
Which makes his bright hammer to rise and to fall.
There's the old Cole and the young Cole and the old Cole of all,
Twanky dillo, twanky dillo, etc.

Here's a health to our King and likewise our Queen
And to all the Royal Family wherever they're seen,
Which makes his bright hammer to rise and to fall,
There's the old Cole and the young Cole and the old Cole of all,
Twanky dillo, twanky dillo, twanky dillo, dillo, dillo, dillo,
And the roaring pair of bagpipes made from the green willow.

Green willow, green willow, green willow, willow, willow, willow,
And the roaring pair of bagpipes made from the green willow.

The lark in the morning she arises from her nest
And she ascends all in the air with the dew upon her breast,
And with the pretty ploughboy she'll whistle and she'll sing,
And at night she'll return to her own nest again.

*The Lark in the Morning*

The lark in the morning she arises from her nest
And she ascends all in the air with the dew upon her breast,
And with the pretty ploughboy she'll whistle and she'll sing,
And at night she'll return to her own nest again.

When his day's work is over, oh, what then will he do?
Perhaps then into some near country wake he'll go,
And with his pretty sweetheart he'll dance and he'll sing,
At night he'll return with his love back again.

And as they return from the wake unto the town,
The meadows they are mowed and the grass it is cut down,
The nightingale she whistles upon the hawthorn spray,
The moon is a-shining upon the new-mown hay.

Good luck, unto the ploughboys wherever they may be,
They will take a winsome lass for to sit upon their knee,
And with a jug of beer, boys, they'll whistle and they'll sing,
For the ploughboy is as happy as a prince or a king.

# Hollerin' Pot

## Admiral Benbow

Come all you seamen bold, landed here, landed here,
It is of an Admiral brave called Benbow by his name,
How he ploughed the raging main
You shall hear, you shall hear.

Last Tuesday morning last, Benbow sailed, Benbow sailed,
What a sweet and pleasant gale when Benbow he set sail
And the enemy they turned tail
In a fright, in a fright.

Great Reuben and Benbow, fought the French, fought the French,
See the boats go up and down and the bullets whizzing round
And the enemy they knocked down,
There they lie, there they lie.

Oh, Benbow lost his legs, by chain-shot, by chain-shot,
Down on his stumps did fall and so loud for mercy called,
Oh, fight on my British tars,
It is my lot, it is my lot.

When the doctor dressed the wounds Benbow cried, Benbow cried,
Oh, pray pick me up in haste to the quarter deck my place
That the enemy I might face
Until I die, until I die.

Last Tuesday morning last, Benbow died, Benbow died,
What a shocking sight to see when they carried him away
They carried him to S'em's'on* church
There he lays, there he lays.

*Selmeston

I am a brisk and donny lad and free from care and strife And sweetly as the hours pass I love a country life —— At wake or fair I'm oft-en there midst pleasure to be seen Though poor I am con-ten-ted And as hap-py as a Queen

## Brisk and Bonny Lad

I am a brisk and bonny lad and free from care and strife
And sweetly as the hours pass I love a country life.
At wake or fair I'm often there 'midst pleasure to be seen,
Though poor I am contented and as happy as a Queen.

I rise up in the morning my labour to pursue
And with my yoke and milking pails I trudge the morning dew,
My cows I milk and then I taste how sweet the nature yields,
The lark she sings to welcome me across the flowery fields.

And in the time of harvest how cheerfully we go
Some with hooks and some with crooks and some with scythes to
    mow,
And when our corn is free from harm we have not far to roam,
We'll all away to celebrate the welcome Harvest Home.

Come write me down ye powers a-bove the man that first cre-a-ted love for I've a dia-mond in my eye where all my joys and com-forts lie where all my joys and com-forts lie

## Come Write Me Down

Come write me down, ye powers above, the man that first created
  love,
For I've a diamond in my eye where all my joys and comforts lie,
Where all my joys and comforts lie.

I will give you gold, I will give you pearl if you can fancy me, dear
  girl,
Rich costly robes that you shall wear if you can fancy me, my dear,
If you can fancy me, my dear.

It's not your gold shall me entice to leave off pleasures to be a wife
For I don't mean or intend at all to be at any young man's call,
To be at any young man's call.

Then go your way you scornful dame since you've proved false I'll
  prove the same
For I don't care but I shall find some other fair maid to my mind,
Some other fair maid to my mind.

Oh, stay young man don't be in haste you seem afraid your time
  will waste
Let reason rule your roving mind and unto you I will prove kind,
And unto you I will prove kind.

So to Church they went that very next day and were married by
  asking as I've heard say,
So now that girl she is his wife she will prove his comforts day and
  night,
She will prove his comforts day and night.

So now his trouble and sorrow is past his joy and comfort has come
  at last
That girl to him always said, Nay, she will prove his comforts night
  and day,
She will prove his comforts night and day.

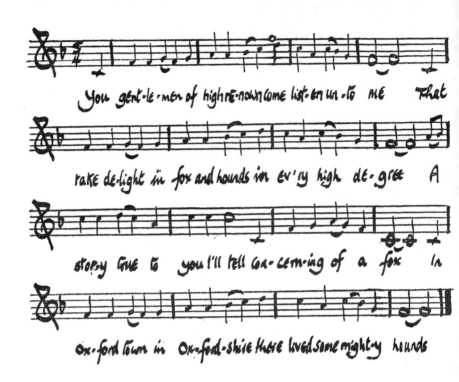

You gentle-men of high re-nown come list-en un-to me That

rake de-light in fox and hounds in ev'ry high de-gree A

story true to you I'll tell con-cern-ing of a fox In

Ox-ford Town in Ox-ford-shire there lived some might-y hounds

## Gentlemen of High Renown

You Gentlemen of high renown, come listen unto me
That take delight in fox and hounds in ev'ry high degree.
A story true to you I'll tell concerning of a fox,
In Oxford Town in Oxfordshire there lived some mighty hounds.

Bold Reynard being all in his den and standing on the ground,
Bold Reynard being all in his den and hearing of those hounds.
I think I hear some joyful hounds thinking for me to kill,
But before they catch me by my brush I'll climb those mighty hills.

Bold Reynard cocked up his head and up the hill he went,
Bold Reynard cocked out his brush and he left a gallant scent.
Your hounds are staunch I know them well, they drive me like the
   wind,
I will step so lightly on the ground I'll leave no scent behind.

We drove Bold Reynard five hours or more without a check of
   speed,
We drove Bold Reynard five hours or more till we came to Oxford
   Green.
There we caught Bold Reynard all by his brush never to let him go,
He has had so many of our feather-ed fowls down in the valley
   below.

Our Huntsman blows his joyful sound, Relope, my boys, fulfil
He will have no more of our feather-ed fowls nor lambs on yonder
   hill.
Oh, pardon, Huntsman, then he cried. No pardon you shall have,
Take off his head likewise his brush and give him three Hurrays.

It was of an hon-est labour-er as I've heard peop-le say He goes out in the morn-ning and he works hard all the day — And he's got sev-en child-er-en and most of them are small He has no-thing but hard la-bour to main-tain them all

## The Labourer

It was of an honest labourer as I've heard people say
He goes out in the morning and he works hard all the day,
And he's got seven children and most of them are small.
He has nothing but hard labour to maintain them all.

A gentleman one morning walking out to take the air
He met with this poor labouring man and solemnly declared,
I think you are that thresher-man. Said he, Yes, sir, that's true.
How do you get your living as well as you do?

Sometimes I do reap and sometimes I do mow
At other times to hedging and to ditching I do go.
There is nothing comes amiss to me from the harrow to the plough.
That's how I get me living by the sweat of my brow.

When I go home at night just as tired as I be
I take my youngest child and I dance him on my knee.
They others they come around me with their prittle-prattling toys
And that's the only comfort a working man enjoys.

My wife and I are willing and we join both in one yoke
We live like to two turtle doves and not one word provoke.
Although the times are very hard and we are very poor
We can scarcely keep the raving wolf away from the door.

Well done, you honest labourer, you speak well of your wife,
I hope you will live happy all the days of your life.
Here is forty acres of good land which I will give to thee
Which will help to maintain your sweet wife and family.

*O, Good Ale*

It is of good ale to you I'll sing
And to good ale I'll always cling,
I like my mug filled to the brim
And I'll drink all you'd like to bring,
O, good ale, thou art my darling,
Thou art my joy both night and morning.

It is you that helps me with my work
And from a task I'll never shirk
While I can get a good home-brew,
And better than one pint I like two
O, good ale, *etc.*

I love you in the early morn
I love you in daylight dark or dawn,
And when I'm weary, worn or spent
I turn the tap and ease the vent,
O, good ale, *etc.*

It's you that makes my friends my foes,
It's you that makes me wear old clothes,
But since you come so near my nose
It's up you comes and down you goes,
O, good ale, *etc.*

If all my friends from Adam's race
Were to meet me here all in this place,
I could part from all without one tear
Before I'd part from my good beer,
O, good ale, *etc.*

And if my wife did me despise
How soon I'd give her two black eyes,
But if she loved me like I love thee
What a happy couple we should be,
O, good ale, *etc.*

You have caused me debts and I've often swore
That I never would drink strong ale no more,
But you for all that I forgive
And I'll drink strong ale just as long as I live,
O, good ale, *etc.*

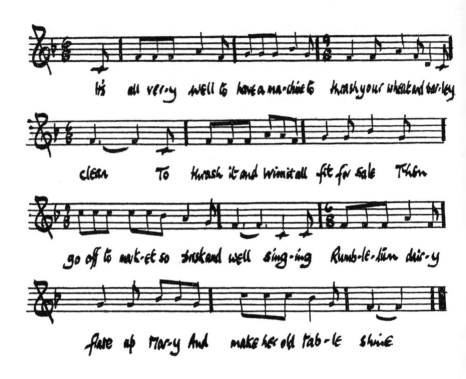

It's all very well to have a ma-chine to thrash your wheat and bar-ley clean  To thrash it and win it all fit for sale  Then go off to mark-et so brisk and well  sing-ing  Rumb-le-tum dair-y flare up Mar-y  And  make her old tab-le shine

## Old Threshing Song

It's all very well to have a machine
To thrash your wheat and barley clean,
To thrash it and wim it all fit for sale,
Then go off to market so brisk and well,
Singing rumble-tum-dairy flare up Mary
And make her old table shine.

The man who made her he made her so well,
He made every cog and wheel to tell.
While the big wheel runs the little one hums,
And the feeder he sits above the drums,
Singing rumble-tum-dairy flare up Mary
And make her old table shine.

There's old Father Howard the sheaves to put,
While old Mother Howard she does make up.
And Mary she sits and feeds all day,
While Johnny he carries the straw away,
Singing rumble-tum-dairy flare up Mary
And make her old table shine.

At seven o'clock we do begin
And we generally stop about nine or ten
To have our beer and oil her up,
Then away we go till one o'clock,
Singing rumble-tum-dairy flare up Mary
And make her old table shine.

Then after a bite and a drink all round
The driver he climbs to his box again
And with his long whip he shouts, All right,
And he drives 'em round till five at night,
Singing rumble-tum-dairy flare up Mary
And make her old table shine.

Sports-men a-rouse the morn-ing is clear the larks are sing-ing all
in the air    Go and    tell your sweet lov-er the hounds are out  Go and
tell your sweet lov-er the hounds are    out    Sadd-le your hors-es your
sadd-les pre-pare we'll a-way to some  cov-er to seek for a hare

## Sportsmen Arouse

Sportsmen arouse the morning is clear,
The larks are singing all in the air. (*Repeat*)
Go and tell your sweet lover the hounds are out, (*Repeat*)
Saddle your horses, your saddles prepare
We'll away to some cover to seek for a hare.

We searched the woods and the groves all round,
The trial being over the game it is found, (*Repeat*)
Then off she springs through brake she flies, (*Repeat*)
Follow, follow the musical horn,
Sing follow, hark, forward the innocent hare.

Our huntsman blows his joyful sound,
Tally ho, my boys, all over the downs. (*Repeat*)
From the woods to the valleys see how she creeps, (*Repeat*)
Follow, follow the musical horn,
Sing follow, hark, forward the innocent hare.

All along the green turf she pants for breath
Our huntsman he shouts out for death. (*Repeat*)
Relope, relope, retiring hare. (*Repeat*)
Follow, follow the musical horn
Sing follow, hark forward the innocent hare.

This hare has led us a noble run
Success to sportsmen every one, (*Repeat*)
Such a chase she has led us, four hours or more, (*Repeat*)
Wine and beer we'll drink without fear,
We'll drink a success to the innocent hare.

'Twas on one sum-mer's morn-ing as my love walked ov-er the plain   He

had no thought of en-list-ing  when a sol-dier to him came who so

kind-er-ly in-vi-ted him to  drink the ale that's brown and ad-

-van-ced      and ad-van-ced      And ad-

-van-ced him a shil-ling all to fight for the crown

## The White Cockade

'Twas on one summer's morning as my love walked over the plain,
He had no thought of enlisting when a soldier to him came,
Who so kindly invited him to drink the ale that's brown,
And advanced, and advanced, and advanced him a shilling
All to fight for the Crown.

So now my love has enlisted and he wears a white cockade,
He is a handsome young man, likewise a roving blade,
He is a handsome young man and he's going to serve the King,
Oh, my very, oh, my very, oh, my very heart is breaking
All for the loss of him.

Oh, may he never prosper and may he never thrive
With anything he takes in hand, this world while he's alive,
May the very ground he walks upon the grass refuse to grow,
Since he's being, since he's being, since he's being the only cause of
My sorrow, grief and woe.

He pulled out his pocket handkerchief to wipe her flowing eyes,
He said, My dear, dry up those tears likewise those mournful sighs,
Be of good courage stout and bold while I march over the plain,
Then I'll marry, then I'll marry, then I'll marry you, my dearest,
When I return again.

Come all you war-like sea-men that to the seas be-long I'll
tell you of a fight my boys on board the Nott-ing-ham it was
of an I-rish cap-tain his name was Som-er-ville With
cour-age bold did he con-trol he played his part so well

## Warlike Seamen

Come all you warlike seamen that to the seas belong,
I'll tell you of a fight, my boys, on board the Nottingham.
It was of an Irish Captain, his name was Somerville,
With courage bold did he control, he played his part so well.

'Twas on the eighth of June, my boys, when at Spithead we lay,
On board there came an order our anchor for to weigh.
Bound for the coast of Ireland, our orders did run so,
For us to cruise and not refuse against a daring foe.

We had not sailed many lengths at sea before a ship we spied,
She being some lofty Frenchman come a-bearing down so wide.
We hailed her off France, my boys, they asked from where we came.
Our answer was, From Liverpool and London is our name.

Oh, pray are you some man of war or pray what may you be?
Oh, then replied our Captain, and that you soon shall see,
Come strike your English colours or else you shall bring to,
Since you're so stout you shall give out or else we will sink you.

The first broadside we gave to them which made them for to
    wonder,
Their main-mast and their rigging came a-rattling down like thunder,
We drove them from their quarter they could no longer stay,
Our guns did roar, we made so sure, we showed them British play.

So now we've took that ship, my boys, God speed us fair wind
That we might sail to Plymouth Town if the heavens prove so kind.
We'll drink a health unto our Captain and all such warlike souls,
To him we'll drink and never flinch out of a flowing bowl.

*When Jones's Ale was New*

Come all you honest labouring men that work hard all the day,
And join with me at the Barley Mow to pass an hour away,
Where we can sing and drink and be merry,
And drive away all our cares and worry,
When Jones's ale was new, my boys,
When Jones's ale was new.

The first to come in was the Ploughman with sweat all on his brow,
Up with the lark at the break of day he guides the speedy plough,
He drives his team, how they do toil,
O'er hill and valley to turn the soil,
When Jones's ale was new, my boys,
When Jones's ale was new.

The next to come in was the Blacksmith his brawny arms all bare,
And with his pint of Jones's ale he has no fear or care,
Throughout the day his hammer he's swinging,
And he sings when he hears the anvil ringing,
When Jones's ale was new, my boys,
When Jones's ale was new.

The next to come in was the Scytheman so cheerful and so brown,
And with the rhythm of his scythe the corn he does mow down,
He works, he mows, he sweats and he blows,
And he leaves his swathes laying all in rows,
When Jones's ale was new, my boys,
When Jones's ale was new.

The next to come in was the Tinker and he was no small beer-
    drinker,
And he was no small beer-drinker to join the jovial crew,
He told the old woman he'd mend her old kettle,
Good Lord how his hammer and tongs did rattle,
When Jones's ale was new, my boys,
When Jones's ale was new.

Now here is Jones our Landlord a jovial man is he,
Likewise his wife a buxom lass who joins in harmony,
We wish them happiness and good will
While our pots and glasses they do fill,
When Jones's ale was new, my boys,
When Jones's ale was new.

### Dogs and Ferrets

I keep my dogs and my ferrets too,
O, I have 'em in my keeping
To catch good hares all in the night
While the gamekeeper lies sleeping.

My dogs and I went out one night
'Twas to view their habitation,
Up jumped poor puss and away ran she
Straight way to our plantation.

She had not gone so very far in
Before something caught her running,
So loudly then she called out, Aunt,
I said, Uncle's just a-coming.

I then drew out my little pen-knife
All quickly for to paunch her,
She turned out to be one of the female kind
How glad I was I'd catched her.

Now I'll go down to some ale-house by
And I'll drink that hare quite mellow.
I'll spend a crown and a merry crown too
And say I'm a right good fellow.